PUMPKINS AND PERIL

THE PERIDALE CAFE SERIES
BOOK 29

AGATHA FROST

Published by Pink Tree Publishing Limited in 2023

All characters and events in this publication, other than those clearly in the public domain, are fictitious and any resemblance to real persons, living or dead, is purely coincidental.

Copyright © Pink Tree Publishing Limited.

The moral right of the author has been asserted.

All rights reserved. This book or any portion thereof may not be reproduced or used in any manner whatsoever without the express written permission of the publisher except for the use of brief quotations in a book review.

For questions and comments about this book, please contact pinktreepublishing@gmail.com

www.pinktreepublishing.com
www.agathafrost.com

WANT TO BE KEPT UP TO DATE WITH AGATHA FROST RELEASES? *SIGN UP THE FREE NEWSLETTER!*

www.AgathaFrost.com

You can also follow **Agatha Frost** across social media. Search 'Agatha Frost' on:

Facebook
Twitter
Goodreads
Instagram

ALSO BY AGATHA FROST

Peridale Cafe

31. Sangria and Secrets

30. Mince Pies and Madness

29. Pumpkins and Peril

28. Eton Mess and Enemies

27. Banana Bread and Betrayal

26. Carrot Cake and Concern

25. Marshmallows and Memories

24. Popcorn and Panic

23. Raspberry Lemonade and Ruin

22. Scones and Scandal

21. Profiteroles and Poison

20. Cocktails and Cowardice

19. Brownies and Bloodshed

18. Cheesecake and Confusion

17. Vegetables and Vengeance

16. Red Velvet and Revenge

15. Wedding Cake and Woes

14. Champagne and Catastrophes

13. Ice Cream and Incidents

12. Blueberry Muffins and Misfortune

11. Cupcakes and Casualties

10. Gingerbread and Ghosts

9. Birthday Cake and Bodies

8. Fruit Cake and Fear

7. Macarons and Mayhem

6. Espresso and Evil

5. Shortbread and Sorrow

4. Chocolate Cake and Chaos

3. Doughnuts and Deception

2. Lemonade and Lies

1. Pancakes and Corpses

Claire's Candles

1. Vanilla Bean Vengeance

2. Black Cherry Betrayal

3. Coconut Milk Casualty

4. Rose Petal Revenge

5. Fresh Linen Fraud

6. Toffee Apple Torment

7. Candy Cane Conspiracies

8. Wildflower Worries

9. Frosted Plum Fears

Other

The Agatha Frost Winter Anthology

Peridale Cafe Book 1-10

Peridale Cafe Book 11-20

Claire's Candles Book 1-3

1

The door of Julia's Café banged against the wall, swinging wide from the gust of chilly wind as the last of the day's customers ambled out. The gale whisked through the café, swirling crispy leaves with the comforting scents of pumpkin spice and cinnamon. Framed photographs of the village lining the wall jittered; one—a shot of the local library—sprung free of its hook and began a quick descent.

Julia lunged towards the wall, clutching a tray with used cups and saucers from those same customers' tables. With uncanny precision, she wedged the falling picture against the yellow wall with her hip before it hit the floor. The half-drunk pumpkin spice latte wobbled on the tray, and Julia's gran, Dot, reached out and steadied it from the nearest table.

"You're never off guard, are you, dear?" Dot chuckled, pouring the last of her teapot into her cup. "Can't let a single piece of Peridale get away from us, even if it's only a picture."

Julia smiled at her gran as she re-hung the frame. "If we don't look out for Peridale, who will?"

"The people of Peridale aren't looking out for our heating bills, are they?" said Sue, her sister, as she closed the door and tapped the 'Please keep the door shut' sign she'd stuck on the glass.

"Might as well lock up while you're there," Dot said. "It's almost closing time. Seems the rush is finally over. Haven't been able to hear myself think all afternoon."

Sue sought Julia's nod of approval, but after a glance at the clock, Julia shook her head. Although the sun dipped low on the horizon, she always preferred to keep the café open until the last minute, especially during the darker months. The thought of someone needing a warm drink on a crisp October night was reason enough for her.

Sue relieved Julia of the precarious tray and inspected the half-finished latte. "Have you noticed for every five pumpkin spice lattes we sell, at least one comes back unfinished?"

"It's an acquired taste," Dot announced, wrinkling her nose before sipping her traditional tea. "One I shan't be acquiring any time soon, thank you very much."

Sue navigated through the tables where only family members lingered. Julia's father, Brian, and his wife, Katie, carved designs in giant pumpkins. Their son, Vinnie, and Julia's daughter, Olivia, focused on the scooping. Across the café, Jessie, still donning her apron, leaned closer to her laptop, her fingers flying across the keys. Julia ruffled Olivia's hair as she walked by before joining Sue in the kitchen.

"I think Gran called it. The Saturday rush seems to be over," Julia said, loosening Sue's apron strings. "There's no need for all of us to stick around with the café being this quiet."

"Are you sure?" Sue replied, removing her apron and hanging it on the hook. "This'll give me time to finish Pearl and Dottie's Halloween costumes—Winnie-the-Pooh and Piglet. Neil's idea," she added with a teasing eye-roll. "Changed your mind about the party tomorrow?"

Julia's eyes flickered to the glossy Halloween party invitation pinned to the kitchen's notice board. For a moment, she considered changing her mind. Judging by how much gossip the invitation had caused, it seemed most of the village would be there. But given the party's host, Julia couldn't bring herself to change her mind.

"We're taking Olivia trick-or-treating," Julia said instead. "I'm sure you'll have a great time."

"It would be better if you were there." Sue offered a soft smile. "But I understand. If you change your mind, you're always welcome."

Sue left through the back door, letting in another gust of the bitter wind. Alone in the kitchen, Julia stared at the unsettling Halloween party invitation tacked next to the bin schedule. A sense of discomfort shivered through her. Julia had nothing against Halloween or Halloween parties. She did, however, have a problem with the party's host—James Jacobson. Shaking her head before he consumed her thoughts like he had been a lot lately, Julia pushed past the beaded curtain and into the café.

Turning her focus towards Jessie, absorbed in her laptop for the past hour at a table closest to the counter, Julia's curiosity got the better of her. She snuck a peek over Jessie's shoulder as she picked up more latte glasses and empty plates. Jessie switched from one window to another without missing a beat, her fingers frozen over the laptop keys.

"How's the article coming along?" Julia inquired.

"Fine." Jessie looked up with a forced smile, tucking a stray strand of dark hair behind her ear.

"Run-of-the-mill stuff. The escalating cost of life in small villages, that sort of thing."

Jessie glanced up at Julia, but she avoided eye contact. Julia had noticed her daughter becoming more withdrawn since her shocking exposé front-page story last month. The headline 'Unnamed Politician Uses Gang to Intimidate Family' sent shockwaves through the village. They'd had a front-row seat in the café, and it was an open secret that the 'unnamed politician' had to be Greg Morgan, their local Member of Parliament. Without the constant drip-feeding of updates, villagers grew bored. The gossip switched back to the usual frivolous topics of 'you'll never believe who I saw doing what they shouldn't' and, of course, the weather.

Since then, Julia could guarantee to find Jessie hunched over her laptop whenever she wasn't needed in the café. She claimed to be working on articles for her part-time job at the paper, yet Julia hadn't seen her daughter's name attached to anything in print for a while. She wanted to press Jessie to understand what was going on. But part of Julia didn't want to know what Jessie was hiding. Change was in the air in Peridale, and few seemed to want to acknowledge it.

"Can't wait to read it," Julia said, opting not to probe further.

Jessie nodded, her tight shoulders easing. The

secretive typing resumed when Julia was out of view of the screen. Setting aside her curiosity, she approached the pumpkin-carving table.

"These are looking great," she said. "Need any help?"

Her dad brandished a wickedly curved carving knife. "No need. We're professionals."

Katie shot him a smirk. "By 'professionals,' your dad means we watched a YouTube video before I closed the salon early."

Julia laughed. Katie's pumpkin face featured round eyes with long eyelashes, pouty lips, and an ornate floral hairdo. She'd never been the craftiest, but owning a nail salon on Mulberry Lane had unleashed her creativity. Brian's pumpkin erred on the traditional side with menacing, triangular eyes and a jagged, toothless grin. Vinnie scooped out pumpkin guts beside them while Olivia did her best to help, tiny fingers covered in strings of pulp and seeds.

Dot shuffled over to the counter, her empty teacup rattling against the saucer on her tray. "The weather has taken a turn for the worse. I won't be surprised if we're shovelling snow next week."

Dot's gaze fell upon a small wooden box between the tip jar and a stack of leaflets for the local food bank. Intrigued, she tilted her head and unlatched the box. Before Julia could utter a caution, the lid sprang open, and an animatronic witch burst free, cackling and swaying wildly on its spring.

Dot yelped, her tray quivering in her hands. Laughter erupted throughout the café—even Jessie chuckled from behind her laptop screen.

"They must've modelled that witch after you, Mother," Julia's dad said.

Unamused, Dot shut the lid, silencing the witch's maniacal laughter. "Honestly, I cannot wait for this Halloween nonsense to be over so everyone can revert to boring normality. This time of year unsettles me."

"That's sort of the point," Jessie muttered, still typing.

Julia's laughter faded as her eyes locked onto something outside the window. Squinting, she moved closer to the condensation-tinged glass. The last fiery burst of the autumn sunset bathed the village green in a hazy glow. Long shadows from the stark, towering oaks on the church grounds stretched across the grass as fallen leaves rustled in the breeze.

A gathering interrupted the peace of the early evening at the edge of the green. Four men in suits huddled around a large sheet of paper. They tilted their heads this way and that, taking turns muttering between broad-stroked pointing as they moved about the green. They faced the café, and Julia's stomach knotted as she recognised the man directing the group.

It was him.

The man throwing the Halloween party at the library. The elusive property developer, James Jacobson.

Unmistakable with his tall, broad frame, James was the epitome of city sophistication in his tailored suit. His swept-back hair somehow defied the wind, and even from this distance, she could almost see the gleam of his unnaturally white teeth as he spoke.

Given he'd sent the invitation to every home in the village, Julia had known it would only be a matter of time before he showed his face again. However, like all his other shady dealings lately, she'd hoped he would host the party from afar.

Surrounded by his well-dressed associates, James gestured at the large sheet of paper. Their heads bobbed, almost synchronised, as they examined the plans. He pointed from the paper towards the alley between Julia's café and the post office, setting off her stomach with an uncomfortable tumble.

Even if she couldn't hear him through the glass, she knew he'd be using persuasive, calculated speech. Words like 'investment,' 'opportunity,' and 'progress,' all coated with a veneer of charm that failed to mask the profit-driven calculations behind his eyes. The men in suits were lapping it up, but the charm had turned cold for Julia.

"If I choose this place," he'd said on that bright summer day outside the abandoned building site at the bottom of Julia's lane over a year ago, "at least I know I'll have two friends up the road?"

"Sure," she'd replied. "Friends."

She now knew too much about James Jacobson to consider him a friend.

Avoiding any interaction with James had just moved to the top of her priority list, though the line between curiosity and apprehension blurred.

A gang of miniature witches, ghosts, and goblins tore past the café window, their Halloween costumes billowing in the wind. The sudden movement jolted her from her watch at the window. The movement caught James' attention, and he lifted his hand in a wave aimed at her. She couldn't bring herself to return the gesture. Instead, she pulled down the blind, locked the café door, and flipped the sign to 'Closed.'

Turning back to the café, the sight that met her was grounding. Olivia and Vinnie shrieked with delight, reaching for a floating, remote-controlled ghost that hovered just beyond their grasp. Katie captured the magic of the moment on her phone while Brian dug out the insides of another pumpkin. Dot flipped through the latest issue of *The Peridale*

Post, and in his basement office below, Julia could imagine Barker typing away on a PI case or his next novel.

This was her world—her family and her café.

She glanced towards Jessie's table, where she was packing up. Julia hoped the timing of her exit was a coincidence, but intuition gnawed at her; when it came to whatever James was planning, Jessie knew more than she was letting on.

Dot, ever the meddler, glanced around the closed blind.

"Well, I never. The wanderer returns," she muttered, her eyes narrowing at the sight of James. "Do you know what he's up to?"

"No," Julia replied, her voice sharper than she'd intended.

"Well, you might want to find out. Don't forget, that swine bought the land behind the café—all fifteen-acres of it!"

Julia exhaled, steadying her nerves. How could she forget? Jessie's article on the 'unnamed politician,' with the eye-catching subheading 'Knight Family Intimidated into Selling Road Access to Undeveloped Field,' hadn't been far from her mind since it had caused the subsided storm in a teacup. She'd been battling the whirlpool of speculation that threatened to consume her, waiting for facts to surface.

"That man needs a reminder of how things work in this village," Dot muttered, letting the blind flap back into place. "We won't be pushed around by *him* again. Not after last time."

Julia said nothing as she adjusted the framed picture of the library, but she couldn't have agreed more. The photograph she'd rescued from a tumble wasn't just of the library's exterior. Julia, her gran, and the rest of the now-defunct Peridale's Ears neighbourhood watch group stood in front of the doors holding 'SAVE YOUR LOCAL LIBRARY' placards. A library they'd saved from being redeveloped at the hands of James Jacobson. He might have retreated into the shadows after conceding, but he hadn't stopped buying chunks of the village from the shadows. Now he was back, strutting around with suited men holding plans, with pockets deep enough to fulfil his wildest ambitions.

And this time, Julia had no idea what he was up to.

2

The smooth tones of lounge jazz filled the office beneath the café as Barker ran his fingers over the soft, matte cover of his recently published book, *The Body in the Time Capsule*. Careful not to crease the spine, he peeled back the cover and inscribed a personal note to the recipient before adding his signature with a flourish. Once signed, he added the book to the growing pile on his mahogany desk, aligning it just so.

With a satisfied smile, Barker scooped up the next book from the box at his feet. A sharp cramp seized his hand, making him wince. His pen slipped from his grasp and clattered onto the floor. He shook out his fingers, flexing them until the ache subsided. His writing hand wasn't accustomed to such extended use these days—unlike during the whirlwind book tour for his debut, *The Girl in the Basement*. He could still envision the snaking queue of excited strangers, each holding a copy of his book at the library, all eager to meet the man behind the words.

How different this modest stack felt in comparison.

There was no fanfare or festivities to celebrate the sequel, just Barker alone in his office, writing the names of those who'd been kind enough to pay a little extra through his website for his inscription on the first page. Tomorrow, he'd put the books in padded envelopes and carry them next door to the post office as sales trickled in a few at a time. He hadn't known what to expect from self-publishing his second novel, but the fun had been in the writing. He preferred being in the driver's seat of his writing career, now a side quest between cases for his private investigator business. No more arguing with publishers about plot changes. No publicists pushing him onto TV and radio. Those days were fun, but they were long gone. His ex-publicist had sent him flowers, now wilting next to the vinyl player. His former publisher had pretended not to notice that he'd relaunched his writing career without them, which suited him just fine.

He finished signing the last few copies and

replaced the pen cap, setting it atop the blank notepad on his desk for when inspiration struck. Lately, he'd felt the itch to begin writing his next whodunit. With no active PI cases on his schedule, now was the ideal time to make headway. He woke his laptop and opened a blank document, willing creativity to flow.

He'd considered writing about last month's George Knight case. The Cotswold Crew gang had burned down his family home and almost ruined his life, while an opportunistic filmmaker captured their downfall for her murderous moon cult documentary. Anwen Powell, the documentary's director, was where she belonged—behind bars for using the confusion of events to murder two people—a gang member and then George's wife—in the name of spicing up her film. Anwen had written to Barker several times to justify her actions, and those letters had gone unanswered into the bin. The dust needed more time to settle, and some aspects of the case remained unsolved.

There was always the case surrounding Ronnie Roberts' callous murder at the Fern Moore food bank. Ronnie, standing in the way of the low-income flats being gentrified into luxury holiday lets, would make for an interesting read. But Ronnie's murder still felt too fresh.

His mind cast back to earlier in the year, to the

allotment case. He'd discovered the body of Henry Foreman himself among the carrots. Henry had protested the destruction of ancient woodland in Riverswick to make way for the Henderson Place housing development. Again, still too recent.

Barker took a steadying breath, willing anything to turn up on the page.

The intercom on his desk buzzed, pulling his attention away before the first word materialised. He silenced the jazz with the remote control and peered at the video screen connected to the doorbell. A broad-shouldered man in a suit stood at the top of the stairs in the courtyard behind the café, hand raised to press the buzzer again. Even through the grainy film, Barker instantly recognised James Jacobson's arrogant stance.

He hesitated to answer the door.

If James wanted to hire Barker again, he could go elsewhere. The case contained within the thick file in the second drawer of the filing cabinet had marked Barker's half-year as a professional PI. Having James as a client had nearly been his undoing. The villagers had been eager to see James locked up, especially after his ill-advised attempt to transform the beloved local library into a restaurant. But the evidence had told a different story—one of James' innocence in the shooting incident at Wellington Manor's final summer garden party. Barker and Julia had pieced it together, proving that James had been framed and hadn't been the one to pull the trigger on the gun that shot his wife. They'd cleared his name and, in a twist of fate, James had abandoned his plans for the library, purchased the manor to convert into apartments, and vowed to make Peridale his home—a changed man.

Since then, summer had come and gone for a second time, and despite the transformation of the manor, James hadn't been seen. And given how many of Barker's recent files, including those vying to be the subject of his next story, involved James' name in some capacity, the wealthy man was far from reformed.

The buzzer sounded again, a drawn-out and insistent hum. With a resigned sigh, Barker pressed the button to unlock the door. As curious as he was to see James on his doorstep, he wasn't surprised to see him back in the village. It was bound to be a matter of time.

"Barker Brown, aren't you a sight for sore eyes?" James proclaimed as he descended the wooden staircase, scanning the office as if touring a prospective investment property. "This place has come along nicely since I was last here. Business must be good?"

"Can I help you with something, Mr Jacobson?" Barker asked, skipping past pleasantries.

James' eyes flickered; a brief cloud of uncertainty crossed his face. Almost as quickly, he squared his shoulders and flashed a practised smile as if brushing off the chill in the room. Barker wouldn't play along if James wanted to act like no time had passed.

"Please, call me James," he said, hesitating by the chair on the other side of the desk. "We're friends, after all?"

Barker didn't reply, nor did he offer James a seat.

"Can I help you with something, James?"

"Just thought I'd pop by to congratulate you on your new book." He pulled a copy of *The Body in the Time Capsule* from his jacket pocket. "Since I have a signed copy of your debut, I was hoping you might give this one a scribble. If it's not too much trouble?"

Barker accepted the book, hiding his true feelings behind a neutral expression. Unlike the pristine copies stacked on the desk, this one had a cracked spine in several places and a curled front cover. He flipped to the title page and scrawled his name with none of the care given to the others.

"I quite enjoyed it," James continued. "Based on a cold case that happened at that little school around the corner, right?"

"That's correct." Barker slid the book back with a tight smile. "Anything else?"

James flicked to the title page with a disappointed tilt of his brows but didn't linger. He traded the paperback for a thick cream envelope, sealed with a monogrammed wax stamp.

"There was, as it happens," he said, tapping the envelope in his palm. "I'm having a party, and I'd like you to attend. Julia, too, of course."

"We've already decided we won't be attending your Halloween party," Barker replied, relieved at the thought of dodging whatever social labyrinth James had in mind.

"Oh, it's not for that," he said with a chuckle, placing the envelope on the desk. "I haven't even decided if I'm going to that yet. No, this is for a little housewarming get-together. *My* housewarming. You might have noticed the house I had built on your old plot is finished?"

Barker nodded, glancing at the envelope. "Months ago."

"Well, I'm ready to move in. Time to make Peridale my permanent home." Barker hesitated, drifting to the filing cabinet across the room. As if reading his thoughts, James interrupted, "I know it's been a while since I was last here. I had a lot of business to attend to elsewhere, but... have I done something to upset you and Julia? I thought we all left on good terms. I waved to her earlier, but she either didn't see me or... chose to ignore me."

Barker narrowed his stare, trying to assess whether James was being earnest. He glanced at the cabinet again, so many unanswered questions burning in his mind.

"You might not have been physically here, James, but you've been making your presence felt," Barker said, choosing his words carefully. "People know you were the one who silently invested in the Fern Moore holiday lets scheme."

"I invest in lots of projects," he replied without hesitation.

"Two people died. Murdered by the man you paid to trick residents into selling their flats for way below market value."

"I wasn't to know Benedict Langley was..." He circled his finger at his temple. "We were only loose associates, and it sounded like a good investment on paper. You can't seriously blame me for those deaths?"

"Your latest purchase," Barker continued, nodding in the direction of the field. "A family were gang-stalked to sell their bordering land, another couple of deaths, and you just happen to end up buying the field at the centre of it all?"

This time, James took a moment to craft a reply. "Unrelated."

"I'm sure." Barker nodded. "And your pal, Greg? How is he doing these days?"

Any hint of expression dropped from James' shiny face, and Barker caught the slight movement of his throat bobbing up and down. "Greg...?"

"Precisely." He returned his attention to the blank laptop screen. "If you want to know why people aren't rolling out the red carpet, there's your answer. I'll discuss the invitation with Julia and let you know, but I wouldn't hold your breath."

James stepped back, his face unreadable.

"Message received," he said, turning on his heels. "I'll leave you to it."

But Barker wasn't finished. He had another question that had kept Julia awake at night since she'd found out about the sale behind her café. As James reached the foot of the stairs, Barker pushed his chair back against the concrete floor.

"The field?" he asked. "What do you have planned for it?"

With his foot on the bottom step, James peered over his shoulder, his eyes not meeting Barker's as a slight smirk lifted the corners of his lips. "Who said I had anything planned for it? I'll see you around, neighbour."

After ascending the steps with calculated precision, James closed the door behind him with a thud. Barker sank back into his chair, staring at the 'JJ' monogram stamped into the wax seal on the envelope. Had James only dropped by for a book signing and to hand-deliver an envelope? Barker wasn't sure, but he had an uneasy stirring in his gut that James might have been trying to gauge how much the local PI knew about his recent activity.

Barker had played right into James Jacobson's hands if that was the case.

He should have kept his cards closer to his chest.

But for Julia's sake, he'd wanted the truth.

Shaking off the urge to start his new novel, he typed 'James Jacobson Peridale planning applications' into the search window. If James wanted to play games, Barker needed to know which board they were playing on, and he was confident it wouldn't be long until he needed to make some space in his filing cabinet for another Jacobson entry.

3

Cinnamon filled the kitchen air as Julia added a generous scattering to the mixing bowl full of leftover pumpkin innards. Pumpkin pie had never graced her menu, so the novelty of having the American staple on the menu would have the autumnal delicacy selling well into November.

As she added a last dash of spice to the orange pulp and set it aside for the pie crusts that she'd bake fresh on Monday morning, her thoughts drifted to James. The uncertainty of what he'd been up to on the village green gnawed at her, unsettling the therapeutic peace she'd whipped up with the mixing bowl.

One look at the party invitation on the noticeboard brought her back to earth. She wasn't sure why she'd pinned it up; she'd had known she wouldn't be attending from the moment she noticed the sender's name. Perhaps her subconscious hadn't wanted to let James wander too far from her thoughts —not that she needed much reminding. She ripped it down and screwed it up, throwing it into the bin with the pumpkin seeds.

Clearing her thoughts with a shake of her chocolaty curls, Julia wiped her hands on a towel as her dad's voice drifted in from the café. He was regaling Katie and the kids with a tale of his latest antique find.

"It's a 1889 mantel clock," he enthused, in the tone that only came about when talking about old relics. "Absolutely pristine condition. You should have seen the detail on it—the Roman numerals, the intricate scrollwork along the base. A real gem."

Julia popped her head through the beads as Katie nodded along, refilling the sugar pots and straightening the menus. Having managed the café during Julia's maternity leave, Katie hadn't forgotten the old routines. Vinnie was trying his best to sweep with a broom twice his size, while Olivia followed him around like a shadow.

Pulling off her apron, Julia was about to join them when an unexpected knock at the door disturbed the peace.

"Sorry, we're closed!" Katie called out.

Pumpkins and Peril

Julia pushed through the beaded curtain as the persistent knocking continued. A man peered between the signs in the door, blinking anxiously behind round glasses.

"Probably someone hoping for a late coffee," Katie said. "I'll send them packing."

"One more brew won't hurt. I'll see what they want."

Julia opened the door, and without needing to ask, she knew the man wasn't there for last orders. His gaze darted about behind his glasses as he clutched a leather briefcase against his tweed jacket.

"Hello?" Julia greeted, hoping to set him at ease. "Can I help you?"

The man opened his mouth, but only a slight croak escaped. He peered over Julia's shoulder into the café, eyes narrowing as Katie and Brian moved closer. The stranger's silence unsettled her, but she resisted the urge to close the door.

"Can I call someone for you? Are you lost?"

"You're Julia, correct?" he finally said, his words tumbling over each other.

"I am. Have we met before?"

He shook his head, eyes still roaming and blinking. "Is it safe to talk here?"

Before she could respond, Brian clapped a hand on the nervous man's shoulder. "Blimey, if it isn't Peter

McBride! Been ages since you dropped by my shop. How are things?"

The man—Peter, apparently—squinted through his smudged glasses at Brian. Recognition flashed across his face. "Brian. Hello. I've been meaning to stop by, but funds have been rather limited of late."

"Say less," Brian replied, tapping his nose. "I had some financial difficulties of my own not too long ago." He turned towards Julia. "Peter here knows local history better than anyone. Would snap up anything in my shop connected to Peridale's past, wouldn't you, old chap?"

"I..." Peter shifted from foot to foot as he clutched his briefcase closer. "I really must be going. Sorry to have bothered you."

"You asked for me by name?" Julia insisted.

Peter wavered as he peered back at the dark village green. "Might I have a quick word? Privately?"

"What's this about, McBride?" Brian asked. "You don't seem yourself."

"It's complicated. I really am here to speak to Julia. *Only* Julia."

Julia sensed her father's rising uneasiness with Peter's behaviour. She gently squeezed Brian's arm, and he backed off a few steps. Arms folded against the night time chill, she joined her visitor on the doorstep.

"Would you like to come into my kitchen?" she suggested. "I could make us some tea?"

"It needs to be somewhere safer," he pleaded.

"I promise, there's no place safer than my café. This place is as good as my home."

"You've no way of knowing that for certain," he whispered, leaning in. "There could be listening devices."

Julia recoiled at the man's paranoia. She studied him closely, and behind the shifty anxiety, his eyes held a glint of determination. He believed what he was saying.

"Perhaps we could meet tomorrow, then?" she suggested. "Somewhere public?"

"It *must* be tonight. I fear lives depend on it."

Lives?

Despite her father vouching for him, she needed more information before agreeing to venture anywhere with this stranger. She offered him the door again, and Peter took tentative steps inside this time. He peered over his glasses at Katie as she tried to distract the children with a sugar-packet puppet show. Arms crossed over his chest, Brian watched from the counter with a suspicious glare. Peter perched on the edge of the chair nearest the door, palms pressed against the briefcase on his lap.

"They can still hear us," he whispered harshly.

"I trust them. They're my family," she assured him, though she was growing impatient. "You came to me for a reason, Peter."

Peter considered her words before giving a terse nod. He took a steadying breath and finally seemed ready to talk.

"You're familiar with the Peridale Preservation Society?" he asked, before answering his own question. "I know you are. You solved the murder of Harriet Barnes, my predecessor and the group's founder. She ran the florist's on Mulberry Lane?"

"Yes, I remember," Julia said with a sad smile. "Harriet was a lovely woman."

"And like many others around here, she cared enough about our local history to stand up for conserving it. When that washed-up actress tried to build that monstrosity of a mega-mansion on your lane, Harriet gave her life to make that stand." He laughed darkly, shaking his head. "Those plans should never have been approved. I should have known then it was just the start."

"Start of what?"

"The era of certain factions of our local government being easily bribed," he hissed. "There are people in powerful positions taking money for things they shouldn't be, for reasons they shouldn't. People who claim to care about history and heritage only until they can benefit. I've had a keen interest in studying and protecting local history and architecture since I was a child. My father was an architect, you see, and his father before him, and his father, and..." He trailed off, his cheeks flushing. "I never had the talent for it myself," he admitted. "But I appreciate the craft and the importance of upholding what came before so others can appreciate it one day." He looked around the café, staring up at the beams in the ceiling, and asked, "Do you know what your café used to be?"

"A toy shop?"

Peter chuckled as he adjusted his glasses. "Yes, I spent quite a few Saturdays and too much of my pocket money here buying those delightful wooden carved toys. What I should have said was, do you know what your café was *originally*?"

"Oh." Julia scratched the side of her head. Before she'd poured her life savings into buying the building, it had sat empty for three years. It had been a mobile-phone shop before that, a travel agent before that, and a toy shop dating back long before she was born. Despite claiming the café was as good as her home, she admitted, "I'm a little ashamed to say I don't know."

"This building once served as an alehouse."

"My café was a pub?" Julia confirmed, surprised.

Peter seemed to relax at her interest. "Built in 1786,

if I'm remembering correctly. Records say it was one of the finest alehouses this village had—a gathering place for many generations, and now you, and—that's not why I'm here." His brief animation at discussing local history faded, replaced by sombre urgency. "Because of my expertise in historical architecture, someone recently commissioned me to consult on—shall we say—the development of an important building. I was brought on to ensure its design properly respected the surrounding landscape."

Julia pictured the newest addition to Peridale's landscape—the lavish bungalow at the bottom of her lane. On the same site where the 'washed-up actress' had tried to build her mega-mansion before fleeing the village almost as soon as she arrived. Where Barker's first cottage had stood, destroyed by a telegraph pole during a wild storm.

"Before you ask," Peter said, holding up a hand, "I'm not at liberty to say. I signed a non-disclosure agreement regarding the specifics of the project."

"Can you nod or shake your head?" she asked. "Was it James Jacobson's new bungalow?"

Peter remained as stiff as a board; his rapid blinking was his only movement. Julia needed no more confirmation than that. New buildings rarely popped up around Peridale.

"They then commissioned me for another project.

But this one was *different*," he said, lowering his voice. "When the project was first presented to me, they assured me the plans I was consulting on were merely hypothetical. Why wouldn't they be? The 1840s plan would never have materialised, even if he hadn't died of consumption." His blinking sped up, and he shook his head as though he'd taken a wrong turn in his thoughts. Julia wasn't sure she was following. "It's not hypothetical. When I realised, I thought my contributions would limit disruption, but now..." His voice faltered and died in his throat. When he spoke again, it was barely above a whisper. "The development is *imminent*, and it's clear to me that this is only the beginning. I want no part in it. I've tried everything I can to stop it, only now, it may be too late."

Julia eyed him intently, foreboding creeping over her. "Too late for what?"

"I've already said too much. There are those who wish for this plan to proceed at any cost. If they found out I was here, it wouldn't end well for either of us."

"Does this have something to do with the field behind my café?"

Julia glimpsed genuine fear flash across Peter's face. He sprang to his feet, clutching his briefcase.

"Forgive me. I shouldn't have come."

"Wait, you can't leave now." Julia rose with him. "What plans? What development?"

Peter's lips parted as he scanned the café; his eyes landed on the beams. Sighing, he clenched his lids and exhaled. "Do you know of Howarth House?"

"In the forest?"

"Good, then meet me there at a quarter to five tomorrow evening. And whatever you do, come alone." He paused, his eyes darting back and forth as if torn between two invisible options. When he spoke, his voice quavered. "The wrong people now have the power to irrevocably damage this community, not just for us, but for—"

As he turned to leave, Peter collided with Katie as she swept near the front door. The impact sent his briefcase flying, scattering its paper contents across the hardwood floor.

"No!" Peter cried, scrambling to gather the documents as Julia moved to help. "Please, I must do this myself."

"What in blazes?" Brian muttered as Peter crawled about. "What's got into you, McBride?"

Katie bent to grab a stray sheet of paper that had slid near her foot. Peter's head snapped up, eyes aflame behind his smudged lenses. In two swift steps, he closed the distance between them and seized Katie's wrist.

"Unhand that!"

"Have you lost your mind, McBride?" Brian rushed over, prising Peter away from Katie with a scowl. "That's my wife you're manhandling!"

Peter stood frozen, the scattered papers like leaves around his feet. Without a word, he dropped to his knees again and resumed gathering them with intense focus. Julia's heart pounded as she struggled to make sense of his bizarre behaviour. He'd said so much, yet so little, and even as his frantic hands shoved the papers into his briefcase, she still wanted to help him.

"Let's all take a deep breath and sit down, shall we?" she suggested. "I'll make us some tea, and—"

"I must go." Peter yanked the case shut with a snap and leapt to his feet. He lunged for the exit, but Katie blocked his path. "Please, I meant you no harm."

"Wait just a second," Katie said, wagging a long, orange acrylic in his petrified face. "I *know* you from somewhere, don't I?"

"I don't think so."

"You visited my father, Vincent Wellington, at the manor before he died."

Peter's eyes narrowed on Katie; something was dawning.

"You're mistaken," he muttered, and with that, he pushed past her, flinging the door open.

For the second time that day, the door crashed

into the wall, and a picture frame sprung free of its hook. This time, it wasn't the library. It was a photograph of Julia standing proud with a rolling pin in front of the café on its opening morning. She wasn't fast enough to catch it before it hit the floor. The glass shattered before the frame fell flat on its face. She closed the front door to the wind and rested her palm on the timber as her father scooped up the picture, while Katie calmed the agitated children.

Julia could only stare out into the night, Peter's cryptic warning echoing in her mind.

"The development is imminent."

4

In the kitchen of her cottage, golden pumpkin pancakes sizzled in the frying pan as Julia manoeuvred the spatula like a pro. Olivia kicked her feet, riveted as she watched her special Halloween breakfast come to life while she bobbed to the spooky pop songs on the radio. Like the pumpkin pie mix the day before, Julia had never made pumpkin pancakes either, so she'd had to follow an American recipe on her phone; her mother's handwritten cookbook had no pumpkin recipes. Rather than the delicate crepe-style pancakes Julia would whip up every Shrove Tuesday, these were thick and fluffy, and smelled like spiced autumnal perfection.

"Almost ready, my little monster," Julia said, her

words creating puffs of breath in the still-chilly kitchen air. The cottage heating had yet to wage war against the early morning chill. "How about some sprinkles and sauce?"

Julia piled the tiny pancakes onto a plate, their steam rising like morning fog. A dash of cinnamon and nutmeg crowned her masterpiece. With a neat flick of her wrist, she distributed a curl of butter over the stack, watching it melt in rivulets down the sides.

"Sprinkles!" Olivia's eyes widened, clutching the jar as Julia handed them over. She placed the plate within Olivia's reach, and the little girl unleashed a flurry of orange and black specks.

Julia savoured a moment with her peppermint and liquorice tea, appreciating the homely mischief that Halloween morning had conjured. Her gaze drifted to the cat-shaped clock that loomed above the fridge, its tail ticking away the seconds.

Thoughts of her later meeting with Peter McBride danced in her mind. She scooped up her phone, switching from the pumpkin pancake recipe to the search results she'd been scrolling through for most of the morning. She was on page three of '1840s plan' and nothing related to Peridale had caught her eye and '1840s plan Peridale' had brought up zero results. She locked her phone at the sound of Barker's footsteps heading from the bathroom. Peter had said many nonsensical things, and she was starting to believe that was one of them.

"Who left you in charge of the sprinkles?" Barker darted to take the jar away, the pancakes no longer visible under a mountain of orange and black. "Don't want a Halloween tummy-ache before we go trick-or-treating tonight."

"Sorry, I was distracted," Julia said, scooping off a handful of sprinkles before Olivia sent them flying around the kitchen. By the bin, she glanced again at the clock, its feline eyes avoiding her as they darted from side to side.

"Why not ask him to meet you somewhere more public?" Barker suggested, reading her thoughts. "Or better yet, don't go at all."

Julia sighed. Even if she wanted to change the location, she had no way of contacting McBride. She'd started her '1840s plan' research on the Peridale Preservation Society website, and they only had an email address.

"I could tag along?" Barker offered, cutting the pancake stack up for Olivia. "I could hang back and watch from a distance."

"He was explicit that I go alone. He's already startled enough without him thinking he's being tricked."

"He could be a complete nutter, Julia," he

whispered. "After everything you said, a lone meeting with this guy in the woods on Halloween sounds like the opening act of a horror film."

Barker ran a finger across his throat in a slicing motion, and Julia didn't disagree. She knew how it looked. The circumstances had an eerie undertone, but she'd felt Peter's desperation and fear. He was scared. Erratic and paranoid, even, but she wasn't scared of him. She was scared *for* him.

"He's the leader of the Peridale Preservation Society," she said with a defensive hint.

"Murderers can appreciate history, too."

Julia tried to think of a comeback, but none came.

"I have all day to decide what to do," she said instead. "I'm not going to spend all Sunday dwelling on it."

As the clock's tail continued to swish, every second ticking closer to the 4:45 p.m. meeting, Julia remained torn. McBride had been on the verge of revealing something significant. Yet the seed of caution Barker had sown weighed on her. Whether she would venture into the woods remained a question mark, though for all the logical doubts Barker could throw at her, Julia wasn't sure she'd be able to resist her curiosity.

A bitter wind swept around Jessie as she ascended the metal fire escape at the back of Katie's Salon, a mischievous grin creeping across her face. Reaching the frosted-glass door to *The Peridale Post* office, she peered inside.

Veronica Hilt, the editor, stood stooped over the radiator, muttering under her breath as she fiddled with the pipes. The cloudy morning light barely illuminated the bright mural of the village spray-painted on the walls, and Veronica hadn't bothered to turn on the lights. Breath held tight, Jessie turned the handle and slid inside, creeping on the balls of her feet.

Finger on the light switch, Jessie inhaled and cried, "*Boo!*"

Veronica jumped and spun around, wielding the wrench with trembling hands as the ceiling lights cast out the morning gloom. "I was seconds away from whacking you, Jessie! What were you thinking?"

"Happy Halloween?" She held out a leftover Halloween cupcake from the café as a peace offering. "I made it myself."

"It's Halloween already?" Veronica grumbled, snatching the cupcake from Jessie. "I didn't think you were coming in today. Pass me that screwdriver and make yourself useful."

Jessie dug out the screwdriver from the toolbox on

Veronica's desk. "I'm here to make myself useful. I thought you were going to call someone in to fix the radiators?"

"I can fix it myself," Veronica grunted as she strained to loosen another stiff bolt. "I only... need... to twist... the right bit."

"Another week of freezing our behinds—"

"I've *almost* got it," Veronica interrupted, finally wrenching the bolt free with a loud squeak. "Is that it?"

As Veronica continued with her tinkering, Jessie pulled her shoulder bag over her head and sat at her desk, still in her jacket. She turned on the computer where a new blinking email awaited her. Jessie's heart skipped a beat, just as it did every time an email came in from the local council's account. Each one could be the break they needed to expose whatever the wealthy developer and his dodgy politician friend were plotting. She clicked the icon, and the little wheel on the screen started spinning. The internet was working as well as the radiators lately.

While she waited for the message to load, she focused on the framed front-page article hanging against the spray-painted sky above her desk. The headline was gigantic next to a photograph of the surviving Knight family members, glum in front of the burnt-out husk of their family home. Tragic, but Jessie had been so proud when they'd published the exposé, finally revealing part of the truth about Greg Morgan's shady dealings—in all but name. The email still hadn't loaded, so she skimmed the front page:

Unnamed Politician Uses Gang to Intimidate Family

A politician, whose identity we have withheld for legal reasons, has been linked to the Cotswold Crew —a feared gang involved in intimidating local university professor George Knight. The politician allegedly conspired with developer James Jacobson to force Knight, a history professor at Oxford, into selling small sections of land. These strips offer the only current road access to a fifteen-acre field recently acquired by Jacobson. Reports suggest the politician facilitated the sale of this land to Jacobson while working in the planning department for the local council before being elected as a Member of Parliament in a recent by-election. It's believed the politician enlisted the Cotswold Crew to pressure Knight into selling, thereby enhancing the development potential and value of Jacobson's land. Knight stated, "I won't be bullied into selling." Despite this paper having photographic evidence of a meeting with a Cotswold Crew member, the politician denies all allegations. Police raids have led to multiple gang-member arrests, but many of the Cotswold crew are still ... Continued on Page Six.

"Are you reading that article again?" Veronica asked between grunts.

"I'm still frustrated," Jessie said—not just by the internet speed; the email still hadn't loaded. "That article should have changed everything, but nothing happened. All we did was scare Greg underground."

"He hasn't been photographed since," Veronica said, a dark pleasure tinging her voice. "Though I'm unsure if that's for better or worse. And we got some of the truth out there, which is our job."

"But it's not enough, is it?"

"Celebrate the minor victories, Jessie," she said. "Which we will be after I get this blasted thing working again."

"How can you be worried about radiators right now? Didn't you get my text last night? James Jacobson's back in the village, which means Greg won't be far away. We need to focus if we're going to figure out their scheme."

"Because we can't write another exposé if we freeze to death, can we?" Veronica peered at Jessie over her gigantic brown tortoiseshell frames. "And it was only a matter of time before my slimy brother and James started stirring up trouble again." With a loud clank, Veronica gave the radiator knob one last twist. Water gurgled in the pipes behind Jessie's desk, followed by a rattling rush towards the radiator. "*Ha!* We have ignition. I told you I could fix it. 'Action is eloquence.'" She paused and added, "Coriolanus, Act Three, Scene Two."

Jessie arched a brow, no longer surprised by the former English tutor's ability to pull a Shakespeare line for any occasion. "Is there a quote along the lines of 'one still cannot believe that one's newspaper editor is really the older sister of that sketchy politician, forsooth whence shocked blah blah blah…?'"

"I can't think of any direct quotes, but sibling rivalries are a common theme—" Veronica cut herself off as she sat at her desk, her feet pointed at the radiator as the chill receded. "That was a rhetorical question, but, you know, since we're talking about the Bard, Greg and James are rather like Iago and Othello. Devious manipulators who'll stop at nothing to get their way."

Jessie furrowed her brow with a shrug.

"Okay, forget Shakespeare."

"If only you'd let me."

"They're like Palpatine and Darth Vader," she

continued. "The evil mastermind and his ruthless enforcer."

"Oh, right," Jessie said, though the reference still confused her. She preferred horror over sci-fi. "The point?"

"The point is, Greg has the political influence to pull all the right strings, while James throws around his investment cash that'll make them both stinking rich. Right now, it seems they need each other. Not that James needs more money. Have you seen that guy's net worth?" She whistled, spinning in her chair to peer out the window as the condensation cleared. "Greed can make fools of us all."

Jessie turned her focus back to her computer screen as the email finally popped up. "Finally. Looks like we have another leak from our council insider."

Veronica wheeled her chair over to Jessie's desk. She skimmed the email with pursed lips. "A special planning committee meeting at the village hall the Friday after bonfire night? That's too soon. There's been no time for anyone to object. There are protocols."

"Object to what? But we still don't know what James' plans are for that land," Jessie said, irritated. "He's put in a dozen different development applications for that field. Public gardens, luxury homes, shops... even a theatre. It's got to be a smokescreen."

Veronica nodded. "No doubt about it. He's keeping the people paying close attention distracted and counting on everyone else being checked out. I had a look into that by-election my brother won in January. The lowest turnout since local records began. I didn't even hear about it when it was happening."

"Me neither," Jessie muttered as she scrolled further in the email to a list of names: Planning Department staff, secretaries, and council members who would comprise the committee. "Who are these people?"

"The people who 'yay' or 'nay' planning applications," Veronica said, pushing her glasses up as she squinted at the screen. "I can't imagine James would have bought that land if he didn't think approval was a certainty. Greg worked in that planning department for years before he moved on up. He'll know which palms to grease."

"And which gangs to hire," Jessie said, examining some names with sloppy circles drawn around them. "Prunella Thompson, Richard Hughes, Alice Adams, Martin Green, and Peter McBride. Okay, but why are these five important?"

"Our insider singled them out for a reason. This is one for you," she said, patting Jessie's shoulder before wheeling back to her desk. "Dig into their backgrounds, social media—anything you can find. If we discover why Greg and James have taken an interest in these five, we might uncover something to throw a spanner in the works before the committee meeting."

"But if the meeting is that soon, we're running out of time. We should bump this to the next front page and warn people something is happening."

Veronica shook her head. "With a dozen plans to discuss? That would create mass confusion, not effective resistance. We find the truth, we can concentrate our attack."

"But there's no—"

"There's no time to waste." Veronica glanced over the top of her giant specs as she peeled the orange casing off the Halloween cupcake. "Dig into those names, find the connections, and I'll—" The strained glugging of the radiator cut her off; the creaking was eerily like the sound that had welcomed in their recent cold snap. "I'll call a plumber."

Glad she hadn't taken off her jacket, Jessie poised over the keyboard, ready to delve into the committee members' lives. She opened a new document, typing the headline: 'The Mysterious Five: Who Holds Peridale's Future?' just in case Veronica changed her mind about that front page.

Julia circled the derelict leftovers of Howarth House for the third time, her boots crunching on the brittle autumn leaves. A rolling fog cut through the stark trees as daylight faded to a murky grey haze, threatening to swallow her in the forest. She shivered, pulling her coat tighter. It was just past five o'clock, and Peter McBride was nowhere to be found. She'd waited nearly twenty minutes; after the bursting-briefcase incident, she'd known in her gut he wouldn't come.

She'd almost skipped the meeting, allowing her better judgement and Barker's words of caution to prevail. But the irresistible pull of untold secrets—that could alter the fate of Peridale—had lured her into the woods.

She stepped towards the house, hesitating at the threshold. Memories of her last visit swarmed her mind—a circle of cultish, flickering candles; a lifeless body lying within; and a documentary film crew hovering over her shoulder to capture every second. Drawing a deep breath, she put a foot over the doorway.

"*Peter*?" Her voice quivered as it broke the stifling silence. "Peter McBride, are you in there? It's Julia. From the café?"

Her call echoed through the dilapidated building, bouncing back to her like a boomerang. Startled birds erupted from the rafters and scattered into the sky, their wings cutting through the foggy air.

Shaking her head, Julia retreated from the doorway. Peter had been an erratic, flighty figure, muttering about not feeling safe; but what could he be so afraid of? What secrets did he guard that might endanger lives?

The sky dimmed further, casting the woods in eerie shadows. She turned her back on Howarth House and quickened her pace along the trail before the way back disappeared into the darkness. Relieved, she caught sight of her beloved aqua-blue vintage car parked on the school lane at the graveyard's edge.

As she drove home, she glanced up at the faint outline of the sliver of a waning crescent moon above. Would the entire village really be at James Jacobson's Halloween party?

Arriving home, she pushed through the door to find Barker in the kitchen, attempting to wrangle Olivia into a pumpkin costume.

"Vinnie's hand-me-down just about fits her," he said, looking up and noting her pensive face. "You're as pale as a ghost, so I'd say you're ready for trick-or-treating. Everything all right?"

"I went to meet Peter in the forest," Julia said,

holding up a hand. "And before you tell me it was a bad idea, I know. He stood me up."

"Probably for the best. Since your shoes are on, should we—"

"Change of plan," she interrupted. "We're going to the party at the library."

Barker arched an eyebrow. "We don't have costumes."

"I'm sure we can think of something."

∽

Jessie sat in her yellow Mini Cooper outside St. Peter's Church, its stained-glass windows reduced to a warm glow by the thickening fog enveloping the village. Leaning against the headrest, she cranked up the car's heating and pulled out her phone. For the second time, she scrolled through the official council website, carefully scanning the bios of the councillors:

> Prunella Thompson serves as the Councillor for Heritage and Culture. With a background in education, she retired as a teacher to focus her efforts on local history and preservation.

> Martin Green holds the position of Area of Outstanding Natural Beauty Representative. He is

an environmental scientist dedicated to sustainable practices and the conservation of the beauty our county has to offer.

Alice Adams serves as the Small Business Councillor. As a local museum owner, she brings first-hand experience to the challenges and opportunities small businesses face along with her passion for history.

Richard Hughes acts as the Councillor for Agriculture. A retired farmer, Richard brings a wealth of experience to discussions about land use and conservation.

Peter McBride serves as the Councillor for Architectural Integrity and Sensitivity. Stemming from a long line of Peridale architects, his passion for preserving the village is both personal and hereditary.

Glancing at the village hall next to the church, she tapped on each councillor's professional headshot, hoping to glean some sense of the people she'd soon be sharing a room with.

Prunella's photo showed a statuesque woman in her late sixties, her silver-grey hair pinned in an elegant bun. A pair of reading glasses dangled on a chain, and she looked like the sort who'd engage in a Shakespeare quote-off with Veronica.

Martin looked every bit the rugged environmental scientist in his early fifties. His beard was greying in patches, and he wore earth-toned casual wear that screamed, 'I hug trees and only buy second-hand but also enjoy a pint at the pub.'

Alice's comforting smile as she posed outside a small museum reminded Jessie of Julia. Dressed in a pastel blouse, her curly brown hair framed her face in a way that made her seem nurturing, even through a photograph.

Richard looked precisely how Jessie would imagine a retired farmer-turned-councillor to look—burly, with a weathered and lined face from years spent working outdoors.

And finally, Peter, whose thin, greying hair, tweed jacket, and round specs made him look like the kind of person Jessie wouldn't mind approaching in a library if she were ever lost, but would probably bore her to tears if he talked for too long.

All in all, they looked harmless and normal—the average people she'd see milling about Peridale on any given day. But as Jessie knew all too well, appearances could be deceiving, especially in a village where scandals and mysteries seemed to blend seamlessly with afternoon tea and village fairs.

Prunella, Richard, Martin, Alice, and Paul were just five of the ten councillors who would make up the scheduled planning committee, although something else connected these five beyond the circles around their names on the insider's email. She'd also found their names listed as the current members of the Peridale Preservation Society, and they met every Sunday at five o'clock in the village hall.

Jessie had always had too many problems in her present life to care much about history, and from their lack of members, she wasn't the only one. She wasn't the typical Preservation Society recruit—what with her being decades younger and averse to tweed—but if the society were the thing that linked the five circled names, she'd give it a go. Their website promised that 'anyone who cares about preserving the village's history is welcome to attend any meeting.' Unless there was some secret initiation on entry, she could fake her way through one meeting for some answers.

Leaving her car, Jessie pushed through the creaky church gate and headed to the village hall next door. The church had been preserved for centuries. The ugly hall had been added in the 1970s. She peered through the window, and there they were—the five circled names in the flesh. Not bad for her first day on their scent. Her hand hovered over the door handle. For a moment, she considered pushing it open and stepping inside, feigning interest in village preservation as she'd planned. But sensing she was about to walk into a war zone, she faltered and waited for someone to make a move.

Prunella Thompson sat still as stone in a chair at a table in the centre. Beside her, Alice Adams seemed flustered, wringing her hands. Martin Green paced, running a hand through his curly mop of grey hair. Richard Hughes's craggy face was twisted in a scowl, perched on the edge of the stage at the far side. And in their midst stood Peter McBride, face red, clutching a leather briefcase to his tweed-clad chest.

"I'm telling you all, this *is* a mistake," Peter implored, his voice strained. "If we go through with these plans, we risk losing the very essence of Peridale. The eighteenth-century bridge alone is a testament to our history."

Jessie's ears perked up, her hand dropping from the handle.

"That bridge hasn't been a safe footpath for decades." Martin threw up his hands in exasperation. "Peter, please, we've been over this countless times. The decision has been made."

"Well, I believe it should be *unmade*, for the good

of the village," Peter replied. "If *we* allow this first phase to go ahead, you know as well as I do that there'll be little to preserve. They won't stop with that field."

Jessie glanced over her shoulder towards the café, not that she could see it through the thick fog. She looked back as Richard kicked away from the stage.

"You always were a sentimental fool," Richard said. "There comes a time for sacrifice, for everyone. I gave up my livelihood so Henderson Place could have road access, and you don't hear me whinging about it."

"You were paid handsomely to hand over your farm," Peter fired back. "And Riverswick lost half of Henderson Vale in the process for that monstrosity of a housing estate to be built. They made no attempt to be sensitive to our traditions, which is why I voted against it. All those trees... all that history. Is that what you want for us?"

"We all agree, change is difficult," Martin said, his voice the kind of forced calm that made Jessie's feet itch. "But it's not as though we're not surrounded by plenty of trees and history and bridges. Think of what there is to gain."

"Money talks, Peter," Richard said. "Best remember that and temper your foolishness."

"My dedication to preserving Peridale's heritage

and future is not foolishness," Peter shot back, "but it seems I'm alone in that now."

"Please, calm yourself," Prunella said, her tone kind but firm. "I detest seeing you worked up like this. We don't want a repeat of last year, do we?"

"Oh, I see," Peter backed away, clutching the briefcase tighter. "That's how you all think of me now. You think my senses have permanently taken leave of me?" He stared around the room, but no one made eye contact. "I *was* being harassed. I *was* being followed. I didn't imagine it. I didn't make it up. And… it's happening again."

A collective groan rippled around the room.

"Peter," Martin said, pinching the bridge of his nose, "have you stopped taking your medication again? You know how you get."

"I'm *not* cracked," he cried, backing away to the door. "Not now, not then. You believe me, don't you, Prunella?"

"Peter, I…" She sighed, her head dropping. "Perhaps you're becoming overwhelmed again."

Shaking his head, Peter continued backing up to the door; their avoidance of looking at him was painful for Jessie to witness. She ducked out of the way and pinned herself against the pebble-dashed wall of the village hall in time for Peter to burst out into the night. She watched him vanish, and a few moments later, Prunella emerged, squinting off into the fog. After a moment's consideration, she set off, sighing as she went. When no more emerged, Jessie returned to the window.

"We could have handled that better," Alice said as she tossed a scarf around herself. "Peter may have a point. I know we've all made our choices, but... what if we *are* doing the wrong thing?"

Richard spat out a harsh laugh as he tapped away on his phone. "You're sounding as daft as Peter now. Don't go soft on us." The phone went to his ear. "Greg? It's me. You were right; we do need to find a new leader for the society straightaway... Yes... Of course, I understand."

"So," Martin sucked the air through his teeth, "which of us shall it be?"

"Does it matter?" Richard shrugged. "Peter was the only loose cannon. The vote will still go our way without him. We should set off. We don't want to miss the party."

A sudden tap on her shoulder made Jessie's heart jump. She turned, half-expecting to see Prunella or Peter's familiar faces. Instead, she found Dante Clarke from the *Riverswick Chronicle* grinning at her.

"Didn't mean to spook you," he said, flashing a mischievous smile. "I'm guessing you were sent the same email. Looks like you connected the dots a little quicker than—"

Without a word, Jessie grabbed Dante's arm and pulled him behind a large bush as Richard, Martin, and Alice emerged from the building, lost in their continuing discussion. Crouching low to stay hidden, their faces drew so close that Jessie could feel the warmth of Dante's breath on her cheek. The scent of recently drunk coffee mingled with the woodsy notes of his aftershave, sending a pleasantly unsettling flutter through her stomach.

Once the trio had moved out of earshot, Jessie released her breath and stepped back, breaking the charged atmosphere.

"You missed the show," she said.

Dante brushed a leaf off his shirt. "Fill me in?"

"What's it worth?"

An amused smile perked up his soft, handsome features. "I see how it is."

"It's good intel."

"I appreciate the hustle." His tongue ran across his lips. Glancing around, he leaned in. "Know where Greg is lying low?"

"Do you?"

"Seems we have a fair exchange on our hands. You going to the Halloween party?"

"Wouldn't miss it for anything."

"Then I'll see you there," he said, backing off into the fog with a swagger. He tripped over the ledge in the wonky paving stones, catching himself before a fall. "I meant to do that."

"Sure," Jessie said with a wink. "I'll see you there."

They parted ways outside the church, and Jessie drove the short distance around the green to her flat above the post office next to the café. Before she headed upstairs, she spotted Peter sitting at the window table in Richie's Bar, glaring out at the misty green. His briefcase was still clutched to his chest. She considered going to join him when James Jacobson walked over and set a drink down in front of him before taking a seat.

Jessie still wasn't sure what was happening in Peridale, but she knew following those circled names had been the right move. Unless there were multiple Gregs in Peridale with interests in local planning, she'd uncovered that he was in bed with the Preservation Society, and now, with James cosying up to Peter, she'd found herself on exactly the right track.

The fireworks had started, and something told her the show would continue at the Halloween party. She ran up the stairs to her flat, eager to get ready.

5

Having spent the week dodging the invitation while listening to her café regulars' excitement for the party, Julia reluctantly crossed the threshold of the Peridale library. The once-quiet space had morphed into a lively party hub. Cobwebs clung to bookshelves as if spun by literary spiders; carved pumpkins flashed their toothy grins from every nook; a dance floor pulsated with colourful lights, beckoning the costumed crowd to its centre.

"Would hardly recognise the place," Barker commented beside her. "Or us, for that matter."

Julia caught their reflection in a nearby window—two ghosts fashioned from white bed sheets accompanied by a giant pumpkin. Olivia wobbled between them, her tiny feet almost tripping in the round foam costume. Her head and arms, the only parts visible from the orange foam, bobbed with each step, mirroring her wide-eyed wonder at the festive chaos around her.

Julia and Barker exchanged glances through their cut-out eyeholes, silently agreeing that their last-minute costumes were the perfect disguise for blending in.

As they navigated through the supernatural zoo, Julia's eyes darted from one elaborate costume to the next, realising they weren't the only ones who would be difficult to spot. Near an extravagant buffet table, Evelyn from the bed and breakfast commanded a small crowd, her vibrating hands suspended over a glowing crystal ball. Dressed in her signature turban and kaftan combination—blood-red for the occasion—she was a beacon of familiarity in a sea of ghoulish decay, vampires swathed in lush velvet, and furry werewolves alongside hook-nosed witches. If Peter McBride was among this masquerade, spotting him would be like finding a needle in a haystack.

By the punch bowl, a zombie nurse with realistic wounds waved to Olivia. It took a moment for Julia to recognise Sue behind the grey and white face paint.

Beside her, a human-sized worm helped itself to a bowl of orange punch.

"Bookworm?" Julia asked.

"Precisely!" the voice of Neil, Sue's husband and the manager of the library, came from the pink-painted face poking out of the foam. "See, Sue. I told you people would get it. Sheets... classic."

"Lazy, more like," Sue said, tugging at Julia's eyehole. "Glad you changed your mind. I knew you would. Great, isn't it?"

"Impressive budget," Barker observed, accepting a bowl of punch from the worm. "That light-up dance floor can't have come cheap."

Neil grinned. "Let's just say when you have a generous co-owner, the cheques turn up blank, and the sky is the limit."

Barker nodded as he pulled the punch through his armhole to sip it under the sheet. Julia accepted a cup from Sue and did the same, watching Barker assess Neil. She could already hear the words on the tip of her husband's tongue.

"So, James has held to his word then?" Barker asked, his forced-casual tone anything but. "No utterings of him trying to turn this place into a restaurant again?"

"None," Neil said, smiling around the room and

exhaling. "After everything he put us through, turns out he's a great guy."

"How times change, eh?" Barker said, forcing a laugh. "The man almost redeveloped you out of a job."

"Yes, well, we've moved past that," Neil replied evenly. "All's well that ends well, right?"

"Right," Barker muttered.

Even through the grey zombie make-up, Julia could see that her sister was uncomfortable with the direction of the conversation as she sipped her punch. When it came to discussions of James Jacobson in the café, Sue's backside must have been marred with splinters from how she balanced on the fence. Before she was dragged into the conversation, she took Olivia off to find her cousins on the dance floor. Julia promised that she'd be right behind, but she had questions of her own for Neil.

"Don't suppose you know a Peter McBride?"

"That Peridale Preservation Society fella?" Neil nodded. "They have meetings here sometimes. I think I saw him earlier."

Julia scanned the thick crowd, but the nervous face of Peter didn't jump out at her.

"He came to see me yesterday," Julia admitted, sipping the punch. "Seemed to want to warn me about something." She paused to investigate the bright orange liquid. Orange sherbet, pineapple juice, and would have tasted tropical if not for the hint of ginger. "I think it was about what James has planned for the field behind my café. Do you—"

"Can we just drop the James topic?" Forcing a laugh, Neil turned to top up his punch. "Like I said, all in the past. It's a party, Julia, so try to enjoy yourself. Eat some food, have a little dance, wander around the haunted maze. Built the whole thing myself around the bookshelves. Can get dark in places, so watch your step."

Neil headed off to mingle, and Barker said, "That's one worm with his head buried deep in the mud."

Julia wasn't sure she could blame her brother-in-law. Nobody had been affected by the fight for the library more than Neil. The place had been dying long before James tried to absorb it into his property portfolio. His change of heart and promise of lifetime investment had breathed a second lease of life into the library *and* the manager who'd worked there since his teen years. And a second lease of life the place had. Julia had never seen as many people in the building since Barker's first novel signing, which'd had a marketing push akin to the flyers and newspaper ads Julia had been seeing for the party all of October.

She peered towards the line snaking through the ivy-arched entrance of the haunted maze. Delighted screams echoed out from between the sheet-covered bookcases. She noticed on a familiar tweed jacket cutting through the line before weaving into the crowd surrounding the flashing dance floor. Was it someone dressed in an uncanny Peridale Preservation leader costume, or...

"Hold my punch," Julia said, yanking up her sheet to thrust the cup at Barker. "I'll be right back."

Julia wove the same path towards the dance floor as the man in tweed rushed through the flashing lights. He almost tripped over Olivia's pumpkin as she jumped around with Pearl and Dottie in their Winnie and Piglet costumes. Julia continued across the dance floor after him, dodging elbows and clawed hands as people danced to 'Thriller' with reckless abandon.

At the library's back door, which led out to a small walled-in courtyard lit by twinkling string lights and used as a makeshift smoking area, the man in tweed looked back, confirming Julia's suspicions.

Peter McBride.

He rushed through a cloud of smoke to a woman waiting in a pointed witch hat. His hand went straight to her shoulder; the witch's back was to Julia. Her old school friend, Roxy Carter, and Roxy's girlfriend, Detective Inspector Laura Moyes, were laughing to themselves about something as they passed a vape device between them. Neither had bothered with a costume, apart from ringing their eyes with liner and back combing their hair a little. Any other day, Julia would have tugged away her sheet and joined them for a chat. Instead, she perched on a tree stump as close to Peter and the mysterious witch as she dared, exhaling and staring up at the sliver of the moon as though she were there to catch her breath.

"... I promise, *he* has it!" Peter was saying. "After all these years, all our searching—"

"You're sure it's *the* painting?" the woman whispered. "It could be a fake."

"I saw it," Peter grinned, unable to hide his excitement. "I assure you, it's real."

"Do you have it?" the witch asked.

Peter sighed. "Not yet. But I will."

The witch nodded, and after a pause, said, "Have you changed your mind about the vote?"

"I'll never vote 'yes' at that committee meeting, but it won't get to that," Peter whispered, his grin stretching. "I think it's time I expose the whole rotten plan."

The witch patted his shoulder. "You're playing a dangerous game, but I respect your bravery. Keep me in the loop?"

"Of course," Peter agreed with a nod, scanning the small courtyard as a group of teenagers burst out from the party. "I need to go. I... I think I was followed here."

"Stay safe, old friend."

Peter hurried inside, and without taking a moment to think about it, Julia pushed off the tree stump and followed him into the party. She patted his shoulder, and he spun around, his eyes wide behind his glasses, his skin a glassy sheen.

"It's Julia... from the café?" She raised the sheet just enough to give him a glimpse of her face. "I waited for you at Howarth House."

"I apologise, Julia, but I should never have involved you. Try not to worry."

"Because you're about to 'expose the rotten plan?'" Julia quoted him, and he blinked in surprise. "I just overheard you talking to your witch friend. What painting were you talking about?"

"Forget you heard anything," he whispered, gripping her arm with tight nails. His eyes widened as he leaned in. "Heed my warning, Julia. They'll come after you next if you try to step in their way."

"Who?"

Peter scanned the party, his fingers unclasping from Julia's arms. Before Julia could respond, he ducked into the crowd. She darted after him, but a foot on the back of her sheet tripped her into a circle of dancing witches. A pair of arms caught her as the sheet ripped off her head, and one of the witches grinned down at her.

"Steady on your feet, Julia," the voice belonged to Shilpa from the post office. "One too many glasses of punch, eh?"

"Exactly." Julia laughed along with her as she searched for the culprit who'd stepped on her costume. They hadn't stuck around to claim responsibility. Shilpa scooped up the bedsheet and shook it out. "Thank you."

"I'm glad I *literally* caught you. I was hoping to talk to you about something," Shilpa said, nodding to the courtyard. "Could use some fresh air after all this dancing if you fancy a breather?"

"I was just on my way to the bathroom," Julia lied, twisting the sheet around her hair until the holes lined up with her eyes. "I'll come and find you?"

"Absolutely. Great party, don't you think?"

"The best."

Leaving Shilpa to continue dancing with her coven, Julia set off in the direction she'd seen Peter run off, but the needle had vanished back into the haystack.

Across the pulsating dance floor, the flashing lights and relentless beats were wearing thin for Barker. Having twirled Olivia and the twins through a few high-energy numbers, his stamina waned. Leaving the girls with Sue, he excused himself and cut to the buffet, where Neil—unmissable in his worm costume—loomed over a tray of devilled eggs transformed into giant spiders. His eyes, however, were fixed on the ever-expanding wall of memories.

Each photograph captured a snapshot of villagers enjoying the library over the years. Conceived during the height of the protests during the library's impending closure, the memory wall served as a poignant homage to the institution's enduring role in village life. He found a picture of Julia in her teenage years, buried in exam revision with her school friends. A more recent addition right next to it showed Julia and Barker there with Olivia during one of Neil's story hours.

"I'm glad these pictures found a place post-Jacobson," Barker said, snagging an empty paper plate from the pile. "Reminds you what's important, don't you think?"

Neil's moves on the dance floor had taken a toll, and his pink make-up had dissolved in patches, revealing his underlying irritation. "Enjoying the party, Barker?"

"I'm having a great time."

Barker picked up some sandwiches shaped like witches' fingers but couldn't seem to stop himself. In a village where nobody could claim to know James well, Neil was one of the few with a window into the elusive man's life. He set down his plate and pulled his phone from his jeans underneath the sheet.

"James came by my office today," he said, and Neil sighed. "Swore up and down that he has yet to make plans for that field behind the café. Didn't take much digging for me to find proposal after proposal to the council. What do you make of it?"

Barker thrust his phone into Neil's hand before he could pick up one of the devilled eggs. Neil grumbled in his throat, but he was too much of a mild-mannered man to not look. His brows furrowed as he scrolled through the endless applications but he didn't seem as concerned as Barker had been when he'd stumbled upon them on the council's website.

"He probably just wants to keep his options open?" Neil suggested, handing the phone back. "People can change, Barker. Look how he saved this place. And don't forget, without him, Katie and Brian would have been dragged under by Wellington Manor."

"It almost ended badly," he said. "As bad as it turned out at Fern Moore when he threw money behind that murderer. And everything that happened with the Knight family, and—"

Neil shook his head. He wasn't taking it in as Barker had hoped. "But it didn't end badly. The library's thriving. Your in-laws are back on their feet. You've got to let this go, Barker. If you're so suspicious, ask the man yourself."

Neil gestured across the pulsating dance floor. Through the revellers, Barker could make out James through the smoke, impeccably dressed as always in one of his fine suits. No costume for the official host, though Neil had been the one networking all night. Barker had kept his eyes peeled for James; he must have been a recent arrival and was deep in conversation with someone draped in a dark, hooded cloak, their face hidden.

"I'm not your flying monkey when it comes to James," Neil said, adding more food to his plate. "Whatever you're up to, just leave me out of it."

Neil continued down the buffet, and Barker sighed, realising no progress had been made. He'd hoped to have Neil as an ally, or at least an informant, given they were married into the same family. But his brother-in-law had made it clear where his loyalties lay.

Weaving his way across the dance floor, Barker moved towards James and his mysterious, cloaked companion. But two familiar faces swooped in before he could reach them, cutting off his path.

"Mr Jacobson!" Dot cried, an accusatory finger outstretched. She looked almost like herself, with a jacket over her usual high-collared white shirt. "I've been looking for you since I arrived."

"Now, dear, let's not cause a scene," Percy urged, hot on her heels. Like Dot, he looked almost like himself—short and bald in a funny bow tie—but he'd also donned a jacket. Unlike Dot, he'd also stuck on a twirled moustache. "We haven't tried the punch yet."

"Up to your old tricks again, I'd bet?" Dot demanded. "What do you have to say for yourself?"

The man in the cloak let the crowd swallow him up as James turned to face Dot and Percy, whose costumes Barker still couldn't figure out as he watched from the side-lines, hidden in his sheet.

"Dot, how *lovely* to see you again," James said, his grin unwavering. "Almost didn't recognise you without a megaphone glued to your lips."

"I *asked* you a question. What are you up to?"

He chuckled. "Attending my party? But it's nice to know you haven't changed. Always shouting about something. One too many glasses of sherry?"

"Excuse you!" Dot huffed. "Don't think I didn't see you earlier, up to no good on the green, looking at plans with those men. If you think that I—"

"If you'll excuse me," he said, giving a slight bow after a peek at his watch. "As always, a pleasure."

James slipped away into the crowd, and it took Percy holding Dot back for her not to follow after him.

"That's quite enough excitement for one night, don't you think, dear? We don't want to get thrown out before we've tried the—"

"We're not here for the punch, Percy!"

Before an argument erupted between the married couple, Barker stepped out from under his ghost disguise, and Dot's eyes narrowed at the sight of him.

"You came," she said, looking around. "Does that mean Julia's here…"

Dot's gaze tapered on something across the room. Barker thought she might have found a matching ghost, but he followed her line of sight to a woman in a costume resembling Dot's. The costume made sense on someone else.

"Oh, you're Miss Marple," Barker said, clicking his fingers together.

"Well observed." Dot's narrowed gaze didn't shift. "And so is that blasted copycat, Ethel White! That woman hasn't had an original thought in her life. I'm going to give her a piece of my mind."

Dot marched off, leaving Percy to push down his moustache against his upper lip as it started to spring free.

"My little grey cells tell me there'll be blood on the dance floor if I let those two battle it out."

Percy, who must have been Poirot, scurried off after the duelling Miss Marples, leaving Barker to pull his sheet back down. He scanned the room again for the man of the hour. Being one of the tallest and few not in a costume, James wasn't difficult to spot now that Barker knew he was in attendance. James glanced over his shoulder before he ducked under the ivy arch and into the darkness of the haunted maze.

Tugging the eyeholes into the right place, Barker swept in after him.

∽

Jessie hadn't intended to be fashionably late. Sculpting her spiked mohawk had taken longer than she'd expected—and more hairspray than she'd ever used. She slammed the car door behind her and shrugged into the studded leather jacket she'd found in the second-hand shop on Mulberry Lane. It was the coolest jacket she'd ever worn, but it did little to ward off the misty chill, and her frayed shorts over fishnet stockings offered even less cover.

As she approached the entrance, she spotted Dante, cosier in his head-to-toe Black Panther superhero ensemble. She noticed his eyes light up when he recognised the shivering zombie punk approaching him. She didn't mean to stare at how the suit clung to his body, but the guy must have worked out.

"Here to shake things up, punk?" he said with a wink. "You took your time."

"Please tell me you haven't been waiting outside for me."

Dante shrugged. "Gave me a chance to scope out the guest list. The whole Preservation Society crew is here. And James, of course. You want my cape? Your knees are knocking together."

"I'm good. Wouldn't want to ruin your look." Jessie glanced into the library, music and lights flashing in the high windows. "Shall we?"

Dante moved to open the door for her, but Jessie pushed through before he had a chance. The inside warmth wrapped around her with the music. She'd been expecting something grand, but she could barely see the library under the trimmings.

"So, you gonna share that intel you promised on Greg Morgan?"

"Straight to business?" Dante half-walked, half-danced by her side as she moved into the party. He had rhythm and he didn't mind looking a little silly showing it off. "Let's at least have a drink first. Reckon the punch bowl has been spiked yet?"

"Let's hope so."

"Ah, not *all* business then." He laughed, scooping the violent orange liquid into two plastic cups. He took a sip. "Seems tame. Shall I spice it up?"

With a roguish wink, he produced a small silver flask from a hidden pocket in his costume and added a splash of amber liquid to their cups as they left the buffet table behind. It looked like people had been picking at it all night, but there was more food than she'd seen at any buffet. She still couldn't believe Julia had turned down the offer to cater, but that's what Jessie loved about her mum. If she believed in something, she really believed.

"Greg Morgan," Dante started after a sharp sip. "As far as I can tell, the last time he was seen in any professional capacity was at that hospital press conference when you confronted him. Right before your big article dropped." Admiration flashed in his eyes. "That took guts, by the way. My editor would have never let that go to print. Mad respect to you and Veronica. How is my old English teacher doing?"

"Knowing her, she's probably at the office. And I'd say it was a medium article. Couldn't even name him. Maybe if I had, it would have made a difference."

"And you'd have been sued."

"You sound like Veronica." Jessie sipped the punch as she scanned the crowd. A ghost in a white sheet waved in her direction. "So, no sign of Greasy Greg since?"

"No, but a little birdie told me he's been spotted hiding in a luxury apartment. Three guesses where..."

"Well, it's not Fern Moore," she said, tapping a mocking finger on her chin. "Wellington Heights, and why am I not surprised? Trust Greg to be hiding out in one of James' properties. Know which flat?"

Dante shook his head. "Only seen a picture of him answering the door to the postman. Looks rough, though. I think you knocked him down a peg or two."

"Good. Still needs a couple more pegs for my liking."

The ghost in the white sheet waved again; this time, Jessie was sure it was directed at her. She waved back uncertainly, wondering who was hidden in the costume. Before she could investigate further, Dante's hand on her shoulder stopped her.

"Ah, ah, *ah!*" he tutted. "Don't punk out on me. We had a deal, remember? Some solid intel in exchange for the inside scoop on that Preservation Society meeting you snooped on."

"A deal's a deal." She relayed all she had overheard during the tense meeting between the five core members. Dante listened, his frown deepening. "There's no doubt about it. Greg has his claws sunk into the Preservation Society, and their members make up a good chunk of that committee meeting."

"Definite corruption there," he said finally. "Bribery, blackmail? Something ugly must be going on behind the scenes."

"But their leader wasn't playing along," Jessie added. "Not that he'll hold that position for much longer. They're ready to oust him."

"Seems like you should get yourself an interview with Peter McBride as soon as possible, but enough business for one night." Dante swirled the drink in his cup, his brows darting up and down. "Fancy taking a few wrong turns in the maze?"

"A maze?" Jessie sighed. "Seriously?"

"It's a party, Jessie," he said, backing up to an ivy arch and beckoning with a tempting hand. "All work and no play, and you'll turn into Veronica."

Despite herself, the *Chronicle* journalist intrigued her enough to take his hand with a playful roll of her eyes. The arch swallowed them up, and beyond it, the library had morphed into a twisting labyrinth. Gone were the familiar spines of the books, now shrouded by dark, oppressive sheets that rose in suffocating walls.

Scattered lanterns cast wavering lights, creating a dance of flickering silhouettes that seemed to lurk just out of sight. From the darkened corridors, automated ghouls sprang to life, their ghostly whispers intertwining with the faint sounds of distant laughter and echoed screams. Dante twitched and jumped by her side; yet Jessie walked with an assured stride, eyes alert but unperturbed—even as a tattered zombie bride emerged from the gloom, her decayed lace brushing against their path.

"You don't scare easily, do you, punk?"

Jessie shrugged, sidestepping a plastic skeleton dangling from the ceiling. "When you've lived through the real thing, cheap tricks don't do much."

"Living on the streets, you mean?" he asked, before quickly adding, "Sorry, I shouldn't have gone there."

"It's fine."

"I just want to get to know you more."

"I said, it's fine, Dante." Jessie reached out to let her fingers trail over the black sheets as they walked. "Sleeping rough can be terrifying. I found a community towards the end, but I was on my own at first. That was scarier than any haunted maze."

"Damn. I don't know how you did it."

"Didn't have much choice," she said with a shrug. "Just had to survive. It was that or another bad foster home to get kicked out of. But now I have somewhere I call home. Somewhere I want to protect."

Jessie couldn't resist work, not when a the

committee meeting timer was ticking in the back of her mind.

"You think James' big plan is to develop something like Riverswick's Henderson Place? All rushed, shoddy work that starts crumbling the minute the last lick of paint dries?"

Dante blew out a long breath, the foggy air swirling around him. "For Peridale's sake, I hope not. We get emails and letters every week from residents who feel abandoned. It's tragic. And a bloody eyesore. All that red brick? It's not like we don't have golden Cotswold stone quarries still operational, but they chose cheap. I don't know how it was ever approved." He paused and caught himself. "Wait, of course I do. You throw money at Greg, and he catches it. It's that simple."

"If only we had enough money to throw at him to make him go away."

They had reached a fork in the maze pathway. Voices echoed from both directions, but Jessie chose the path to the left on instinct. The bookcases narrowed, forcing Dante and Jessie closer. She tried to place where they were in the library, but she'd lost all sense of the place. Even the pounding music seemed miles in the distance now.

Beside her, Dante cleared his throat. "You know, I was glad to run into you today. After that conference at the hospital, I'd hoped maybe you'd want to, you know… call or text. You owe me that drink, after all."

Jessie stared ahead. "I think my exact words were, 'I'll think about it.'"

"And did you?"

She had, but she hadn't had much time between working at the café and digging into the Greg and James case. Maybe she *was* turning into Veronica.

"We're having a drink now, aren't we?" she said.

"Good point." He toasted his cup to hers. "Maybe when we get out of this maze, we can—"

An animatronic skeleton leapt out right next to them with an electronic cackle. Dante jumped, his toasting cup colliding with hers and spilling the spiked punch all over her punk costume.

"Jessie, I'm so…"

Laughing, Jessie took his cup from him and sloshed the remainder of his drink onto his chest.

"There. Now we're even."

The punch soaked into the material, outlining the defined muscles beneath. Jessie found her gaze lingering once more. Dante huffed out a laugh as he ran his hands along his chest. When he lifted his head, Jessie realised how close they were standing in the narrow pathway. The humour in his eyes shifted into something more heated. He leaned in slowly.

Pumpkins and Peril

Jessie's breath caught, her heart kicking faster beneath her sodden costume.

Before anything happened, two children in matching astronaut suits raced around the corner, forcing Dante and Jessie to spring apart. Jessie joined Dante's rueful laughter, willing her flushed cheeks to cool.

"Come on, this way," she said, choosing the opposite direction from the astronauts. "Let's get out of here. I'm bored of the cheap scares."

They walked in a charged silence, their easy conversation left behind in the last corridor. What would have happened if those kids hadn't torn them apart? Would they have kissed? Would she have wanted to? Clenching her eyes, she was glad her warm cheeks were hidden behind her vibrant pink and orange blush.

Jessie opened her eyes, wondering if they should talk about what almost happened, but she stopped in her tracks. Dante bumped into her, and she stumbled forward, her foot landing in a patch of something wet and sticky.

Up ahead, a body lay on the ground, an axe protruding from between their shoulder blades.

"Reckon that's part of the maze?" Dante asked. "We must be near the exit."

Dread sat heavy in her gut, wishing she could have

been as oblivious as Dante at that moment. She lifted her Doc Marten and dabbed at the side of her boot. Rubbing her fingers together, an unmistakable coppery scent filled her nose.

Blood.

"I don't think this is part of the maze," Jessie said.

6

The pounding bass of the Halloween party throbbed through the shadowy walls of the library's maze as Julia stood at a fork in the road. She had no idea where to turn; she was sure she'd seen that plastic skeleton hanging from the ceiling twice already.

Rounding a corner, she collided with a huddle of costumed figures murmuring in the darkness. She recognised Barker's voice instantly, even through the sheet pulled over his face. Beside him stood Dot and her rival, Ethel White, dressed as Miss Marple, deep in their usual bickering. Percy, as Poirot, trailed behind, holding a moustache to his face that didn't seem to want to stick for more than a couple of seconds at a time.

"Barker, you have a copycat too," Dot exclaimed.

"For the *final* time, Dorothy," Ethel snapped, elbowing past her. "I didn't copy you! *You* copied *me*."

"Of course, you didn't. Just like you didn't follow me into this maze."

"*You* followed *me* into this maze," Barker muttered, pulling off the sheet. "Julia, please tell me that's you under there."

Julia joined him in unveiling herself, and they shared a sigh of relief. She didn't know how long she'd been wandering around the maze, but she'd started to doubt she'd ever see a familiar face again.

"I followed James in here," Barker said, looking around. "Seen him?"

"I haven't seen many people," she admitted. "I followed Peter in here."

"Onwards, I say!" Percy exclaimed, charging ahead with the two Marples fighting for second place behind him. "I'm sure we've come down this tunnel twice already."

Julia wrapped her hand around Barker's and the group crept deeper into the shadowy maze. Distant shrieks and eerie sound effects echoed through the passages, but she remained focused on the mission at hand, keeping her ears strained for any hint of Peter or James up ahead.

"I need to tell you something," Barker whispered,

squeezing her hand. "I found some stuff online. I wanted to tell you, but I didn't want to scare you before I knew the details."

Julia's stomach lurched.

"Details about what?"

"That field behind your café," he said. "I'd say the chances are slim to none that James is going to leave it as it is."

Rounding the next bend, they almost banged into the back of Dot and Ethel, who were held back by Percy's outstretched arms. Up ahead, two crouched figures blocked the path. One was dressed in tattered punk garb with a spiked jacket. The other cut a sleek silhouette in a black costume. As Julia watched, the punk spun around, her spikes almost touching the ceiling.

"Mum?" Jessie croaked. "Dad?"

Jessie's face flooded with relief at the sight of her family. She rushed through the Christie trio to sweep Julia into a tight hug. As they embraced, with the spikes embedded into Julia's shoulders, she peered past her daughter's shoulder, her smile freezing on her lips.

A crumpled form lay on the ground, face-down on the floor. Something long and sinister jutted from the man's back. With a sick lurch in her gut, Julia recognised the tweed jacket and wispy grey hair.

"We just found him lying here like this," Jessie's haunted whisper confirmed Julia's worst fears. "It's Peter McBride. He's... he's dead."

Not too long ago, Julia had been perched on a tree stump listening to Peter talk about finding some painting, ready to expose a 'rotten scheme.' Now, he lay lifeless, bleeding out on the floor of a maze while a party boomed behind them, his secrets dead alongside him.

Dot and Ethel swooped in, magnifying glasses in hand as they scrutinised the scene. Percy crouched to examine the axe lodged in Peter's back, while Barker muttered into his phone.

"My little grey cells tell me he's dead," Percy confirmed before ripping off the moustache.

Ethel tutted. "Honestly, Percy, even an idiot could see..." Her voice trailed off as she focused on a book under his torso. "Would you look at that? My first clue!"

Dot elbowed her aside. "*My* first clue."

After several minutes of them swarming around the dead man like buzzards, their amateur forensics were interrupted by pounding footsteps, followed by a winded, gruff voice.

"Who designed this thing? I... I passed that damn skeleton twice." Detective Inspector Laura Moyes ground to a halt after barrelling around the corner, face flushed from her sprint through the maze. "My favourite family, at the scene of another crime," she said, not bothering to conceal her sarcasm. "I might see if we can hire you as sniffer dogs."

But Julia wasn't in the mood for jokes. As DI Moyes set to work clearing the gawking geriatric gang away from the body, Julia couldn't tear her eyes away from the axe. Peter's desperate pleas for safety and privacy echoed through her mind, his certainty that lives would be at stake if he didn't do something to stop the wheels already in motion.

Given his enthusiasm talking to the unnamed witch in the courtyard, he'd thought his life was safe. Somewhere out there, a killer now roamed free. And Julia feared the worst was yet to come for her beloved village.

"Barker," she whispered. "What if this was James' doing?"

~

The music and flashing lights had been extinguished, leaving an eerie silence hanging over the library. Partygoers, now shedding their costumes, mingled about as police officers took statements under the stark ceiling lights. The children were growing restless, and Barker was glad Olivia had fallen asleep, now free of her pumpkin costume. He handed her to Julia as DI Laura Moyes made a beeline for him.

"Quite a party this turned out to be," Moyes said, her gruff voice as soft and measured as ever. "I'd ask if you're alright, but at this point, this is just another day in Peridale for you."

"I'm glad I'm not the one having to wave a badge around," he said, pulling up two of the chairs scattered around the place. "How's being Peridale's new resident DI treating you? I heard you went on a cruise."

"I needed it after that moon cult mess, which tells you how I'm finding the job." She offered a dry smile as she turned the chair around to straddle it backwards. "Guess you being in that maze wasn't a coincidence?"

"I was following our host, James," he said, his throat parched. The punch had long since run out, and so had James, given his absence. "Julia was looking for Peter. He visited her café yesterday evening, desperate to tell her something but too afraid to fully confide in her. She was supposed to meet him in Howarth Forest today, but he didn't show up. We only came to the party to talk to him."

Moyes sighed and took a drag from her electronic cigarette, ignoring the 'No Smoking,' signs dotted around the walls. "Knowing Julia, she's probably blaming herself. I just spoke with your daughter, and from her recollection, it seems Mr McBride was either losing his marbles or..." She glanced at the ivy arch as forensic officers rushed back and forth. "Given the circumstances, it's safe to say Peter was tangled up in something dangerous."

"Julia said he was paranoid, talking about 'they,' as if 'they' were following him."

"Do you think it could be the Cotswold Crew gang?" Moyes weighed the option with another puff of spicy smoke. "Jessie mentioned her Riverswick reporter friend saw all the members of Peter's society here."

"Julia didn't mention them," he said, spotting Jessie across the room deep in conversation with the lad in the Black Panther costume. "How did Jessie know who they were?"

"She gate-crashed one of their meetings earlier and heard some suspicious things that I'll be looking into. Unless they're among the last few to have their statements taken, none of the members were present when Peter was axed."

"But we don't know how long he was in there before Jessie found him," he pointed out. "They could have slipped out before the alarm was raised."

"Good point, Brown," she said, rubbing her clenched eyes. "I'm going to need another holiday after this. There's been no sight of Jacobson since you saw him going into that maze. Julia seems to think he swung the axe?"

Barker considered whether he agreed with her. It had been his initial gut reaction too, but now that he knew Peter's fellow society members had been in attendance—along with any number of masked people invested in seeing Peter's secrets die with him—he wasn't as confident under the harsh strip lighting.

"Julia overheard him talking to a witch outside about some painting."

"What painting?"

"She doesn't know, but it sounded important. 'He has *the* painting,' Peter said. Then something about a 'rotten plan.'"

"What plan?"

"I don't know," he said, his voice sharper than he'd intended. "I wish I did. I've been digging all weekend and hit a dozen dead ends. If I knew, this would all make a lot more sense. If I did, I could have—"

"Got an axe in your back too?" Moyes ducked to meet his eyes. "I know your family well enough now to know you're not going to let this go, so I won't waste my breath. But it goes without saying that you need to watch your back, Brown. Whatever Peter McBride knew was worth killing for. If you figure it out before I do, I'd hate to see you or your wife become their next targets. Call me if you uncover anything concrete. And if you think 'they' show up, I can have undercover officers on your tail in seconds. You have my number."

DI Moyes' caution sounded as much a threat as it did a warning, but her eyes were filled with nothing but earnest concern. Barker thanked her with a smile and promised they'd catch up at the pub soon. He'd grown to like the village's new DI quite a lot, and not just because she was dating Julia's old school friend. Moyes headed towards Roxy across the library, who was using her schoolteacher skills to keep the restless children distracted with a reading circle.

Barker thanked her, and after an officer confirmed they'd seen the 'punk and the superhero' leave five minutes ago, he headed for the exit with Julia. Holding Olivia tight as they walked to Julia's car outside the darkened Comfy Corner restaurant across the street, his daughter's warmth soothed his unsettled nerves while his mind echoed with the warning Julia had relayed to him.

"Peter said there were those who wanted the plan to proceed at any cost," he reminded her once Olivia was in her car seat and they were driving away. "If that's the case, I don't think you should—"

"Why did Peter come to *me*?" Julia cut him off, her

mind somewhere else. "He knew my name before he met me."

"You've got quite the reputation for solving mysteries."

"If he wanted a mystery solved, he could have hired the village's top PI," she said, turning the corner. "He came to warn me about something, which can only mean one thing: I must be part of this 'rotten plan,' whether I like it or not."

Barker sighed, holding back what he really wanted to say. His warnings would fall on deaf ears. Julia had that look in her eyes, and it wouldn't go away without some answers. She slowed to a crawl as they passed the glowing lavish bungalow buried in the fog, and Barker knew one answer—no matter which angles he looked at the mystery from, all roads led back to their new neighbour, and they had done for quite some time.

~

Jessie climbed the creaky stairs to *The Peridale Post*'s office and found the door unlocked. She discovered Veronica slumped over her desk, asleep on a pile of paperwork. Walking over, Jessie noticed that the documents were pages from Veronica's extensive file on Greg. She lived in that file most days.

His bank records lay splayed open, and a highlighted transfer of £100,000 from Jacobson Holdings Ltd caught Jessie's eye. The reference read 'public-speaking engagement' and was dated from last week.

Jessie sighed, imagining the toll this obsession was taking on Veronica. She placed a gentle hand on her editor's shoulder.

Veronica stirred with a groan as she lifted her head. "What time is it?"

"Just past midnight. I knew you'd be here when you didn't answer your doorbell."

"You were at my cottage at midnight?" Veronica grumbled, dabbing at the damp corners of her mouth. "What if I'd been asleep?"

"It's about our circled five."

"Have you found something?"

"It's Peter," Jessie said, swallowing the lump in her throat. "He's been murdered."

Veronica paled, sitting up straight. "Peter's dead? But how...?"

"Axe through the back at the Halloween party."

Veronica removed her glasses, massaging her temples. "This changes things. Given what you told me earlier, the committee has lost their stick in the mud. We don't have much time." She shuffled the paperwork scattered on her desk, filing it away. "But we can't give up hope yet. Peridale is depending on us, and we have a new front page to make before the printer's run with our cost-of-living piece. I need to know everything that happened at that party."

"Do you think—"

"That my brother came out of hiding to sink an axe into the man kicking up the dust?" Veronica shook her head. "Trust me, that's not his style. Put the kettle on. This is going to be a late one."

7

Heavy rain lashed against the café windows in angry slashes as Julia rolled out the buttery pastry dough against the stainless-steel island. The weather matched the gloom that had settled over Peridale since Peter McBride had been found murdered at the Halloween party a mere twelve hours earlier.

She lined the scratched tart tins with the dough, her thoughts far from pumpkin pie. The axe protruding from Peter's back was etched in her mind, oozing crimson through his tweed jacket in dark stains. She shuddered, forcing the grotesque image away.

The bell above the door jingled, startling Julia from her dark daydreams. She peeked through the beaded curtain to see Barker stomping rainwater off his boots, his trench coat dripping onto the welcome mat.

"What a lovely first morning of November this is turning out to be," he said, pulling down his hood and looking around the empty café. "I was half-expecting to see this place full."

Julia wiped her floured hands on her apron. "I have a feeling it will be once the rain calms down. You saw how many people were at that party last night. They're going to want somewhere to rehash every painful detail until there's nothing left to say." She sighed. "I'm not sure I'm ready to spend the day reliving it."

Barker gave her a sympathetic smile. "You'll handle it like the pro you are. They'll be talking about something else tomorrow."

"I hope you're right." She glanced at the clock; the café had been open for an hour, and she was quietly pleased she hadn't heard the bell before Barker's arrival. "Fancy a coffee while I finish the pies?"

Barker followed her through the beads and into the kitchen. As the coffee brewed, he recounted his morning of dropping Olivia off with Julia's dad before popping his head into Jessie's flat next door.

"She didn't seem like she'd had the best night's sleep," he said. "Made her a coffee and some toast while she filled me in on some details between her yawns. You were right—she has been digging into this story for a while."

Julia's interest piqued as she lined the pastry shells with baking parchment. "Go on."

"One of the newspaper's contacts clued them in about an upcoming planning committee meeting. Seems to regard the fate of James' mystery development for the field."

Julia nearly dropped the parchment. "She kept that to herself?"

"I think she's still processing the information," Barker said, leaning against the counter next to her. "You know how Jessie is—she won't ring alarm bells until she's absolutely sure of the facts. She doesn't want to worry you."

Ironically, Jessie's secrecy seemed to be doing anything but calming Julia's nerves.

"Five names were highlighted on the document," he continued, lowering his voice despite being alone in the café. "Prunella, Alice, Martin, and Richard. All members of the Preservation Society, and they're all on that committee. That's why Moyes told me Jessie crashed their meeting yesterday. She didn't know about Peter coming to see you until I told her."

"'The wrong people have the power,'" Julia remembered aloud. "Peter said that when he was here. I wonder if he was talking about the society members. When's the meeting?"

He hesitated. "Next Friday."

"*Eleven* days?"

"Jessie's determined to expose the corruption on the committee and put a stop to it before it gets that far. She's convinced Greg Morgan is puppeteering the society members to sway the vote with bribes—bribes likely paid for by our new neighbour."

Julia processed this new information as she scooped the pumpkin purée into the waiting shells. Greg Morgan, their local MP who'd been hiding from the public eye, was influencing the planning committee from the shadows? It was underhanded, but after the Knight family harassment, she wouldn't put it past him.

"There's something else." He retrieved a creased envelope with a broken wax seal from his coat pocket, his smile apologetic. "James visited my office on Saturday. He was trying to keep up appearances, acting as though we were best friends. We've been invited to a housewarming party at his new place."

"More secrets?"

"I was always going to tell you," he assured her. "But after Peter's visit and then everything that happened yesterday at the library, it never seemed like the right time. We could go to question him, but I don't think we'll get a straight answer. I tried to ask what he had planned, and he acted as if he had nothing planned. So, I dug into the public records and found something."

First her daughter, now her husband?

"I don't know what he's building," he added quickly. "I think that secret lies with the committee members for now. But James has been submitting planning applications for all sorts of things since the day he bought the field. Jessie said the first application was submitted an hour after the sale, so whatever it is, he's been planning it for a while."

"And Jessie's known about this for a month?" Julia sighed, unable to mask her disappointment. "Am I that fragile, Barker? She could have kept me in the loop."

"You'd have felt more helpless than you already do." He gave her shoulder a reassuring squeeze. "And she certainly doesn't think you're fragile. She looks up to you. But you've seen how she gets when she's working on investigations for the paper. She's laser-focused."

Julia nodded, even as doubts nagged at her. She tried to keep the lines of communication as open and honest with Jessie as she could. Had recent events created a distance she'd failed to notice? She pushed the thoughts aside as she slid the pies into the oven.

There were more pressing matters than her daughter's evasiveness.

"If Jessie's investigating the corruption side of the society," Julia said, taking a steadying breath, "then I'll focus on their relationships with Peter."

"You think they could be suspects?"

"Peter was their leader and against whatever plans are in motion. All the society members were seen entering the party, yet none of them were around when Peter's body was found. If Jessie is right and they're being bribed to sway the vote, James isn't the only one with something to gain by getting Peter out of the way."

Barker took a thoughtful sip of coffee. "Can't argue with your logic, but... I can't help feeling you should take a backseat this time. Like you said last night, it seems as though Peter saw you as part of the plan. If Jessie is focused on the society, I'll focus on James, and you can—"

"Watch on from the café?" Julia arched a brow over her shoulder as she checked on the pumpkin pies. "Not a chance, Barker. You know I can't sit idly by. Peter cared about this village the same way I do. The same way many people do. I have to finish whatever he started."

Barker sighed in resignation. "It was worth a shot.

I wouldn't be a caring husband if I didn't try. Just... be careful."

"You too," she said, crossing the kitchen to open the back door. "Now, if you're investigating James, there's no time like the present."

After Barker took his coffee down to his office, Julia lingered on the back doorstep for a moment, her gaze drifting across the small yard behind her café. The wind sent the gate swinging back and forth in a creaky dance. Beyond it, the thick sheet of relentless rain soaked the empty field, a patch of wild grass that stretched out to the horizon. It was nothing much to look at: somewhere locals had picnics on sunnier days when the village green was filled with tourists; where people walked laps with their dogs; and where Julia stared out after busy days, feet tired from running the café. Untouched nature—that was the point. Now, it was a battleground in a struggle she couldn't fully grasp yet.

With a sigh, she closed the door.

Eleven days to throw a spanner in the works, to unravel whatever web of deceit and corruption had ensnared their village. She wouldn't be a bystander.

The oven pinged, and after cutting off the crust edges and sliding them onto plates, she set the finished pumpkin pies under the glowing spotlights in the revolving display case. They looked perfect, but a sense of melancholy seeped through her. So much had changed since she'd whipped up the purée just a few days ago. She'd baked the pie cases on autopilot, her thoughts as lost in the maze as she had been twelve hours ago.

The bell above the door announced the first official customer of the day. Julia smoothed her apron and forced a cheerful smile, bracing herself for the inevitable questions about the party.

But the woman lingering on the front doorstep wasn't one of Julia's regulars there for gossip and tea. Dressed in an elegant black coat and heels, she carried herself with graceful poise. Her steel-grey hair was arranged in a tidy bun. Behind stylish glasses, her eyes were as sharp as they met Julia's.

"Hello there," she said in a polished voice as she stepped inside, closing her umbrella with precision. Her gaze swept the empty café before settling back on Julia. "Such dreadful weather we're having. I thought I might stop in for a warm drink." She moved closer. "Unless you're otherwise engaged?"

There was an intensity in the woman's stare that felt like more than polite interest.

"Not too busy at the moment," Julia said, gesturing to the deserted room. "Have a seat wherever you'd like."

The woman's smile didn't reach her eyes. "You're too kind. It's Julia, isn't it?"

"That's me," she replied, taking her place behind the counter. "Can I make you some tea? The pumpkin pie is fresh."

"Oh, how... American." She cast a sideways glance at the orange pie spinning in the display case and shook her head. "I'm actually not here for tea. My name is Prunella Thompson."

It was Julia's turn for a scrutinising gaze. Barker had mentioned a 'Prunella' in connection with the secret planning committee.

"You're on the Preservation Society."

"That's correct. Among other things," Prunella said. Her eyes clouded over as she maintained a polite smile. "I've been elected as the interim leader of the society while we figure out our next steps following Peter's untimely demise. I understand you spoke with Peter McBride recently?"

Julia stiffened. Her first customer of the day was there to fish for information, and she'd already labelled Prunella as a suspect. She hadn't yet devised a strategy to infiltrate the society, but fate seemed to be tipping the scales in her favour by delivering its new leader right to her doorstep. Julia would have to choose her words carefully.

"Peter stopped by the café on Saturday," Julia said,

not revealing his reason for being there. "He had some things he wanted to discuss with me."

"I see." Prunella watched her closely. "Did he share anything... noteworthy? Anything peculiar on his mind that might suggest what could have led to his murder?"

Julia met her gaze, resisting the urge to glance away. "He seemed rather preoccupied in general."

"I see." Prunella's stare remained fixed, as if searching for any hint of deception. After a tense moment, she relented with a polite smile. "I can see you're busy, but I'd love to discuss this more with you later." She scribbled an address on a notepad page, tore it out, and passed it to Julia. "Could you meet me at my cottage once your workday has finished? I'm keen to get to the bottom of what happened to my old friend."

You and me both, Julia thought, looking at the address.

"I think I know where this is. I'll be there."

"Then I'll see you later," Prunella said, her eyes settling on the beams like Peter's had. "Eighteenth century. How quaint."

Prunella left the café and hurried around the village green towards the church. As Julia watched from the window, Prunella's voice echoed in her ears.

"Old friend?" she murmured.

The woman dressed as a witch at the party had used the same term to refer to Peter, her face hidden by a pointed hat. Could it have been Prunella? The poised, controlled tone seemed to match.

Drawing away from the window, Julia headed to the counter, searching for a pen and notepad in her apron pocket. She served herself a large slice of pumpkin pie and made a pot of peppermint and liquorice tea. If no one else was going to savour the café's delights, she might as well indulge.

Settling at her preferred table by the counter, she flicked past her notes on Peter and started on a blank page. At the top, she wrote 'Society', followed by the four names Barker had shared. Taking a sip of her tea, she noted down everything she recalled about her conversation with Prunella.

Prunella's invitation hinted at an intent to question Julia regarding Peter's visit. However, Julia was set on using the encounter to gather her own information about the elusive society. With her pen gliding across the page, she began formulating the questions she'd pose to Prunella during their next meeting.

~

Jessie zipped up her jacket against the autumn chill outside the café. She was looking forward to warming up with a coffee while she did some digging into the society, but not here. Not today. She'd expected the café would be busy, but there wasn't an empty chair in the place, and the wall of chatter sounded like a peak-summer Saturday. Julia was behind the counter, her 'everything is absolutely delightful and I don't mind answering five hundred questions an hour' smile glued into place while the gossip swirled.

Jessie almost wanted to save her, but Mondays were *Post* days, and Sue had forgone her day off to weave in and out of tables. Besides, Jessie needed to focus without her mum looking over her shoulder every time she thought Jessie wasn't paying attention. She should probably tell her how reflective the screen was.

She pivoted to Richie's, the closest place to grab a coffee. Before she reached the door, she spotted a familiar figure crouched behind the bins in the alley.

"Dot? I thought you'd be in the café steeping in the gossip."

"I have better things to do," Dot said in a loud whisper. She pointed to the end of the alley where none other than James Jacobson was crouched. To Jessie's surprise, a ginger cat was dancing around his hand with loud purrs. "He's going to snatch that poor thing up and turn it into a pair of slippers. I'd bet my pension on it."

"How long have you been following him?"

"All day. I'm not letting him out of my sight. He'll slip up. Any minute now…"

Jessie suppressed a smile. "You keep up the good fight, Dot. I'll see you later."

She left Dot to her surveillance and slipped into the bar.

Inside, she found her usual booth and settled in with a steaming mug of coffee. The mellow afternoon light filtered through the windows as a Blondie song played softly in the background.

With the warmth of the coffee spreading through her chilled fingers, she watched Richie laughing with customers at the bar, pouring drinks and cracking jokes. He had an easy charm about him, unlike his father, the infamous James Jacobson. Jessie had yet to meet the notorious property developer face-to-face, but everything she'd heard painted him as superficial and self-interested at best.

Richie felt real in a way his father didn't: approachable and genuine, despite his family name. She wondered if it was even worth asking him about James' dealings around the village. Richie seemed to want little to do with the family business, from what she could tell.

Jessie opened her laptop and started her research. She typed each name into a separate search window and scrolled through until something jumped out. Martin Green, the society member who sat on the planning committee as the 'Area of Outstanding Natural Beauty' councillor, caught her eye first. Outside of the society and committee, his social media listed him as an 'environmental scientist.'

On his feed, he'd posted pictures of his 'new house,' so extravagant it made Jessie choke on her coffee. When she'd seen the picture of him on the council website, she'd thought the scruffy-looking guy in his fifties looked like a tree-hugger who only bought second-hand clothes. After a quick reverse-image search, she found the original listing. The two-million-pound 'eco-house' looked more like a luxury resort, complete with solar-panelled roofing, naturally heated pools, and floor-to-ceiling windows overlooking sprawling, rural views of the Cotswolds. At the basement level, which was as big as the house above, Martin could enjoy a home theatre, fully equipped gym, sauna, and wine cellar.

For a man who supposedly cared so deeply about reducing humanity's carbon footprint, Martin's extravagant home seemed a walking contradiction. Jessie wasn't an expert, but the costs associated with building, maintaining, and operating such an immense property must have been astronomical from an environmental-impact perspective.

Doing a deep dive into his professional background, Jessie landed on his personal website, showcasing his environmental consulting firm. Martin offered specialised services to councils and businesses seeking guidance on sustainability practices and environmental-impact assessments. He touted expertise in hot topics like climate-change mitigation and sustainable development. Judging by some of his previous clients, business was booming.

Jessie dashed off a text to Veronica, summarising her findings:

JESSIE

> Found records of Martin Green consulting for Wellington Heights and that Henderson Place development in Riverswick. Serious £££ with James and Greg. No wonder he can afford that ridiculous 'eco-mansion.' Think he'd take a bribe?

VERONICA

> If he's in bed with Greg and James, you can bet on it. Greg steps on anyone to get his way—nature included. Henderson Place was as sustainable as an umbrella made from candy floss. Keep digging...

Before Jessie could reply, the bar door opened, and she glanced up. Dante strolled in—a bit rumpled, but still unfairly good-looking, as always. He slid into the booth across from her, dropping his satchel onto the table.

"Sorry I'm late. Got held up on a story." He ran a hand through his tight, dark-curls and rubbed his eyes.

Jessie reviewed him with a tilt of her head. His shoulders sagged under his wrinkled t-shirt, and his trademark easy smile seemed dimmer than usual.

"You okay?" she asked. "You seem off."

"I'm good. Just busy with work."

Jessie levelled him with a knowing look. "You don't have to do that with me. Drop the mask, Dante."

He dropped the smile and sighed, leaning forward on his elbows. "Yeah, you're right. I'm still pretty shaken up. Not gonna lie. I know it's part of the job, but... I've never seen a dead body before."

His honesty resonated with Jessie. She'd built up her own tough exterior when it came to the grim realities of life, but she couldn't expect the rest of the world to be as hardened as she was.

"Stuff like that isn't supposed to be easy," she said, matter-of-factly. "You'll be fine, and if you're not, I'll help you through it."

Her attempt at reassurance seemed to put him at ease, though a tinge of awkwardness still lingered—residual tension from their near-kiss? She wondered if they'd ever acknowledge it or if it had even happened. Maybe she'd misread the moment? She hadn't given it much thought, but now that they were face-to-face, it was her only thought. But work beckoned, and Jessie didn't have time to dissect mixed signals. Not with the crucial planning meeting looming.

Richie chose that moment to swing by their table, setting down a basket of chips.

"On the house," he said with a dimpled grin. "You two have fun scheming."

"Thanks, mate," Jessie replied. Once he'd returned to the bar, she nudged the basket towards Dante. "Here. You look like you could use these."

Dante gave her a grateful smile and grabbed a chips. Jessie followed suit as she recapped her research on Martin so far. Dante listened intently while steadily depleting the chips, clearly comforted by having food in his system.

"So, Martin's living the high life on James' payroll," Dante mused, chin resting on his fist. "And Richard used to own a farm over in Riverswick. Sold it to the developers of Henderson Place. Found some sketchy stuff there. The farm was worth a third of what he was paid for it. Looks like a bribe disguised as a property sale to me, but good luck proving it with all that legit paperwork."

"Proof and Greg Morgan don't really go together,

do they?" she muttered, sipping her coffee. "Always hiding behind something or someone."

"I've heard James has been consulting with the same shoddy construction company behind Henderson Place," Dante offered. He rifled through his leather satchel and pulled out a bulging manila folder overflowing with papers. "Cut every corner possible. Churns out shabby work as fast as they can. We get complaints sent into the *Chronicle* several times a week."

"My Auntie Sue lives there," Jessie said as she flipped through page after page of water damage, electrical shorts, and cracked foundations. "I'll ask her how her place is."

"After Henderson Place got shoved through planning, Greg must've seen it as confirmation of what he could make happen for the right price. Rumour has it he took huge bribes from Phil Henderson. But with Henderson dying during those allotment murders, Greg was lucky to slink away."

"And now he's got a new developer in James to buddy up to," Jessie said bitterly, passing the bulging folder back to Dante. "Ready to build something shoddy in Peridale."

Dante nodded, sliding the complaints back into his bag. "I might see if I can get an interview with James to get his side of the story." Before Jessie could respond, Dante's phone buzzed. He checked it and sighed, shoulders slumping. "Well, duty calls. Need to cover a sponsored knit-a-thon over at the nursing home."

"Riveting stuff."

"Only the hard-hitting stories for me." He winked as he stood, hoisting his bag over his shoulder. "You're lucky Veronica lets you loose on the real stuff."

"The glamorous life of an investigative journalist, right?"

"See you around?"

"Not if I see you first."

Dante flashed her a proper smile, and she was glad to see him in a better mood. The door swung shut behind him, and Jessie dropped her forehead onto the table.

"Not if I see you first?" she repeated to herself.

She wasn't that cheesy, was she?

"You did that last time I saw you in here with that cutie," Richie said, his cloth appearing near her face. "Must be love."

"Shut up." Jessie rolled her eyes as she lifted her head; she usually liked Richie's sarcastic brand of humour. "He's just a friend."

"And I'm the King of England."

"You might be as rich as him, Richie."

"My *father* might be," he said, whipping her with

the cloth before scooping up the empty basket. "He named me after his favourite thing, after all."

Richie returned to the bar, but Jessie wasn't going to let an open dialogue about James run away from her, especially since Richie had brought him up.

"So, your dad's really settling down here for good?" she asked, slipping onto a bar stool. "Must be nice having him close by again."

Richie let out an exasperated huff. "Oh yeah, it's great. Amazing. Best. Thing. *Ever*."

"Ah."

"A leopard doesn't change its spots," he said, leaning against the bar and folding his tattooed arms. His eyes glazed over. "He's just as he's always been."

Jessie nodded along, hoping Richie would open up more about James' return if she offered a listening ear.

"I really thought he'd turned over a new leaf, you know?" Richie continued. "After my mum got shot, he was certain we were going to be a 'proper' family. I'd hear about that at boarding school."

"Is that what I missed at boarding school? Mother shootings?"

"Divorce, I mean," he said, his sulk lifting into a smile. "She's been putting a dent in her divorce settlement, showing off her scar in Ibiza ever since. Maybe I'd be doing the same if I was shot by my dad's financial advisor, but... I thought that whole ordeal changed him. Just for a moment, it was like he finally realised family comes first." He shook his head, tossing the cloth into a bucket with more force than necessary. "Just a blip."

"I'm sorry," Jessie offered. "That must be really disappointing."

Richie shrugged, busying himself with lining up bottles on the shelves. "It's whatever. I'm used to him by now."

Jessie let the conversation fade, sensing she'd gleaned as much as she could for today. She thanked Richie again for the coffee and chips before gathering her things and heading out into the late-afternoon drizzle.

As she walked, she mulled over everything she'd learned. The shoddy builders being carried over from the Henderson Place disaster. Richard's suspiciously inflated farm sale. Martin's lavish lifestyle and susceptibility to temptation. One property developer with all the money in the world. And two councillors who seemed happy to take a slice to have their votes influenced. The planning-committee meeting inched closer every minute, and Jessie still didn't know what they were voting over.

8

The rain slowed to a light drizzle as Julia navigated the narrow country lanes leading out of Peridale's village centre. Dense hedges and skeletal trees lined the one-lane road, their slanted branches forming a natural tunnel overhead. She switched on the headlights and squinted to make out the cottage numbers in the fading light on Thistlebrook Lane.

At last, she spotted 16 from Prunella's note, barely visible in the gloom. She turned down the gravel drive bordered by leafless rose bushes. The wheels crunched along until Prunella's cottage emerged from the early-evening fog. Ivy crawled over the stone façade, trimmed neatly around the windows. It was the picture-perfect vision of a Cotswold cottage, and at least three times bigger than Julia's modest dwelling.

She cut the engine and looked up at the diamond-paned windows, glowing with warm light against the dreary dusk. She inhaled, prepared for any outcome as she stepped out into the rain.

Prunella answered on the first knock, almost as if she'd been waiting right behind the oak door. "Julia! How good to see you. Do come in. You're just in time. My little meeting was just coming to an end."

Further down the hallway, three people emerged from a room, pulling on their coats. Julia hadn't had much time to herself throughout the day, but she'd managed to find some pictures of the society members on the council website, and here they were.

Martin turned his collar up against the drizzle, hands shoved in his pockets. He avoided meeting Julia's gaze as he rushed past.

"I'm sorry for your loss," Julia called after him. "I know you worked closely with Peter."

Martin paused, looking flustered. "Oh yes, well... thank you. It's been difficult, as I'm sure you can imagine. Peter and I didn't... didn't know each other well outside of council business. Our interactions were purely professional."

Martin seemed eager to avoid any further discussion about his relationship with Peter. She made a mental note of his apparent discomfort as he hurried to his car.

Next, Richard strode past, his burly frame casting a shadow in the glow of the carriage lights. His flannel shirt and work boots were speckled with raindrops. She offered her condolences again.

"Hmm. Known the man since school. We had our fair share of disagreements over the years, both personal and political. Can't say I'll miss dealing with him, but yes, very sad."

Julia found Richard's bluntness as peculiar as Martin's evasiveness.

Alice followed, dabbing at her eyes with a handkerchief, mascara smudged under her lashes.

"Peter was a pillar in this community," she said before Julia had to say anything. "We'll all feel his loss deeply. I wish there was more I could have done to help him."

Of the three, Alice was the only one displaying outward grief, but that didn't rule her out either.

"If you'll follow me, Julia," Prunella said, offering the hallway.

Julia shook the rain from her coat and followed Prunella down a long hall, panelled with dark wood. The floors gleamed under ornate rugs, and bouquets of white lilies adorned every available surface. Julia eyed the paintings lining the walls—

portraits of stern, unsmiling faces and stormy landscapes.

"What a lovely home," Julia said.

"How kind. I like to fill it with things that bring me joy," Prunella's voice rang with brittle warmth. "Let me take your coat."

Julia slid her arms from the damp sleeves, skin prickling as Prunella's hawk-like gaze swept over her. She hadn't had time to change after the long day at the café and didn't need to look down to know tea and coffee stains had made their way around her apron. Handing the coat off, she asked, "Have you lived here long?"

"My whole life." Prunella draped the coat on an antique rack. "I'm not sure how much longer I'll be here." Her smile tightened. "It's rather big for one, and I can hear Westminster calling. I've been reflecting lately on how I might take a more active role in shaping policy around issues I care about. The arts, education, heritage preservation... there's only so much that can be done at a local level. And if Peter's death has taught me anything, it's that none of us knows how long we have left."

Prunella led the way into a sitting room glowing with lamplight. Plum-coloured wingback chairs surrounded a stone fireplace containing a roaring fire. Julia perched on the edge of a seat, back ramrod-straight. A tea tray waited on the low table between them, atop a newspaper; wisps of steam rose from the china pot. Prunella busied herself preparing two cups.

Julia accepted the delicate teacup and took a tentative sip, letting the heat thaw her rain-chilled bones. Across from her, Prunella watched and waited. After a prolonged silence, Julia set down her cup, realising her host was waiting for her to take the lead.

"Thank you again for inviting me," Julia said, wishing she'd scanned her notepad before leaving her car. "I know you wanted to discuss Peter's visit to my café?"

"Yes, I did. Let's get right to it, shall we?" Prunella set her tea down without drinking any. "What exactly did Peter say during this visit? He was in a peculiar mood in the hours leading up to telling me he was on his way to your café."

Julia recounted the bare facts of Peter's cryptic warnings and claims of being watched. She omitted any mention of the overheard painting conversation. Time to see how much Prunella would reveal without prodding.

Prunella sighed. "Poor Peter. It seems his troubled state of mind was worse than I realised. All that nonsense about being followed—such a shame he convinced himself it was real."

"But he seemed so adamant," Julia pressed. "What

if someone really was harassing him?"

"I understand your concern, but Peter hadn't been himself lately, not since..." Prunella pursed her lips, looking pained. "Not since his wife, Joanna, passed last year. He'd become paranoid, convinced nefarious forces were out to get him. He even claimed men in black suits were tracking his every move! Can you imagine?" Prunella shook her head, a lock of hair coming loose from her bun. "It was a shame to watch his mind break down like it did."

Julia's thoughts raced. "Men in black suits? Ever heard of the Cotswold Crew?"

"Can't say I have."

Julia glanced down at the paper under the tea tray; she'd recognise the corner of the latest issue of *The Peridale Post* from even less. She'd seen the 'Macabre Maze Murder' headline on every table in the café. Perhaps Prunella didn't read the paper cover to cover. If she had, she might have seen the 'Three More Crew Members Arrested' headline a few pages in.

"I wouldn't dwell on his wild stories if I were you," Prunella said, reaching out to pat Julia's hand. "Peter always tended towards colourful fancies, even before grief unbalanced him. I'm sure his mind simply concocted phantoms to explain his troubles."

Julia wasn't convinced Peter had been unhinged, but she nodded, biding her time. She'd try a different angle. "Peter also mentioned an old plan from the 1840s coming to life, but I couldn't find anything online. Does that ring any bells? Something about a man who died of consumption?"

"Old name for tuberculosis," she said in a flash. "The 1840s, you say? Nothing rings a bell. Our society focuses on preserving what already exists in Peridale, not chasing old, obscure plans."

"He also insinuated I was part of this 'rotten plan,' though he didn't explain how," Julia pressed. "Have there been any society discussions involving my property or the café?"

"You part of a plan?" Prunella let out a startled laugh. "Goodness, no. The society hasn't had any dealings regarding your café, I assure you. My old friend always did have an exaggerated flair for the dramatic."

"'Old friend,'" Julia picked up, her notepad scribblings pushing forward. "You called him that at the party. You were in a witch hat." A statement rather than a question. "I happened to be in that little courtyard while the two of you were talking."

Prunella took the moment to have her first strained sip of tea. Julia wondered if she was considering a flat-out denial.

"Yes," she stated. "I was there, as were you, evidently. And what did you overhear?"

"Peter told you he knew where some painting was," Julia said, watching Prunella closely. "You replied with '*the* painting.' What did he mean by that?"

Prunella's composure finally cracked. She recoiled, nearly upending her teacup. "That was... rather different circumstances than it might have seemed. I come from a long line of artists, you see. Landscape painters, mostly." She motioned to the many paintings lining the walls in thick, gold frames. "I was an art teacher for most of my professional life, and I've spent much of my retirement hunting down several of my ancestors' works of art. Over the years, Peter has helped with that endeavour. We met at an auction, and it was obvious to me he had quite the nose for finding antiques,. There's one painting that continues to evade me. A sentimental piece of the view from the top window of this house. My grandfather would talk about it. His father painted it, and it was lost to time. Peter had a habit of..." Sighing, she sank into her chair a little. "I'm not sure if he did it on purpose, or whether it was a feature of his condition, but whenever his erratic behaviour started to push me away, he'd promise he'd found *that* painting."

"I see," Julia said, echoing her host. "And do you know who 'he' was?"

"An art dealer, perhaps? Your father is in antiques,

no?"

Julia nodded, sipping her tea and wondering how much research Prunella had done on her. Or, like Peter, was she just a frequent customer of Brian South's on Mulberry Lane?

"Your response after Peter said he was going to acquire the painting," Julia continued. "You asked if he'd changed his mind about the vote?"

Prunella laughed. "Oh, no. Yes, I can see why it seems like that, but they were separate topics. It was a pivot to ground him back in reality. I did pause, if you'll recall." Arching both brows, Prunella waited for Julia to nod; she did remember the pause. "I've yet to decide which way my vote will swing, but Peter was intent on changing everyone's minds. But votes are highly personalised, are they not? One person's point of view isn't another's."

Julia narrowed her eyes. Prunella's flustered response didn't mesh with her polished veneer. She decided to switch gears again.

"And this vote is about...?"

"I'm afraid I'm not at liberty to say," she said, a hint of amusement on her lips. "But I can assure you, all will be revealed in due course."

"But it relates to the field behind my café? It must be something big if Peter was so against it?"

"Preservation and progress can go hand in hand,"

Prunella said, her smile thinning. "Since you're so curious about society matters, perhaps you'd like to join us at our next meeting? It's in three days at the village hall. Today's get-together was a more informal affair to grieve our collective loss. We're meeting to discuss how best to advance forward, and it would be the perfect time for us to welcome in a fresh perspective. You seem to care a great deal about this village."

The invitation caught Julia off guard. Joining the society could grant her critical access, yet fraternising with potential suspects made her uneasy. She weighed her options under the scrutiny of Prunella's stare.

"I'd be delighted to attend."

"Wonderful. We gather at five o'clock. I look forward to officially introducing you to everyone, though it seemed you were already rather acquainted with them today. Strange, because when I asked them about you, none of them had the faintest idea who you were." Her tone made it clear the interview had concluded. "Now, I must see to dinner preparations, but please do finish your tea."

Prunella rose in a fluid motion and glided from the room. Alone, Julia gulped down the rest of the tea and stood, pulse racing. She had wasted enough time playing the role of the polite guest. Careful of the creaky floorboards, she crept into the central hallway, keeping an eye out for Prunella. Voices drifted from a room down the corridor, just out of sight. Julia tiptoed closer, ears straining.

"...no, I don't believe she knows anything concrete... She agreed to attend... Yes, understood. I should go. She's still here... Right, see you then."

Julia darted back to the sitting room, heart pounding. She had just settled back in the chair when Prunella returned, holding Julia's coat.

"Thank you for the invitation," Julia said, rising from her chair for a second time. "I look forward to attending the meeting. I'll bring some cake along."

"How thoughtful. I'll see you then."

The oak door shut behind Julia with a firm thud. Back in her car, she cranked up the heat and rested her head against the seat, exhaling hard. The conversation she'd overheard cancelled out Prunella's genteel pretence, though she hadn't bought too much into it before that. Julia had no doubt Prunella was hiding something, and after her brief interaction with the rest of the members, Prunella wasn't the only one.

Peeling out onto the country lane, Julia knew one thing for certain—she would get answers out of the society. She'd play along with them for as long as she needed to, but for Peter's sake, and for the sake of Peridale itself, she would uncover the truth.

9

Sunshine streamed through the windshield of Barker's car, putting him at odds with his gloved hands cupping his thermos of coffee. He fidgeted in his seat, his stakeout in front of Wellington Heights crawling into its second hour.

The luxury apartment building was a mammoth structure, its pale Cotswold stone glinting in the morning light. Barker scanned the rows of identical balconies. According to the listings, every single apartment had sold—a remarkable feat, given that all he'd heard since the building was finished was that they were struggling to sell. Good things came to those who waited, it seemed, and James Jacobson's 'manor-to-apartments' gamble had paid off in spades.

His phone buzzed with a new text message. It was

from his brother Casper, letting him know that he and his wife, Heather, wouldn't be able to make it to Peridale for Barker's birthday meal at the Comfy Corner. He'd forgotten Julia had booked them all a table. Turning forty-three in two days didn't seem like much cause for celebration, given everything happening in the village. He fired back a quick 'No worries' reply just as the front door of the apartment building swung open.

Barker slid to the phone's camera setting, ready to snap some shots of James finally emerging. But it was just the woman he'd watched have a single cup of coffee delivered half an hour ago, now wrapped in a scarf and still sipping her coffee. Barker had checked: the nearest place delivering coffee was nine miles away, and the delivery had cost her £7.49 for a £6.99 coffee. Life at Wellington Heights couldn't be too bad. Stifling a yawn, he sipped the boiling coffee from his thermos and sank back into his seat as the woman wandered off down the lane.

Now, it was just him, his camera, the icy sunshine —and his mounting frustration at James' failure to re-emerge. Barker leaned forward again, phone in hand, resuming his watch.

The creak of a car door made him sink further. The electric car had snuck up on him. Barker smiled as Detective Inspector Laura Moyes stepped out, followed by her shadow—or pet—Police Constable Jake Puglisi. Barker had preferred to have his Detective Sergeant tag along during his days in Laura's shoes.

"Fancy seeing you here," he said as his window slid down. "Out for a morning stroll?"

"And I suppose you're just bird-watching?" Moyes replied wryly. "Wouldn't be following James, would you? Your wife said you were digging into him when I had lunch at her very busy café yesterday."

"Guilty as charged," Barker admitted. "I've been on him since the crack of dawn. Followed him here from his house. Hasn't come out yet, though. What brings you both here?"

"Routine questioning," Moyes answered vaguely. "We need to speak with one of the residents."

"A suspect?"

"Perhaps."

"Richard Hughes," Puglisi confirmed in a gossipy whisper. "How's the next book coming along?"

"Haven't started it yet."

"You're not getting that one for free," Moyes said, shooting Puglisi a sharp glance. "Come on, then. What do you know?"

Barker filled her in on Prunella's strange behaviour during Julia's visit to her cottage, along with Jessie's research on the extravagant Martin

Green. Puglisi jotted down notes until Moyes gave him another look.

"Since you brought them up," Moyes said, glancing around as she leaned in. "Prunella doesn't seem like the most trustworthy person. Did some digging and found a scandal from her days as a university art lecturer. She was accused of forging art research papers that she published through the university. Caused quite the stir. And Mr Eco Mansion out in the countryside has more loans than I've had hot dinners."

"Not the squeakiest of characters," Barker agreed. "And Richard?"

"I pulled CCTV footage from the Halloween party," Puglisi admitted, rocking back on his heels. "The fella's clothes don't match up. He enters wearing a leather jacket but leaves later in a denim one. Makes you wonder why he changed his outfit, and if the original had any... incriminating stains."

"Blood stains?" Barker suggested.

Moyes' expression remained neutral. "Richard also has a past conviction related to his old farm. Let's just say he wasn't choosy about who rented space in his old barn."

"Stolen goods," Puglisi whispered.

"Right, well, that's quite enough of that." Moyes puffed clouds into the air as she scanned the building.

"Don't want to hold Barker's hand the whole way, do we? Though, I think you'd quite like that, Puglisi."

"I'd love to read your new book when it's finished," Puglisi said, before leaning in and adding, "Any chance your Jessie is still single?"

"Steady now, Puglisi."

Moyes rolled her eyes and headed into the apartment building, Puglisi following behind.

After taking the time to write down Moyes' revelations about Prunella's scandal, Martin's loans, and Richard's sketchy barn, the front door creaked open again. Barker perked up, wondering if Moyes and Puglisi were finished with their questioning already. But instead of the detectives, James Jacobson emerged, accompanied by another man.

Barker lifted his phone and snapped a couple of pictures as James spoke with the bearded stranger wearing a baseball cap. After a brief conversation, the two men shook hands. The bearded man gave a small wave and glanced around before disappearing back inside the building.

James straightened his suit jacket and climbed into his glossy sports car parked at the side of the manor. Barker slipped as far under the wheel as he could as James revved his engine like he was playing with a toy. Then, all at once, the car sped off like a bullet.

Barker peered down at his phone, zooming in on the blurry photos. He squinted at the bearded man's face, sure his eyes were deceiving him.

Shaking his head in disbelief, Barker started his own engine and drove home. He arrived back at the cottage to find Julia bundled up, manoeuvring Olivia's pram out the front door.

"We're off to the library for Neil's story hour," Julia explained, before adding, "And I'm going to do a little research before my first society meeting. I want to be as prepared as possible. Find anything interesting staking out Wellington Heights?"

Barker filled her in on Moyes' revelations before pulling out the photographs of James meeting with a mysterious bearded man on the doorstep.

"Does this look like Greg Morgan to you?"

Julia squinted at the picture. "Perhaps his down-and-out cousin? Hard to tell. I'll see you later."

"Be careful around those society people. Don't take anything they say at face value."

"Believe me, I don't trust them one bit," Julia assured him. She leaned in to give him a swift kiss. "Wish me luck. The 1840s, here I come."

Barker watched them go, hoping Julia would get the answers she sought. He cracked open his laptop in the dining room and opened a blank word document, still lacking a first word to his next novel.

He wrote 'Chapter 1' and waited.

Before he knew it, he was back online, searching to back up DI Moyes' claims.

~

Later in the afternoon, lively chatter filled the café as Jessie worked behind the counter with Sue. The place was moderately busy, but there were no customers waiting to order, so Jessie sat on a stool with her laptop open while Sue flipped through a magazine.

Near the front window, Dot held court at a table with Evelyn, Amy, and Shilpa. Dot was deep in spirited conversation, but the other three women looked less engaged.

Behind the counter, Jessie took a forkful of pumpkin pie and savoured the sweet, spicy flavour. "This is a winner for me. Did you make this?"

Sue smiled. "Based on the recipe your mum found, but I tweaked it a bit."

"Your baking gets better every day," Jessie said. "You seem to be really enjoying working here. How's it going?"

"Oh, I love it," Sue said, her eyes lighting up. "It's so nice not to feel so swamped, and your mum is a joy to work for—the easiest boss I've ever had."

"She's a proper pushover. Veronica cracks the

whip far more," Jessie noted. Sue's enthusiasm seemed genuine, so Jessie decided to probe further, Dante's manila folder on her mind. "How are things otherwise? Do you like living at Henderson Place?"

At the mention of her new home, Sue's expression faltered. "It's lovely. The kids are thrilled, Neil is very happy, and it's nice having a brand-new home."

Despite her words, Jessie detected a false note in Sue's voice. Her aunt was clearly hiding some doubts about the controversial housing development.

"No issues with the house, then?" Jessie pressed.

Sue shifted, looking uncomfortable. "Well, I suppose there are a few minor things—draughts, plumbing noises, some cracks here and there. But that's to be expected with new builds, isn't it?"

Jessie nodded, but suspected there were greater problems than Sue was letting on. "Did you buy or rent?"

"We bought," Sue said, arranging the empty mugs on the counter with more force than necessary. "Anyway, I should clear those tables. Excuse me."

As Sue hurried off with her head lowered, Jessie wondered what Sue wasn't saying about the house. She watched her aunt gather the cups for a moment, her eyes avoiding Jessie at all costs. Hoping she wasn't burdened too much, Jessie returned her focus to her laptop screen and the link Barker had sent about Prunella Thompson's university scandal.

The link sent her to a website that screamed 1999. Jessie had to squint for a good minute to figure out what she was even looking at. Once she sussed out that it was a forum post from a University of Gloucestershire student, she was still in the dark—until Prunella Thompson's name popped up. As it turned out, the student had caught their art history lecturer, Prunella Thompson, faking an academic paper on some long-forgotten nineteenth-century painter named Catherine Thompson.

Unmasking the Fabricated Legacy of Catherine Thompson: A Deep Dive into Prunella Thompson's Research Misconduct

While researching Catherine Thompson for my thesis, I found significant disparities between various reputable sources and the research paper published by our very own art-history lecturer, Prunella Thompson. Upon digging deeper, I discovered that most of the claims made in her paper about Catherine painting 'lost' royal portraits were baseless. No records or mentions of such portraits exist in any other credible source. What's even more shocking is the audacity to fabricate such a legacy, especially when the supposed ancestor is directly related. Is the goal to elevate one's status by riding on the coattails of a fabricated illustrious past? It's disappointing to see educators whom we trust to shape our academic journey, resort to such deceitful practices.

According to a user who posted in 2000, Prunella Thompson wasn't a lecturer at the university. However, another user who posted in 2001 confirmed that she had returned. This user stated that the university had allowed Prunella to retract her falsified research and continue lecturing after serving a suspension.

Not exactly evidence that she could be easily bribed, but perhaps the forgery could have led to blackmail? She forwarded the link to Veronica.

Jessie closed the laptop lid as Dot approached the counter to return her empty tea tray. Evelyn, Amy, and Shilpa had already left, and Dot was in a sour mood.

"Useless," Dot grumbled. "I was trying to reunite the neighbourhood watch, but no one's interested. Amy's too busy with church, Evelyn's thinking of swanning off to India for a winter yoga retreat, and

Shilpa flat-out said she can't be bothered. We need people looking out for this village now more than ever." Taking a calming breath, Dot asked, "Any updates on the field out back?"

Jessie shook her head. "Not yet, but don't give up hope. Perhaps you could team up with someone more like-minded? Even people you don't always see eye-to-eye with..."

Jessie nodded at Ethel White, who'd shamelessly eavesdropped on Dot's meeting from the next table over while slurping her pumpkin spice latte.

Dot scowled. "Work with that insufferable woman? I'd rather walk on hot coals barefoot, thank you very much!"

"That's probably what Evelyn will be doing at her retreat." Noticing Sue staring out the front window, Jessie changed topics. "Does Sue seem all right to you lately?"

"I don't have the foggiest," Dot replied, lowering her voice. "I tried asking about Jacobson earlier, and she nearly bit my head off, insisting he's 'not that bad.' He could have bribed her into silence, for all I know." Then, in a conspiratorial whisper, she added, "And rumour has it, Jacobson has made another offer to buy the post office from Shilpa, but she didn't say as much. I hope you don't lose your flat."

"Another offer?"

"He tried when all that stuff was going on with the library," Dot said, wafting her hand. "Jacobson was snapping up properties all over the place. She was quite torn about it but decided to stay put in the end."

Jessie glanced at the wall adjoining the post office next door.

"You could always stay with Percy and me in our spare bedroom if push comes to shove," Dot offered. "I won't see you out on the streets... again."

Jessie's thoughts were already racing ahead; losing her flat was the last thing on her mind. She thanked Dot for the offer and excused herself, returning to her laptop. She pulled up the map that had accompanied her exposé on Greg Morgan. It delineated the strips of land that George Knight had been pressured to sell, thereby blocking road access to the field behind the café. On the left side, the field stretched out towards the school. On the right, it extended all the way to a group of cottages near Mulberry Lane. The back way in was obstructed by the land George Knight had refused to part with. The only other access point was where she stood, and she hoped her mind wasn't running away with her down the wrong road.

10

Julia wandered through the quiet aisles of the library, unable to shake the lingering unease that clung to her like cobwebs. Without the decorations, the library should have felt like an altogether different place, but she could still feel the lingering horrors of Halloween night.

She rounded the corner of the 'World History' aisle and caught a glimpse of the children's corner where Neil's energetic storytelling enchanted the giggling group of toddlers gathered at his feet. Julia spotted Olivia's bouncing curls among them as Uncle Neil brought *The Very Hungry Caterpillar* to life. The sheer joy grounded Julia in the present, brightening the dark shadows.

She turned the corner onto 'Local History', the feelings of being lost in the maze echoing from that fateful night—the panic, the confusion, the dread. The body. The axe. The blood. Julia shook her head, trying to clear the vivid flashbacks clouding her mind. She focused on why she was here—to unravel the tangled threads of Peridale's mysterious past.

She scoured the thick spines of the history books, pulling out any that related to architecture, planning, even sheep farming. Anything that might contain knowledge of Peridale's history.

With a precarious stack balanced on her forearms, Julia rounded the corner and almost collided with a woman standing in the middle of the aisle. She was staring at the floor, as still as stone. It took Julia a moment to recognise the stranger.

"Alice?" Julia said, breaking the woman's trance. "We met yesterday? At Prunella's?"

Alice's eyes flickered with a delayed recognition. "Oh, yes. Julia, isn't it? Forgive me. My mind's been... elsewhere."

Julia glanced at the spot Alice had been so captivated by.

"This is where Peter died," Alice confirmed Julia's suspicions, her eyes welling. "Struck down, right here."

Julia glanced around, struggling to reconcile this

sombre spot with her journey through the library's maze that night. The black sheets had obscured this tucked-away corner, nestled in the shadowy recesses.

She joined Alice in staring, remembering Peter's body splayed across the cold floor, blood pooling around him from the axe. The warm library seemed to drop a couple of degrees, though there seemed to be a draft. She noted the fire escape disrupting the flow of books, a stone's throw from them.

Alice sighed, regaining her composure. "Peter was a misunderstood soul. Genteel and caring, passionate about the things that mattered, and incredibly intelligent. And now he's..." Her voice broke, but she steeled herself, glancing at the books in Julia's arms. "History books?"

"I'm conducting a little research."

Alice's face brightened at the topic change. "Anything I can help with?"

"I'm particularly interested in the 1840s," Julia revealed, watching Alice closely for any telling reaction. For a fraction of a second, Alice's eyes widened. "Old plans for the village, perhaps?"

"I can't say I know much about any building plans from the 1840s," Alice responded, a touch too hastily, adding the 'building' detail Julia hadn't.

Julia considered her approach. Like Prunella, Alice was hiding something, but a direct confrontation could jolt her. She decided a gentle, roundabout approach was best for now. Unlike Prunella, Alice didn't have spikey edges hidden behind a tight smile. She was the only one who seemed shocked by Peter's demise.

"If you still want to help," Julia said, holding up the stack, "two sets of eyes could be better than one?"

They made their way to an empty table and split the books between them. Alice flicked through a thick volume about Cotswold planning history like a person who was at home.

"The present has never captivated me quite like the past," Alice said, inhaling the musty pages of the book. "I must have caught the history bug from my grandparents. They worked in the museum when I was a little girl."

"I didn't realise Peridale has a museum."

"It didn't until I opened mine," she corrected. "The one my grandparents worked at closed a long time ago. Funding. Lack of interest. The usual story."

"Where is it? I'd love to visit."

"My place is on Mulberry Lane. I don't get many visitors."

Julia scanned the shops on Mulberry Lane in her mind's eye. She'd been there last week to drop off some leftover cakes for Katie and her clients to share, but she couldn't recall seeing a museum. She picked up a weighty volume titled 'Architecture of the Cotswolds,' while Alice fumbled through a glossary in another.

"Is that how you came to be in the society?"

Alice shook her head. "My museum hasn't been open for long. Don't think it'll be open for much longer either, given how things are going." She sighed, but didn't elaborate. "I was one of the original members who protested that actress's house a few years back." At the end of the glossary, she closed the book. "I can't find anything specific about the 1840s in this one."

Julia had been skimming through a book on Cotswold architecture, so she moved to the glossary pages at the back. She was about to scan for entries related to the 1840s when her tracing finger swept past 'alehouses and inns.' Recalling Peter's comment about her café, she brushed to page 32. After a few flicks through the pages, an all too familiar sight stopped her in her tracks.

"Oh, hello you," Julia whispered. Her fingers traced an intricate pencil drawing, immediately recognisable. "Peter was telling the truth."

The sketch sucked her in, depicting her café as it looked centuries ago when it first opened as a small alehouse in 1786. The square-paned bay window was identical, as was the wooden front door. An ornate sign swung above the entrance where her café's sign hung today.

It had been called The Shepherd's Rest.

Wooden tables dotted the cobblestones, occupied by chatting farmers with earthen jugs. Horses and carts peppering the edges. A little boy chased a hoop with a stick, and a small dog with floppy ears chased him. Their distant laughter echoed through the ages, no different from her lively weekend crowds. For an instant, Julia longed to step through the page into that world, so far away, yet so familiar.

"Magical, isn't it?" Alice broke the spell. "My little museum used to be a blacksmith."

"I wish I'd known this sooner," Julia said, reading through the description under the image. "If Peter hadn't visited me, I might never have known."

Alice shifted in her seat, busying herself with another glossary.

"It's not like people are still around from back then," Alice said. "We mostly pass down what we remember. Maybe a little before that, too. Otherwise, the past is a different country, and yet, the older I get and the faster the years race by, I don't think days like that are as long ago as we all think." Alice leaned over, and Julia was back to staring at the alehouse. "All the surrounding fields were sheep pastures back then. Wool was the thriving local industry during the medieval period until the spinning machinery technology brought along the factories."

Julia's ears pricked up. "Around the 1840s?"

Alice hummed agreement in her throat, giving away that she knew about that period after all.

"I don't think it's in that book, but as the wool industry evolved, The Shepherd's Rest became a tearoom by the mid-1800s," Alice said, flipping through a book without paying the pages much attention. "The concept of afternoon tea emerged around the 1840s, becoming all the rage among the upper classes."

As interesting as that was to know, she wasn't sure that's what Peter had been trying to tell her.

"So, the field behind my café was a sheep farm?" Julia commented, flipping to the next page where there were similar drawings of The Plough pub, still intact up the road from the green. "There used to be a market hall on that land too, or so I've heard."

"Ah, now we're getting into more recent memory," Alice said, engaged once again. "It was a latecomer to the market hall game, popping up in the late-1800s. I suppose the sheep farmers who owned that land held out longer than most before selling it on. The market hall burned down in the 1960s."

"That's when the council purchased the field,"

Julia recalled. "To protect it from development. For £3,000 in 1969?"

Alice studied her with a curious smile. "You've done your research."

Julia didn't admit the research had been Barker's during the George Knight case, but since they were on the topic, she decided to risk a more direct approach.

"James Jacobson recently paid £165,000 for that land." She shut her book and looked Alice straight in the eyes. "Quite the turnaround for the council, and rather a bargain for James, I'd say."

"When adjusted for inflation, it's—"

"Still £100,000 profit in the council's back pocket," Julia interrupted with another of Barker's researched facts. "You're a councillor. You're on that planning committee. What's the plan, Alice? What's going to become of that old sheep pasture behind the long-forgotten alehouse?" The atmosphere grew tense, and Julia's hopes of playing into Alice's love of history didn't inspire the truth to tumble out. "What's to become of the field behind my beloved café?"

Alice slammed her book shut, the slap of pages echoing in the silence. "I cannot discuss council matters. It's been lovely, Julia, but I must be getting back to the museum. I've long overstretched my lunch break. Good luck with your research."

Julia stood up, not wanting the first society

member who'd shown her any decency since Peter to run off. Alice hovered on the spot, her gaze evasive. As she passed Julia, she paused, her hand resting on Julia's shoulder.

"Hold out..." Alice whispered, but with the resonance of a gunshot. "Hold out for as long as you can."

Baffled, Julia could only watch as Alice hurried away, leaving her in a cloud of unanswered questions. As Alice disappeared around a bookshelf, Julia noticed a man in a black suit stand up from another table and follow after her. His movements were slow, but Julia's senses were on high alert. She pulled out her phone and snapped a photo of the man before he vanished from sight.

Julia stared down at the blurry image of the back of a man on her phone screen, wondering if she was now as paranoid as Peter. She looked around the library at the other scattered villagers. One of the librarian's smiles seemed a little too forced, and the man reading the newspaper had it open just a bit too wide. Julia shook her head, trying to push the theories out of her mind.

When she finally returned to the children's area, Neil's story hour was wrapping up. Olivia clapped along with the other toddlers, but the words and the laughter buzzed around Julia like white noise.

Hold out for *what*?

~

Barker scanned the quiet library aisles, his trained eyes hunting for evidence the police wouldn't have been foolish enough to leave behind. The fluorescent overhead lights washed the evidence-scavenged shelves in an aseptic glare. He almost preferred the shadows and flickering lanterns of the maze.

Rounding the corner, he found Neil tidying up the oversized cushions scattered across the rainbow rug. Barker resisted the urge to help search for stray fibres or shoe prints. This was no longer his crime scene, and that was no longer his job, but old habits die hard.

Neil tensed up when he noticed Barker hovering nearby. The gulf created by the murder lay between them, a chasm filled with the lingering tension from their last strained interaction. Barker held up his hands in a peaceful gesture as he approached.

"No arguments today, I promise," Barker said. "Just had a few questions I was hoping you could assist me with."

Neil sighed, his posture softening. "I suppose we're family, after all. What's on your mind?"

Pumpkins and Peril

Barker glanced around before lowering his voice. "Any updates from the police about the case?"

"You think they're keeping me up to speed?" Neil forced a laugh, throwing the last cushion into the basket with the rest. "Last I heard was them explaining how I could claim compensation to cover the costs of ordering another copy of the book they took for evidence."

"The book found under Peter?"

"An art history book," Neil said with a solemn nod. "I didn't think anyone would pull books out from behind the sheets."

Given that Barker had spent his afternoon digging into a university scandal from the 1999, he wasn't sure it could be a fluke.

"Did you order a replacement copy yet?" Barker asked. "I'd be curious to look at it."

"Funny you should ask. The new one arrived just this morning." Neil gestured for Barker to follow him. "Still needs cataloguing, so I haven't put it on the shelves yet."

They made their way to the front desk, where Neil retrieved a thick, leather-bound book from a box behind the counter.

"*Picturesque Past*," Barker read off the gold-embossed cover. He flipped through the glossy pages filled with full-colour prints and illustrations of unsmiling faces painted in dark oils. "Do you know if Peter showed any interest in this book before?"

"He spent most of his time in the history section," he said, his fingers bouncing on the computer keyboard tucked under the desk. "Doesn't look like he ever checked this book out, but he rarely did. Do you think he went into the maze to look for a book? At a party?"

"Stranger things have happened." He skimmed the table of contents, spotting a familiar name. "Ah, Catherine Thompson. Made her way into a history book, at least." Neil arched a brow. "Her name cropped up earlier."

Barker turned to the section on Catherine Thompson, a landscape painter from the 1800s. He scanned the chapter, finding no mention of royal portraits or the acclaim mentioned in Prunella's discredited research paper.

"A single paragraph and no examples of her work?" Neil said, reading over his shoulder. "A footnote in history. Her name doesn't ring any bells, but Peter..." A touch of sadness entered his voice at the mention of the deceased historian. "He'd know more if he was here."

Barker closed the book, gears turning. Between the scandal and Catherine's near-absence from art history, he grew more suspicious of Prunella by the minute.

"You're a smart guy, Neil," Barker started. "How serious is it for someone to fake a research paper?"

Neil stiffened, dropping his gaze. "People lie for many reasons. Sometimes it's saving face, or hiding embarrassment." He glanced around the empty library before leaning in. "Barker... Can I tell you something in confidence?"

Barker nodded. "Always. Is this about James, by any chance?"

"No, it isn't." Sighing, Neil looked like he was wondering if he should continue. He swallowed hard and said, "It's about Peter's death. I think I made a fatal blunder."

"Did you sink the axe into his back?"

"What? No! Never."

"Then it can't be *that* fatal," Barker said, his attempt at a joke not having the desired effect; Neil had always taken himself far too seriously for Barker's liking. "What happened?"

"It's about the axe... The police asked where I thought it came from. I lied and said I didn't know. Suggested someone must have smuggled it into the library under costume. But that wasn't the truth."

Barker remained silent, allowing Neil to confess.

"Let me show you something," Neil said.

He led Barker across the library through the armchairs and trolleys where the light-up dance floor had been. Pushing through the glass door, they emerged into a small courtyard enclosed by brick walls.

Neil patted a small tree stump near the back wall. "There used to be a tree right here. It blocked the sunlight into the library, and there's nothing like reading in natural daylight. I chopped it down weeks ago. And I'm almost certain I forgot all about it and left the axe out here afterward."

Barker eyed the fresh stump. The implications whirled through his mind. The courtyard had three ways in and out—the glass doors they'd just come through, and two fire doors.

"Are there cameras back here?" he asked.

Neil shook his head.

"Would you mind if I inspected?" Barker gestured to the doors.

"It'll set the alarm off," he said. "I'll disable it for a moment."

Neil hurried back inside, and Barker crossed the mossy flags and crouched to examine the tree stump. The cut wood still bore the faint outline of an axe head, the grove fresh and pale next to the rest of the yellowing stump.

Barker pictured James slithering out to the

courtyard, yanking out the axe before pocketing it in his expensive suit jacket. It was all too easy to visualise.

The scuff of approaching footsteps made Barker straighten. Neil reappeared, a deep frown weighing down his face.

"The security system was unplugged that night," he admitted. "I borrowed the socket for one of the fog machines. This is all my fault, isn't it? If I hadn't left that axe lying around..."

"The fault lies with whoever stole your axe to commit murder."

Barker examined the first of the fire doors. It opened almost precisely where Peter had been struck down with an axe. The second door led to a narrow alley, sandwiched between the library and Mulberry Lane, that extended in both directions—an easy escape route that bypassed the maze.

"I should confess the truth to the police," Neil said. "Shouldn't I?"

"Let's not jump to any rash decisions until we know more," Barker advised. "Your lie might have been to avoid implicating yourself. For now, keep this between us."

Neil nodded, seeming to relax. "I appreciate that, Barker. Let me know if there's anything else I can do to help. Anything at all." After a breath, he said, "As long as it doesn't involve James. I still think you're wrong about him."

Likewise, Barker thought.

∼

As Julia drove up the winding country lane back to her cottage, she replayed the library conversation. Alice had initially seemed open to discussing local history, even hinting at her knowledge of obscure plans from the 1840s. But the moment Julia had broached the subject of the impending council vote, Alice's demeanour changed. The abrupt departure only fuelled Julia's suspicions that Alice was hiding something important.

And that cryptic parting remark.

"Hold out for as long as you can."

Julia gripped the steering wheel, her knuckles white as she passed James' bungalow. Hold out against what? So many tangled threads. Peter's desperate pleas for help, cut short by the axe that ended his life. Prunella's civil veneer barely concealing her evasiveness. Martin and Richard's avoidance at any mention of their dead colleague. And Alice—conflicted, warning Julia to resist while being light on the details.

Distracted by her swirling thoughts, Julia almost

drove past her cottage. She pulled up alongside the stone wall and killed the engine. For a moment, she stared ahead, unable to unfasten her seatbelt. It took Olivia yawning in the backseat for Julia to get moving.

Inside, she put her sleepy toddler in the nursery for a nap before settling in the dining room with a cup of peppermint and liquorice tea. Not long after, Barker returned.

"We must have just missed each other at the library," he called as he hung up his coat. "Any breakthroughs?"

Julia recounted the highlights—and lowlights—of her afternoon research session with Alice. She attempted to muster the same excitement she'd felt when discovering her café's origins, but Alice's warning lingered like a bloodstain soaked into tweed.

"This grows more complicated by the day," he said, taking the seat across from her. "The society knows something big is happening on that field, and it seems Alice wants no part of it. So why not just tell you the plan?"

"She seems as scared as Peter," Julia said, dropping into the chair across from him with a sigh. "Maybe I'm just as paranoid as he is, but I think I saw someone following her—a man in a black suit." Saying it aloud, she wondered if she had been imagining things after all. "Any luck with James?"

Barker clasped his hands behind his head, leaning back. "I wish I could say yes. All I've got are dead ends and loose threads, so I followed your lead and returned to the scene of the crime."

He filled Julia in on the art history book found under Peter's body and his conversation with Neil about the murder weapon. Julia absorbed this new information, as unsure as Barker about what it could mean.

"You think James stole the axe from the library courtyard?"

"It's seeming more possible with each passing day," he admitted. "Nobody has more to gain than James. The murder took place at *his* party. He could have slipped outside, grabbed the axe when no one was looking, and then followed Peter."

Julia weighed this theory. As much as she distrusted James, an act of cold-blooded murder didn't seem as likely as it had when she'd been lost in the maze. Given how controlling he was of his secrets, would he risk such an act in public?

"Something doesn't add up," she thought aloud. "This seems too sloppy for someone like James. Maybe he hired someone else to do it?"

"Men in black suits, perhaps? The Cotswold Crew could have easily blended in at the party," he suggesting, scratching the dark stubble covering his jaw. "But you're right. Stabbing someone at your own party without an alibi does sound a little sloppy."

"We're still missing some of the picture," she said, rising with her teacup. A refill might help.

"Or maybe we're just looking at the picture from the wrong angles."

In the kitchen, she stared out the window above the sink as she waited for the kettle to boil, Mowgli dancing around her ankles. She scooped him up; his purring was a tonic as daylight began to fade in her drizzly back garden. If they were looking at things from the wrong angle, what was the right one? The shriek of the kettle jolted her, sending Mowgli springing from her hold to the breakfast bar. She dropped a teabag into her mug, staring at the cream envelope under Mowgli's paw.

"James' housewarming party is next week," she pointed out. "Think we'll still be welcomed guests?"

Barker's eyes widened, a hint of a smile tugging at the corners of his mouth. "I thought you wanted to steer clear of him?"

"I did. But we're running out of options, and he did hand-deliver the invitation." Julia moved the teabag up and down in a hypnotic rhythm. "Either that, or we pay our new neighbour a visit right now. It's only polite to welcome him to the lane."

"Not a bad idea. Any leftover cake?"

With Olivia asleep in her pram, and three-quarters of a Victoria sponge cake in a box, Julia and Barker strolled down the lane after the rain had eased off.

They followed the winding stone path to James' single-storey home. Nestled behind a low Cotswold stone wall, its large glass windows and stretches of golden limestone radiated opulence. Yet the simple garden and solar panels lent it a utilitarian touch, a garage concealing his sports car from view.

Their cottage looked like a crumbling shack compared to this modern marvel, but it was a sight better than what had come before it. Julia wasn't certain how much Peter had influenced the final design, but the result reflected well on him. For all James' shortcomings, he had succeeded in blending elements of the past, present, and future seamlessly. Perhaps that was his intention in Peridale: to blend in.

Struck by an unexpected wave of nostalgia, Julia knocked on the front door. She couldn't be sure, but the door might have been in the same spot as Barker's old cottage door.

"Must not be home," Barker said, cupping his hands against the expansive windowpane. "Crikey, it's bigger on the inside. Should we poke around?"

"Terrible idea. He probably has cameras everywhere. Let's come back later."

"No use getting arrested over someone like James."

Weighing up the cake box, she wondered whether she should leave it on the doorstep for when he returned. She'd welcomed Barker when he first moved in—to a mixed reception—and had done the same when Veronica moved in further up the lane, as well as for Leah Burns before her. Before overthinking it, she placed the cake box on the polished-stone doorstep.

As much as she hadn't wanted to interact with James upon first seeing him, she didn't see what choice she had. If their paths didn't cross in the next week, she'd be attending the housewarming party.

Until then, Julia resolved to make the most of the calm evening ahead, hoping she wouldn't become too lost in the maze of the case for another restless night.

11

The next morning, Julia darted about the café kitchen, whipping up a quick batch of pumpkin spice scones. She'd been adding the blend to everything since the early sunsets had crept in and —like the lattes—there had never been such a divisive flavour on the menu. The villagers who disliked it made their opinions known, but those who loved it were turning up every day for their pumpkin spice fix. If only arguments about the autumnal spice were her biggest headache of the season.

Sue hurried in fifteen minutes late. "Sorry. Had to wait for a guy to sort out a thing at the house."

"A guy and a thing?"

"Not important," Sue said, cramming her apron over her head. "Ready for another day, Captain?"

"As ready as I'll ever be."

They worked in the comfortable rhythm of Sue refreshing the display case while Julia popped the scones into the oven. The warm scent of cinnamon, nutmeg, ginger, and cloves filled the air—the secret to pumpkin spice was that, unlike pumpkin pie, it didn't contain a drop of pumpkin. She set the timer and, with no customers yet to serve, swapped her apron for her coat.

"I'm off to the post office before we open," Julia said, flinging a chunky knitted auburn scarf around her neck. "Need to buy some stamps."

Outside, a brisk wind nipped at Julia's cheeks as she hurried next door. In the post office, she stepped inside, but the usual friendly face of Shilpa was nowhere to be seen. Ethel White leaned against the counter, gossiping with Shilpa's son, Jayesh.

"I'm telling you, it was *no* accident Peter ended up with an axe in his back," Ethel proclaimed. Jayesh nodded as he sorted through envelopes, disinterested. "I inspected the scene myself. Wouldn't be surprised if we hear that our new permanent resident was behind it. I heard he's going to build skyscrapers as far as the eye can see. Soak up the sun while you can, I say."

Ethel spun around, her suspicious gaze sizing Julia up and down.

"You must know what he has planned," Ethel remarked. "In on it, no doubt."

"If I were, Ethel, do you think I'd be able to keep something like that secret in a village like this?" Julia picked out a bar of chocolate and placed it on the counter. "No Shilpa today?"

"Mum's got a cold."

"Hmm," Ethel grumbled. "Well, I hope she gets well soon. And you heard it here first, folks. *Skyscrapers!*"

With that, Ethel hurried out of the post office, no doubt ready to accost every passer-by with her wild theories.

"She didn't even buy anything," Jayesh muttered as he scanned the chocolate. "Anything else?"

Julia had wanted to ask Shilpa about the supposed offer James had made to buy the post office. Her gran's late-night gossip phone call had pulled her away from *Breakfast at Tiffany's* and their Chinese takeaway. As curious as she was, she didn't want to put Jayesh in an awkward position by prying into his mother's business if she hadn't told him.

"Book of stamps, please," Julia said. "And tell your mum Julia said to get well soon."

She left the post office with a polite smile, wondering about the alleged offer while she ate the chocolate. She cast her mind back to the party when her ghost costume had been yanked off her head. Shilpa had caught her and said she needed to tell Julia something, and Julia had promised to be right back. Three days later, and their paths still hadn't crossed.

Looking across the green to the village hall, she thought ahead to that evening's Preservation Society meeting. It was a chance to pry into James' secretive movements further. She wouldn't miss it for the world, but she needed to eliminate some of the question marks first. With the café still quiet, Julia boxed up some of the morning's earlier scones, pulled her scarf tighter, and walked to Mulberry Lane.

The salon bell jingled as Julia entered. Katie looked up from her acrylic desk in the middle of her pink palace with a girlish grin, and her client, Roxy, turned around.

Julia held up the box. "Fresh scones, still warm from the oven."

"You're an angel," Katie said with a giddy wiggle in her chair. "It's like you knew I missed breakfast."

"I'm as psychic as Evelyn," Julia said, setting down the box and pulling up a chair. She'd also brought plates, knives, cream, and jam, and enough to share on the off-chance Katie had a customer. Julia had hoped Katie would be alone, but her only customer being an old school friend was even better, given whom she was in a relationship with. "Didn't have you down as the manicure type, Roxy."

"Laura's always moaning about me biting my nails," Roxy said, rolling her eyes. "Bad habit, apparently. Like she doesn't have that smoke machine always sandwiched between her lips." She assessed her finished hand; the French manicure was subtle enough to pass as perfect, natural nails from a distance. "Got the morning off from school thanks to some senior staff meeting they didn't invite me to. Seemed only right that I treat myself."

"Self-care," Katie muttered, licking cream from her plump lips after a huge bite of scone. "Very important. My self-care is that whenever Julia's father talks about antiques for more than sixty seconds, I allow myself to fully tune out. I imagine myself on a nice, hot beach topping up my tan."

"I might try that one when Laura gets an hour deep into her case notes," Roxy said. "It's like living inside a true-crime podcast that you can't switch off."

"Any updates from DI Moyes on the case?" Julia asked.

"DI Moyes," Roxy chuckled. "I might start calling Laura that to see how she reacts. And if I divulged the contents of our pillow talk, I'd simply have to kill you."

Julia slid a scone to Roxy. "Not even for your oldest friend?"

"A valid point," Roxy said, considering her options while trying to pick up the scone without smudging her nails. Julia picked it up and fed her a bite. "Okay, you didn't hear this from me, but she's struck your new neighbour off the suspect list."

"Oh."

"You sound disappointed," Katie said, dunking the brush into the varnish with force. "James isn't *that* bad."

"They fixed Peter's time of death at around quarter past eight," Roxy explained. "Multiple witnesses confirmed James left the maze at least twenty minutes before then, and he was in for only a couple of minutes at most."

"Maybe he went in there to make a phone call?" Katie suggested.

"Or slip away from Barker's tail," Julia murmured.

If James had an alibi, pursuing his true motives would prove even more difficult. Ruled out of Peter's death, but not innocent by any means.

Soon, Roxy's nails gleamed with a shiny topcoat. She flexed her fingers, admiring Katie's handiwork. "You've got good at this, Katie. Might have to start self-caring more often. I should head back to deal with the school crisis. Let's hope those men with the tape measures were there to size up my windows to fix those draughts."

After Roxy paid and left, Julia took the warmed chair and let Katie drag her fingers across the desk.

"Oh, dear. Forget the school, Julia, your cuticles are in *crisis*. Let me see what I can do before my next client gets here in ten."

"I did want to pick your brain about something."

"Well, I assumed you weren't here just to deliver scones," Katie said with a playful smile. "Though I wish you'd drop by more often so I don't have to keep bringing your nails back from the brink. So, what is it? Husband, baby, café..." She tilted her head, buffing faster. "Axe?"

"Axe. Remember when Peter collided with you at the café? You were sure you recognised him from somewhere. Given it any more thought?"

"A little," she admitted. "I recognised him from all the blinking, and I'm certain he visited the manor a handful of times back in my past life. I remember arriving home from the airport after a tricky glamour shoot on a freezing beach in Malta in the middle of winter." She nodded at one of the many modelling shots lining the walls between the shelves of polishes. "Peter was there, ranting and raving. Going on about how he knew my father had 'it' and wouldn't leave until he got whatever 'it' was. I was in such a bad mood after being flown home economy class, I marched him out myself."

"Any idea what 'it' might have been?"

Katie pursed her glossy lips. "Well, Peter dropped by again after my father's second stroke. It wasn't long before he passed. You know what he was like during that time. Communicating wasn't the easiest thing for him. But Peter was even angrier, insisting my father tell him where 'it' was. The nurse kicked him out that time."

Julia took a stab in the dark. "You don't think 'it' could have been a painting?"

Katie thought about it, buffing away as she squinted into the distance. "Hmm, you know, it could have been. My father loved his art collection. He didn't care about art, but he liked how much they were worth." She sighed, deflating a little. "I sold all of them off during the bankruptcy nightmare before we lost the manor. Although..." she trailed off, lost in thought.

"What is it?" Julia asked.

"My brother, Charles, was adamant our father had a secret safe somewhere in the house. He'd go looking for it whenever Father wouldn't give him another trust-fund top-up. He never found it, and believe me, I searched high and low during my lowest lows at the manor. I'd dream about pressing a panel and finding a room filled with gold blocks and rubies to save us from having to sell." Her distant gaze snapped back to the nails, and her shoulders shimmied with a shiver. "All gone now. And if there was a secret safe, I sold the building with the remaining contents to James. Maybe he found it."

The name hung heavy between them. Julia's mind spun with questions. Had James got his hands on the painting Peter had desperately wanted? Had he tried to use it as leverage to influence his vote?

Katie finished Julia's nails with an expert flick of the wrist. "Much better. Might have time to de-bush those brows too if—" She leaned to the side to look around her desk. "Oh, maybe next time. Mrs Coggles is here for her weekly moustache wax."

Julia followed Katie to the counter as Mrs Coggles, a woman Julia sometimes saw in her café with a raw top tip, climbed out of her car. Julia slotted a fiver into the tip box and left the rest of the scones.

"Thanks, Katie. I know more than I did when I arrived."

"You're very welcome," Katie said, before peering around Julia to call, "Take a seat, Mrs Coggles."

"What did you call me?" the woman barked.

"Take a *seat*!" Katie motioned to her ear, and Mrs Coggles turned on her hearing aid. "Take a seat."

"No need to shout. I'm here for my... treatment."

Mrs Coggles shuffled to the waiting chairs, and Katie leaned across the reception desk, the neon tubing tinting her blonde hair bright pink. "There was another thing. After I bumped into Peter, I saw something strange on that piece of paper I picked up. It was only for a split second, but it looked like a sketched map of Peridale. I recognised the manor on there right away, only... it couldn't have been Peridale."

"Why not?"

"Because it looked like half of it was just... gone," she whispered. "My geography has never been the best. It was probably nothing."

"I don't think anything is 'nothing' anymore," Julia said, her tone heavy. She searched Katie's face. "This may sound strange, but your family have been around forever. Do the 1840s ring any bells to you? Any stories passed down?"

Katie frowned. "Hmm. The manor would have been built before then. Sorry, my history is as good as my geography. Is it—"

"*Kathy!*" Mrs Coggles demanded. "I'm waiting."

"My name is..." Katie didn't bother finishing her sentence and flashed Julia an apologetic smile. "It's literally written in flashing neon on the sign, but it's better than last week. I'm sure she called me Keith. I should get on with her whiskers. She leaves a review after every visit. You'd think she hated the place, but she's never missed an appointment."

Julia left the pink glow of the salon and Mrs Coggles to her wax with 'Kathy.' She buttoned up her coat on Mulberry Lane and scanned the familiar shops for Alice's museum, but it was nowhere to be seen. If Alice had made it up, it was a strange thing to fabricate.

About to set off back to the café, she spotted her father outside his antique shop in the barn at the bottom of the lane. He looked like he was trying to sell a faded armchair to a disinterested man waiting in line for coffee at Vicky's Van. Julia waited for the man to fully turn his back on her father before she approached.

Brian's face lit up when he saw her. "Ah, my favourite daughter."

"Sue sends her love."

"*Equal* favourites," he corrected, his cheeks glowing red. "Don't tell her I said that. What can I do for you?"

"I need some local history knowledge."

"Ah, you've come to the right man." Rubbing his hands together, he wove through his wares displayed around the edge of the barn. "Shall we voyage through the refined waters of the Georgian period, or perhaps stroll through the splendours of the Victorians? The elegance of the Edwardian period? Dazzling Art Déco, or the laid-back charm of mid-century modern?"

Julia stifled a smile. Refocusing him would prove challenging.

"Anything from the 1840s?"

"Ah, Gothic, Rococo, and Classical inspirations. I like your style."

"Anything more about the history," she asked, "and less about the furniture?"

Holding his hands up, he said, "You caught me. I'm a fraud. Your father is simply a walking catalogue. Sorry I can't help you, dear."

"That was only my first question," she said, following him into the warmer interior of the shop. "Peter McBride was a customer of yours. You said he loved anything related to local history. What sorts of things did he like?"

"Literally anything if I could prove it had a history within a ten-mile radius. Pottery, farm tools, textiles, spinning wheels, prints—"

"Paintings?"

"*Painting*," he said with a nod. "Just the one."

Feeling like she might be onto something big, she wondered why she hadn't visited her father first.

"I overheard him talking about '*the* painting' before he died."

"That'll be the portrait of Duncan Howarth," he said with so much confidence that Julia was really kicking herself. "Howarth's the chap who tried industrialising our little village. There are no surviving photographs of him, but a rumour has persisted over the years that there's an oil painting. He'd always ask about it when he stopped by, but I've never seen it, and I don't know anyone who has. Still, McBride was convinced it existed. It was his white whale."

"Any chance James Jacobson has it?" she asked on a whim. "Katie said Peter was sure Vincent Wellington had it at the manor."

Leaning against a wardrobe, he considered his answer. "I couldn't say. If he did, he didn't buy it from me."

"Who painted Duncan Howarth's portrait?"

"Again, I couldn't say. The painter is as lost to time as the portrait. If you ask me, I don't think it exists outside of local lore." Brian checked his watch, pushing away from the wardrobe with a start. "I could chat about this stuff all day, but I'll be late for a valuation if I don't get my skates on. Got a minute to help me pack up?"

It took more than a minute, but Julia was happy to help her father carry the furniture inside the barn.

He'd answered a question that had been bugging her since eavesdropping at the party.

But how could a portrait of Duncan Howarth be important now? Maybe Prunella had been telling the truth about the context of the painting being unrelated to their conversation about the committee vote.

Yet a gut feeling assured her there had to be a connection.

Peter had been so focused on James' plans, he wouldn't have let a side quest distract him if it wasn't important.

~

Jessie's foot rapped against the pavement in a recurring rhythm, her eyes darting to her watch before scanning the empty lane. The sinking feeling in her gut had a question attached: had she been stood up? With a little over a week to go until the committee meeting, every minute counted.

Just as she was about to give up hope, Dante came jogging around the top of the street. Seeing him dishevelled and out of breath, Jessie's impatience vanished. He didn't have a face she could stay annoyed with for long.

"I know, I know," he said, slowing to a walk as he approached Jessie. "Got held up investigating a story."

"What was it this time? Old people skydiving? Sponsored dancing dogs?"

"Haunted house that turned out to be rattling pipes in the attic," Dante replied, with a sheepish smile. "With everything going on, the *Chronicle* are spending their resources well."

"It's fine. I was late too." She'd been ten minutes early. "Shall we get down to business?"

They walked to the bottom of Mulberry Lane and turned the corner, where a small sign read 'Peridale Museum' above a narrow door. Jessie had lived in Peridale for more than five years and had never noticed these tucked-away shops before. It seemed few others had either, given how deserted the row was.

"Have you found any dirt on Alice yet?" she asked.

"Not much to go on. Seems clean so far."

They entered the museum, which was little more than a narrow corridor. Dusty bulbs hung from the low ceiling, barely illuminating the space. The walls were crammed with faded photographs and old agricultural tools competing for space. Despite the dreary interior, Alice's shoulders lifted as she caught sight of them.

"Welcome, welcome!" she cried, shuffling out to greet them.

Jessie looked around, taking in the lacklustre exhibits. A moth-eaten wool jumper slumped on a mannequin in the corner. The glass display cases were smudged and mostly empty, save for a few shards of pottery and textiles. Alice stood before them, wringing her hands, practically giddy despite the museum's shortcomings. As she beamed at them, Jessie felt a smile tugging at her own lips, despite her reservations. She felt guilty for considering this place a waste of time. It was clearly a passion project for Alice, even if the execution was lacking.

"Would you like me to give you a guided tour, or would you prefer to have a look around yourselves?"

"A tour would be great," Jessie answered before Dante could reply. This would give them a chance to question Alice under the guise of innocent museum patrons.

Alice's eyes lit up. "Wonderful! Right this way."

They followed her through the first exhibit detailing Peridale's rich wool history. Alice spoke at length about spinning techniques, weaving practices, and the importance of sheep farming in the local area over the centuries. Jessie tried to feign interest as they moved from display to display, each containing paraphernalia related to wool and sheep.

"Riveting," Dante whispered.

"I know everything there is to know about wool," Alice proclaimed proudly. "Ask me anything."

Jessie wracked her brain for a wool-related question. "Umm... how long did it take to shear a sheep in the olden days?"

Instead of directly answering the question, Alice launched into an elaborate explanation about 'the olden days' being too broad a term to give a simple answer. Jessie caught snippets about 'manual hand shears' and 'half an hour per sheep,' and something about 'mechanical shears' drastically reducing that time in the late 19th century. But she found herself less focused on the specifics of what Alice was saying and more on the way her eyes sparkled, her hands shaping the air as she outlined the history of sheep shearing.

"This is brutal," Dante whispered.

"At least she's passionate?"

They continued through the small museum, past cabinets full of faded photographs of unsmiling villagers alongside postcards of Peridale through the ages. The camera quality changed. The fashion changed. The village looked the same.

Finally, they reached the end of the museum, a section devoted to Duncan Howarth. A large portrait frame hung on the wall, empty except for a plaque reading 'Duncan Howarth.'

"As you can see, there are no known images of

Duncan Howarth," Alice explained. "He's a rather mysterious figure."

Jessie read through the information on the exhibit while Alice gave them a summary of Howarth's life and his grand but unfulfilled vision for transforming Peridale into an industrial centre.

According to the plaque, Howarth was born in 1805 into a wealthy family that owned textile factories in London. From a young age, he was transfixed by the rural beauty of his family's ancestral home in the Cotswolds village of Peridale.

However, unlike others who saw only pastoral charm in the region's lush green fields, Howarth envisioned an industrial future for the Cotswolds, with Peridale at its heart. He dreamed of converting the quiet pastures into a sprawling complex of wool factories, the rural calm replaced by the endless clatter of machinery.

"Howarth might have remained obsessed with his industrial ambitions had he not been distracted by romantic passions," Alice said with a wistful sigh. "He fell in love with a local woman named Clarissa Wellington, daughter of Earl Philip Wellington. Consumed by desire, Howarth constructed an elaborate home deep in the forest as a gift for his beloved Clarissa."

"I think I'm sort of related to Clarissa," Jessie said,

unable to work out the complicated connection off the top of her head. "My adopted mum's dad's second wife is a Wellington."

"Really?" Alice's eyes lit up. "Oh, how fascinating!"

"Wait till you see my mum and step-grandmother in the same room if you want complicated," Jessie said, before adding, "Same age. Don't ask."

"How delightfully... complicated," Alice said, her eyes dimming slightly despite her politeness. "Well, it's very loose, but on a family tree, given how many generations it's been and that Clarissa didn't have children, your connection would be through her brother, Jonathan, so you'd technically be her great-great...great-great—maybe one less great—but some kind of niece."

"Check you out," Dante said, rocking back on his heels. "Impressive."

"Thanks, I always knew I was descended from greatness," Jessie said, hand on her chest. "I guess I stole the right woman's cakes from the right café all those years ago. Had myself adopted into nobility via the in-laws. It was meant to be."

"Between us, I think Earl Philip was no more an Earl than you or me," Alice whispered, "but the villagers of the time would have seen him as such, fake title or not. Unfortunately, before Howarth

House could be completed, Clarissa tragically passed away from influenza."

"Oh," Jessie said. "Bummer."

"Quite. It broke his heart, and Howarth became a recluse in the house he built for them. He was a total outcast, shunned by the villagers of the time. Some say he went mad, wandering the shadowy forest until his final days. In the end, Howarth's untamed vision for Peridale died with him when he succumbed to consumption in 1852. The house remains to this day, though it was abandoned decades ago. In the years following his death, Howarth's name became synonymous with thwarted dreams. For instead of a bustling industrial empire, all he left behind was a village forced to speculate about the course it might have taken if his grand plans had come to fruition."

Maybe the museum wasn't so boring after all.

"So, he just gave up his dreams for love?" Jessie asked.

"Oh no, it was much more than a doomed romance," Alice said. "Howarth faced opposition from the first day he arrived. We Cotswold folk can be a stubborn lot, reluctant to embrace change at times. Many locals wanted to preserve their way of life, even back then. He had a lot of opposition from Henderson in Riverswick, too."

Jessie noticed a small plaque at the bottom of the exhibit.

"'Sponsored by James Jacobson,'" she read aloud, meeting Dante's eyes.

"How... generous of him," Dante remarked.

Alice nodded. "Yes, James has been very supportive of my little museum. He covered the costs of this entire room, actually."

Before they could question her further, the front door banged open. Two men in crisp suits strode in. Jessie tensed. She'd seen their type before, usually right before being dragged off to a new foster home.

"Cotswold crew?" Dante asked.

"Debt collectors," she whispered to Dante, knowing he must have had a comfortable life if he didn't recognise them from the way they sauntered in.

The collectors cornered Alice, speaking in hushed tones that Jessie strained to hear. She caught phrases like 'missed payment' and 'demand notice.'

Jessie's protective instincts flared. She wanted to yell at them to leave Alice alone, to stand up for this woman who clearly loved history more than money. She took a step towards them, her hands balling into fists. But Dante's gentle grip on her wrist stopped her.

"I think I'm figuring you out enough to know what that look means," he said, his tone firm. "We shouldn't interfere. As journalists, we have to document things objectively, observe without getting involved, like a nature documentary."

Jessie sighed, the fight draining from her stance.

"Besides, if she's drowning in debt," he continued, miming rubbing his fingers together, "she'd be pretty susceptible to a well-timed bribe, don't you think?"

In her desire to protect the woman who'd just told them a story about the past, Jessie had overlooked the potential motives unravelling in front of them. With the museum failing and debt collectors at her door, Alice was the perfect mark for threats and temptations.

"You're right," Jessie agreed. "We need to keep an eye on her."

"Now you're thinking like an investigative journalist."

Jessie managed a small, remorseful smile before going back to reading the exhibit. She had to look at the bigger picture so the ugly truth could reveal itself. Her instincts told her Alice wasn't the one who'd axed Peter, but she was still one of the circled names on that committee.

After a brief exchange, the men exited the museum empty handed. They must have offered a rare extension. Alice stood alone, blinking back tears as she stared at a dusty old wheel.

"Are you okay?" Jessie asked.

"Oh yes, I'm fine, dear," Alice said, with false brightness. She smoothed her blouse with trembling hands. "Don't mind me. Now, would you like to see this eighteenth-century spinning wheel? It's one of my prized pieces."

Jessie exchanged a look with Dante. Neither of them was eager to continue the wool tour after what they'd witnessed, and she didn't feel like pushing Alice further than she'd already been pushed.

"We should get going," Dante said, apologetically. "But thank you for the lovely tour."

"Of course, of course," Alice replied, deflating. "Well, it was wonderful having you. Please do come again. If I'm still here, that is..."

Outside the museum, Jessie felt sympathy for Alice's situation. She understood now wasn't the time to play the hero, but that didn't mean she didn't want to lob a brick at their van as they drove away.

"Quick drink?" Dante asked, digging his hands into his pockets. "My treat."

She checked the time on her phone. "I should head to the office. I promised Veronica I'd drop by. Sounded like there was another council leak."

"Cool." Dante paused, shifting his weight. For a moment, she thought he might go for a hug, but he stepped back with an awkward shuffle. "Another time, then."

"I'll see you around."

"Not if I see you first."

She laughed to herself as she watched him walk away, then set off for the office. Whatever that feeling was bubbling in her chest, she wasn't sure she liked it very much. Shaking it off, she cut through the nail salon—where Katie had Mrs Coggles pinned to the waxing chair—and climbed the narrow staircase to the office.

Veronica was stooped over her computer, the office freezing despite the plumber's ongoing work.

"Any leads at the museum?" Veronica asked without looking up.

Jessie relayed everything she'd learned about Duncan Howarth and his thwarted industrial vision for the village.

"Interesting," Veronica murmured. "Another ambitious man foiled by the people of Peridale. Some might call that a pattern."

She swivelled her screen to show Jessie an official-looking document sent through by their insider contact. It was titled 'Preserving Tradition, Embracing Progress.'

"What's this?" Jessie asked.

"A very sanitised report claiming any potential future developments would respect Peridale's heritage while allowing necessary improvements that residents strongly support." Veronica's eyes blazed behind her glasses. "Utter rubbish, of course. Our contact didn't send any context, as usual, but someone in the department is clearly under pressure from above to make the project sound amenable."

"Does it mention the field behind the café?"

"It's all very vague, but that seems to be the implication." Veronica smiled despite the lack of concrete evidence. "Don't look so disappointed. I may have found us a way in. You'll never guess who agreed to an interview with our little publication."

"Duncan Howarth via a Ouija board?" Jessie asked. "Oh, by the way, I'm related to his corpse bribe. Sort of. Kind of. If you squint…"

"Try to make sense."

"Try to stop building suspense." Jessie kicked the table. "Who?"

"James Jacobson himself," Veronica announced. "This could be our chance to get some real answers straight from the horse's mouth."

"I don't know if he looks like a horse…"

"Figure of speech." Veronica squinted over her glasses. "Are you alright? You look all flushed, and you're acting… odd."

Jessie cleared her throat. "It's just cold in here. I'm fine."

"Hmm." She glanced at the plumber. "How much longer, lad?"

"Think I'll need some different parts," he said, digging through a toolbox without looking up. "Might have to come back tomorrow."

"Disaster." Sighing, she waved a dismissive hand at the plumber. "Remind me what Jessie is short for?"

"Jesseriah."

"Are you sure you're okay?" Veronica shot her a sharp glance. "I've never seen you looking so pink."

"It's Jessika with a K."

"Well, Jessika with a K, you might want to adopt that for your interview." She pushed her glasses up and returned to typing. "You said you've never met the man, so let's hope he doesn't know that your parents are the local super-sleuths. Start preparing your hard-hitting questions for Mr Jacobson. He's being non-committal about the time and place, so it could happen any minute. Be prepared for anything."

"I'm always prepared for anything."

Jessie retreated to her desk and cracked open her laptop as the plumber tinkered with the ice-cold radiator. A text message popped up on the screen.

DANTE

Let me know when you want to hit up
another museum, noble woman.
Can't wait to see more exhibits of
your famous ancestors.

Jessie bit her lip. She had no idea what to reply, and no idea why she was smiling.

Prepared for anything.

But maybe not this.

"Are you researching over there? I don't hear typing."

"Yes, Master."

JESSIE

Not sure I can stare at another
spinning wheel, but how about that
drink, minus the maze?

DANTE

I like your thinking ;)

Jessie was sure that if Veronica could see her, she'd be commenting on her pink cheeks again.

Switching to a search window, Jessie started her research. For all she'd heard about James, she'd never done her own personal deep dive. She wanted to be ready for James, but she also wanted to make sure James was never ready for Jessika.

12

The next day after closing the café, Julia, Barker, and Jessie were gathered around the stainless-steel island in the kitchen, eating from a giant double chocolate fudge cake with forks. The forty-three candles had already been blown out and lay discarded to the side.

"I get why this is your favourite, Dad," Jessie remarked, taking another bite of the rich cake. "It's incredible, Mum."

"Well, it's the least I could do for your birthday," Julia replied, smiling at Barker. "I know it's been overshadowed by everything, but I promise we'll have a nice dinner at the Comfy Corner tonight to celebrate properly."

Jessie winced. "About that... I may have double-booked myself tonight."

"With?" Julia asked.

"Um, just Dante from the *Chronicle*," Jessie mumbled, a shy flush creeping over her cheeks. "Super-casual drinks."

Julia's eyes lit up, exchanging knowing glances with Barker.

"Why don't you invite Dante along to dinner with us?" Julia suggested. "It would be nice to get to know your new... friend?"

"Way too weird."

"Go and enjoy your drink with him," Barker assured her. "I have a birthday every year, and who am I to stand in the way of young love?"

"Keep it up, old man, and you won't be having a birthday next year," Jessie warned, gathering up her laptop and notepad. "I should get going. Need to do some more research on James before my interview. Can you believe he grew up over on the Fern Moore estate? It doesn't make sense how he turned out like he did."

Julia nodded, the memories coming back to her. "He told me about his upbringing when we first met. His mother died when he was quite young." Her brow furrowed, and she busied herself digging some more chocolate cake onto her fork. They'd bonded over losing their mothers young. "Maybe that little boy from Fern Moore is still in there somewhere beneath the flashy suits."

"He's got a funny way of showing it," Barker pointed out. "But if things go as badly as we think they might, maybe we can appeal to that hurt child inside him."

"Oh, things are *definitely* going to go badly if James and his politician pal are sneaking around as much as they are," Jessie said darkly. "You don't make well-intentioned plans in the shadows, do you?"

"Speaking of Greg…" Barker pulled out his phone to show Jessie the blurry photo he'd taken at Wellington Heights. "I snapped this shot of James talking to someone I'm almost certain was Mr Morgan. You've met him up close. What do you think, Jessie?"

"No way."

"Wrong guy?"

"Oh, no, that's definitely him." Squinting at the screen, Jessie zoomed in on his face. "He looks like he's been through it. You might have snapped the first picture of him in public. Can you send me this? I had intel that Greg was hiding out in one of those apartments."

"Why am I only just finding out about this now?" Barker sighed, taking his phone back. "We should be pooling our information if we want to get to the bottom of this."

"We'll have a sharing circle tomorrow," Jessie said, waving as she hurried to the back door. "There'd better be leftover cake."

"Enjoy your date," Barker called.

Jessie left, muttering to herself, and Julia and Barker shared a smile. Neither of them said anything, but she could tell Barker was as happy for Jessie as she was. It was nice to see their daughter distracted by something other than newspaper intrigue for once, even if Jessie seemed to want to talk about anything but her drinks with Dante.

"I need to leave too, or I'll be late for my first Preservation Society meeting," Julia said, kissing him on the cheek. "I'll meet you at the Comfy Corner at seven." She moved her lips to his. "Since it's just the two of us, dress up nicely."

"Birthday date night?" Barker grinned, pulling the apron over her head. "I like your thinking, Mrs South-Brown. Enjoy the meeting."

Feeling a blush of her own prickling her cheeks, Julia scooped up the cake she'd set aside after making Barker's favourite. After locking up the front of the café, she rushed across the village green, cake box in hand, when a voice called out to her. She froze, her heart sinking.

James Jacobson stood outside Richie's, regarding her with a charming smile.

"Julia?" he called again. "I wanted to thank you for the lovely cake you left on my doorstep the other day. I assume it was you? Thought it might be some kind of threat at first, but then I realised it had to be from you."

Hope you didn't choke, Julia thought.

"Hope you enjoyed it, neighbour."

"I'll be dropping by your charming café for a chat very soon."

Thrown off balance, Julia struggled for words. The friendly, engaging man before her reminded her so much of the James she'd grown to like last summer, before everything that happened with the Fern Moore flats and the field sale. Yet she couldn't forget his shady actions, no matter how harmless he appeared in this moment.

Spotting an opportunity, she fixed him with a steady gaze. "You're welcome anytime, James, as long as you're actually ready to talk." She tried to keep her tone light, but she heard an underlying hint of warning in her voice.

James' easy smile faltered. He gave her a small bow. "Then I shall see you very soon."

With that, he ducked into Richie's, leaving Julia conflicted in the middle of the village green. Had her cake delivery really come across as threatening? She couldn't recall her exact mindset when leaving it there, but the idea of catching the elusive James Jacobson off guard—of making him feel apprehension and uncertainty, even fleetingly—did give her a sense of grim satisfaction.

After the months of secrecy surrounding the field sale, of feeling like a powerless bystander in her own community, the notion that she'd cracked James' suave exterior with three-quarters of a Victoria sponge felt like a minor victory.

The curtains twitched at her gran's cottage, pushing her to continue to the village hall before she was held up any longer.

Inside, she found Prunella, Martin, Richard, and Alice seated around a table in the middle of the polished wood floor. Was it the stark lighting, or did they all look a little wearier than they had when she'd seen them together at Prunella's cottage?

"Julia, welcome. Do come in," Prunella greeted, though her tone held no real warmth—only thinly veiled irritation. "You're late."

Alice avoided Julia's gaze, preoccupied with adjusting her chair. It didn't move an inch. Martin and Richard slumped low in their seats, eyeing Julia with unveiled contempt.

Julia took a seat, smoothing her skirt. "Before we

begin, I was hoping to get to know you all better." She scanned their stony faces, steeling her nerves. "So, how did you all come to join the society? Alice told me she was one of the founding members alongside Peter."

Prunella's eyes narrowed. "It seems the two of you are well acquainted already?"

"We bumped into each other at the library while I was researching the history of my café. Mid-eighteenth century, you were right." Julia kept her tone light despite the tension thickening the air. "So, what brought you to this club, Prunella?"

"Society," Prunella corrected. "I joined two years ago, soon after its inception. Peter and I went back many years before that. We met at an art auction." She gave Alice a sharp look.

Julia's eyes flitted to Alice. An art auction. Likely for the Duncan Howarth painting, she deduced.

"Same," Martin mumbled, not meeting Julia's eye. "Two years ago."

"Last year," Richard grunted.

Prunella flipped back the lid of the box Julia had placed on the table and scowled at the contents.

"What a... quaint cake," Prunella said, acid in her tone. "What is it?"

"Pumpkin spice sponge cake with cinnamon buttercream."

"How rustic." Prunella slid it onto the table as though it carried the plague. "You shouldn't have gone to the trouble. We don't even have forks or plates."

Julia pulled paper plates and plastic forks from her bag, arranging them neatly, ignoring Prunella's poor attempt to unsettle her. She caught Alice suppressing a smile as she helped herself to a small slice, though Prunella declined outright.

"Shall we just get on with this?" Richard grumbled, shovelling cake into his mouth. "It's fine. Not too sweet."

"Thank you," Julia said, waiting until all had some cake before continuing. "But I have a couple more questions. You were all at the Halloween party but left early. None of you were present when Peter was killed. Did you see him there at all?"

Richard and Martin tensed, their faces darkening. Alice's gaze dropped to her lap. Prunella's jaw clenched so tightly Julia thought she heard her teeth crack.

"I had another party to go to," Martin muttered after a stretch of silence.

"Me too," Richard echoed, avoiding Julia's eyes.

"I don't care for late nights," Alice admitted.

"I needed to feed my cat," Prunella said.

If Peter hadn't ended up dead at that party, she might have believed them.

"Since we're on the topic of the party," she continued, "I wanted to ask you about that painting Peter mentioned again, Prunella. I've been researching, and it seems Peter was hunting a 'white whale'—a portrait of Duncan Howarth?"

At this, Richard let out a derisive guffaw. "Peter was obsessed with that old crackpot, but he would've hated Howarth's guts if the man were alive today. And Howarth would have despised his spinelessness."

Prunella shot Richard a subtle warning glare before turning back to Julia and smoothing over her icy exterior. "As I've told you multiple times now, Peter was helping me hunt for an ancestor's painting. A sentimental family piece."

Julia leaned forward. "Are you absolutely certain? Because it seems Peter was completely fixated on locating this specific portrait of Duncan Howarth—the only one in existence, if the rumours are true."

Prunella met her gaze steadily. "I can assure you, the existence of that painting is a myth. Peter became irrationally convinced this imaginary painting held a deeper meaning and obsessed over it. But it was a delusion, nothing more." Her tone rang with finality.

Julia wasn't convinced, but changed tack, turning to Alice. "The history exhibit on Duncan Howarth at your museum was quite informative to my daughter. Sponsored by James Jacobson, of all people."

Alice kept her eyes lowered.

"James has an affinity for old Duncan," Martin offered, then recoiled as Richard kicked his shin under the table. But Martin pressed on, "He and Peter should've been best mates with their shared obsession. No wonder James got Peter working on those old plans—"

Richard elbowed Martin hard in the ribs, cutting him off.

But it was too late. Martin's slip confirmed the existence of the plans. Between Peter's clues, Alice's exhibit, and Jessie's research, the puzzle was coming together.

"You and Prunella both denied knowing anything about those plans," Julia said evenly. "But Peter tried to tell me the truth. He just couldn't break his contracts. Maybe you all signed gag orders too?"

She scanned their faces. Martin looked ready to crack.

"Let's get on with the business of this meeting, shall we?" Martin blurted out. "I think we should discuss the bus stop restoration—"

"What a wonderful idea," Prunella interrupted, seizing the diversion. "We should fundraise..."

As they prattled about mundane village affairs, Julia observed cynically. This show of civic duty reeked of deception. She wouldn't fall for their pretence.

Eventually, Prunella glanced her way. "As you can see, most of our business is rather dull. We focus on pragmatic community needs."

"So, you haven't been meeting to discuss James' plans?" Julia countered. "Those could change this village drastically. More than a crumbling bus stop."

"My dear, you've let Peter's ramblings infect your imagination," Prunella dismissed with a hollow laugh.

Sensing she'd hit close to the mark, Julia turned to the others. She looked at Richard. "You changed clothes after the party. Had stains to hide?"

"I spilled my drink, that's all," Richard growled, fists clenched.

She turned to Martin. "Quite the mansion you just bought. Expensive."

Martin reddened. "Paid for fair and square!"

She glanced at Alice, who seemed to shrink under her gaze. "Financial troubles at the museum?"

"Every new business has growing pains," Alice whispered, head bowed.

Finally, Julia turned to Prunella. "And those doctored research papers. Must have damaged your reputation. Wouldn't be good for you if they came back to the forefront."

Prunella sucked in a sharp breath, trembling with

rage. "How dare you! My students simply objected to poor marks. Their accusations were untrue. Nothing more!"

Richard slammed his fist on the table. "That's enough! Who do you think you are, coming here and—"

Martin grabbed his arm. "Settle down."

Prunella stood. "I believe it's clear you are not a fit for our society, Julia. This meeting is over."

Just then, two men entered carrying something large concealed under a velvet purple cloth. Richard and Martin exchanged conspiratorial smirks, while Prunella feigned ignorance. Alice sank lower in her seat.

As the men moved to arrange the object on stage, Julia rose from her seat.

"What is that?" she asked. "What are you bringing in here?"

The men didn't so much as glance in her direction, continuing about their task as if she hadn't spoken.

Julia looked to Prunella for an explanation, but the older woman avoided her gaze, sipping her tea with affected nonchalance.

Frustrated, Julia turned her attention back to the object as the men positioned it at the centre of the stage. It was wide, perhaps three feet in height, and relatively long. In her mind, she saw a model. But of what? The velvet cloth revealed nothing, not even the faintest outline to hint at the mysterious object's identity.

As the men stepped back, Julia seized her chance. She hopped onto the stage before anyone could stop her and gripped the fabric.

But Prunella's sharp voice halted her. "I wouldn't do that if I were you. That's private property."

Julia froze, the velvet slipping from her fingers.

As the others hurried out and the men in polo shorts sporting the council logo lingered on the stage watching Julia like a hawk, Julia slipped into the bathroom. She climbed atop the toilet and waited.

Jessie sat huddled in her coat at her desk in the newspaper office, fingers frozen and stiff as she typed up interview questions for James Jacobson. The space heater sputtered in the corner, barely taking the edge off the bone-chilling air. In an hour, she'd be thawing out in the warmth of Richie's with Dante; but for now, she was shivering in her puffer jacket.

Nearby, Veronica rifled through a stack of papers while munching on steaming, vinegar-soaked chips wrapped in newspaper. The tempting aroma of hot grease and salt made Jessie's empty stomach growl.

"Want some?" Veronica asked. "Can't let good chips go cold."

Jessie grabbed a few piping-hot chips as her eyes drifted to the dartboard Veronica had put up, sporting the blurry photo of James and Greg on the doorstep of Wellington Heights.

With expert aim, Veronica flung a dart, hitting the bullseye square between the men's faces. "When do you think he last saw sunlight?"

Jessie leaned in for a closer look at the haggard, unshaven man she couldn't believe had been a clean-shaven, camera-ready, shiny-faced politician—always ready for a photo opportunity—only a month ago.

"Maybe it's part of an upcoming rebrand?" Jessie suggested. "He's done with politics and ready to open a microbrewery with a passion for IPAs."

"If only," Veronica replied. She held out the darts to Jessie. "Have a go if you fancy. It might make you feel better before the big interview."

"I don't think I'm that psychotic yet. Give me a couple more years. How did you get so good, anyway?"

"The staff room at the college had a board. Passed the time and stopped the other tutors from boring me to sleep," Veronica fired another dart, barely looking, yet still hitting the bullseye. "They all thought I'd wind up some spinster recluse obsessed with Shakespeare and five cats."

"How wrong they were," Jessie said, half under her breath. "You don't have the cats."

Jessie clicked through the pages of James' personal website, skimming over the details of his many successes. Wellington Heights was just one of the lavish properties he had acquired over the years. He owned manors, estates, and mansions up and down the country. His party trick seemed to be buying impossibly expensive buildings and dividing them into luxury flats to quadruple their value. It was hard to believe this was the same lad who came from such humble beginnings in Fern Moore.

She paused on the 'Early Years' section, which featured a photo of James as a young boy. He sat on a swing set in the small metal playground that used to be in the centre of the Fern Moore courtyard, back when the equipment was still shiny and new. The boy's clothes were too tight on his pudgy frame. Behind him stood a pencil-thin woman in a long leather jacket; one hand pushed the swing while the other held a lit cigarette. Neither of them looked happy in the captured moment.

Jessie stared at the image, transported back to her own childhood—hopping around families, homes, schools, towns, then doorways, bridges, industrial estates. If there were pictures of her looking miserable on swings, she'd never seen them, but she understood that look on his face. To have nothing where others have so much. He must have felt that same envy growing up poor. Yet here he was now. The puppy fat was gone, and he had to be one of the richest men in the country, still chasing more wealth and power. She wondered if he was any happier for it, or if that boy swinging with a scowl in old hand-me-downs was still driving the car.

"Jessie…"

"Hmm?"

"New email."

Spinning away from her laptop, the sight of Veronica's thousand-mile stare chilled her more than the lack of a decent heater.

"What is it?"

"It's from our council insider," Veronica said, her voice croaky. "It's tomorrow."

"The committee meeting?"

Veronica shook her head. "They're publicly unveiling the development plans."

"Just like that?" Jessie's heart dropped. "But there's been no advertising."

"I think that's the point. Minimal attendance means fewer objections." Veronica's stare hardened like flint. "They couldn't have a committee meeting without publicly announcing their plans. There'll be nobody there. The timing reeks of my brother's handiwork."

Rage simmered within Jessie. She should have known they'd try something so underhanded. Gripping a dart from the board, she hurled it at the bullseye with focused fury.

"There'll be people there," Jessie said, dragging her chair back to her desk and pulling her laptop close. "I'll make sure of it."

Jessie rushed to pull up the newspaper's design software, her fingers shaking as she clicked through the layouts. All she needed was a simple flyer, and she knew exactly what to write.

Minutes later, she saved it on a USB stick and left the office. Fighting against the swirling wind, Jessie ran around the corner to the library. Barker was waiting outside the Comfy Corner in a fancy shirt and tie, preoccupied with his phone, and Neil was locking up the library.

"Jessie? Everything alright?"

"Neil, I need to use the printer," she said, breathless. "It's urgent. Please."

Though confused, Neil unlocked the door. "Of course. Help yourself."

While Neil turned the lights back on, Jessie sprinted straight for the printer and got to work. The old machine sputtered to life, firing out flyer after flyer at surprising speed. As the papers piled up, Neil wandered over, peering at the bold text.

"Is this... are you sure this is accurate?"

"My source is solid," Jessie said, her tone leaving no room for doubt as the printer spat out another page.

When she had a hefty stack, she thanked Neil for the help and rushed out into the night. She headed straight for the first person she knew would be able to help her get the message out. She pounded on the door of Dot's cottage. The door flung open, and the dogs barked behind Dot as she squinted into the night.

"What's happened, Jessie? Where's the fire?"

"The village hall, tomorrow at 2 p.m." Jessie thrust a flyer at Dot. "I need your help to spread the word. Exhaust your phone book, get your megaphone back out—whatever it takes. People need to know about this."

Dot scanned the heading: 'FIND OUT WHAT YOUR LOCAL MP AND HIS PROPERTY DEVELOPER FRIEND DON'T WANT YOU TO KNOW. VILLAGE HALL. 2.P.M.'

"Those devious snakes! Don't you worry, I'll rally the troops. But how did you..." she trailed off as another figure appeared behind her.

To Jessie's astonishment, Ethel White emerged from Dot's sitting room, teacup in hand.

Dot shot Jessie a weary look. "Turns out you were right. We do have quite a lot in common. We buried the hatchet. Ethel, it's happening tomorrow."

Dot handed a flyer to Ethel, who slammed her teacup on the side table. Dot sighed at the spilled tea on the wood, snatching up a tissue to dab it up.

"Why haven't people been talking about this?" Ethel demanded.

"I have the inside scoop." Digging into her bag, Jessie pulled out hundreds of flyers and split them. "How many houses do you think you can get these to?"

"Every house?" Dot's eyes gleamed with determination. "What do you think, Ethel?"

"Easily. I know these streets better than anyone. I'm sure I'll hit twice as many houses as you."

"Impossible. My legs are much longer than those little stumps you have." Leaning on the banister, Dot hollered up the stairs, "Percy! Out of the bath. We need all hands on deck. Battle stations!"

The two women continued exchanging competitive banter as Dot's husband, Percy, appeared at the top of the stairs, clad only in a towel and a shower cap covering his bald head. "Where's the fire, dear?"

Leaving them to mobilise, Jessie scooped up some

flyers and headed out into the night. She forgot all about her date until she noticed Dante waiting outside Richie's, dressed to the nines and checking his breath in his palm. Jessie peered down at her puffer jacket, baggy jeans, and scuffed Docs. He looked through her for a moment as she approached him before his eyes snapped. The smile that crossed his face made her feel like she was dressed in her best outfit.

Rather than explain, she handed him a flyer and saw the same reaction she'd been seeing in the short time since she'd created it.

"Got that hip flask on you?" she said, pulling more flyers from her bag. "We might need to take that drink on the move. We're needed."

∾

Julia waited in the bathroom stall, listening as the chatter faded away to perfect silence. When all was finally quiet, she crept out and made her way back to the main hall.

Her phone buzzed in her pocket.

BARKER
At Comfy Corner. Everything alright?

JULIA
I'll be there soon. Sorry, ran over.

She'd explain later.

The village hall was shrouded in shadow as Julia crept back inside, the click of her heels echoing across the wooden floorboards. Moonlight streamed through the high windows, casting an eerie glow over the cavernous room.

Julia's heart raced as her eyes landed on the stage. Something large lay concealed beneath a velvet cloth. She glanced around warily before moving closer, holding her breath. Each creak of the floor sounded deafening in the empty silence.

Reaching the stage, Julia hesitated, her fingers hovering over the plush fabric. Curiosity battled with caution, but she had come too far to turn back now. With a deep breath, she gripped the cloth and yanked it away.

Julia staggered back, her hand flying to her mouth. There before her sprawled a detailed model of Peridale—but not the Peridale she knew. The quaint village green and familiar shops remained, yet behind them, crammed together in James' beloved field, were hundreds of identical suburban homes.

Julia circled the diorama. The historic pasture was unrecognisable, swallowed entirely by this sterile sprawl. She shuddered at the clinical precision with which centuries of untouched greenery had been erased.

Sudden voices outside made Julia jump. Darting underneath the model, she pulled the cloth back just as the door creaked open, she didn't dared breathe. Heavy footsteps crossed the hall, and with a surge of dread, she recognised James Jacobson's cultured tones —accompanied by the oily voice of Greg Morgan.

"...don't see how they can refuse, the greedy sods," Greg was saying. "The vote *will* go our way."

"Perhaps, but without the road access, it's all for nothing," James replied.

Julia pricked up her ears.

"Leave that to me," Greg said. "I can pull some strings in Westminster, get a compulsory purchase order pushed through. It's only those Knights causing a fuss over their measly strips of land."

"No, no more using intimidation tactics with that family," James said sharply. "The last incident caused too much negative publicity."

Julia tensed. They were openly discussing harassing the Knights. She fumbled for her phone to record it but accidentally knocked it against the stage.

"What was that?" Greg asked.

"Oh, don't be so paranoid," James cautioned. "You're as bad as Peter these days."

They both laughed coldly. Julia held her breath, willing them to leave.

Instead, James walked over and yanked the cloth

completely off the model. Julia squeezed further under the model, drawing her knees in tight.

"It will all be worth it in the end," James said, surveying the miniature community. "They won't know what hit 'em."

"We're going to be so damn rich," Greg chuckled.

"My friend, I'm already so damn rich," James replied. "But I'll be happy to make you richer."

"Right, well, when I'm Prime Minister, you'll get whatever government role you want. Secretary of State for Housing, perhaps?"

James laughed, and kept laughing. "Oh, you delusional fool. With all the scandals you've been involved in, you'll be lucky to win the next local council election. Now, do be a good man and shave that scruff off your face before the hearing tomorrow. Can't have you looking like a Fern Moore peasant for your big comeback."

Greg sputtered, but no comeback materialised. Julia held her breath, praying again they would leave.

"I'll handle the access road issue," James continued. "I have interests in surprising places."

Finally, their footsteps receded, and the door banged shut. Julia sagged with relief but remained frozen in place. Her mind reeled from all she had heard. This went far deeper than she could have imagined. She knew she had to expose their corrupt plans. But who would believe her word alone against two of the village's most powerful men?

Slowly, Julia crept from her hiding place. She stood staring down at the sprawling model community destined to replace the old sheep field. She looked at her café in the shadow of the high wall closing in the unnamed estate and noticed something in the middle. An opening. A new square with shops. The blocks were grey, but she could imagine what they would become. A chain coffee shop. A supermarket. Luxury high-end boutiques.

Rural village killers.

No wonder James had wanted to keep his plans secret for as long as he could.

~

Moonlight pierced the gauzy clouds, illuminating the foggy field behind the café with an icy sheen. Julia and Barker, huddled in their coats, leaned against the weathered fence. They passed the fork between them, taking turns eating chunks of the leftover double chocolate fudge chocolate cake balanced on the fence post. Their movements were deliberate, unhurried, like they had all the time in the world.

After a long moment, Julia broke the silence. "We should enjoy this while it lasts."

Pumpkins and Peril

"You can bake another cake."

"I'm not talking about the cake."

"I know." He sighed, the cake on the fork not reaching his mouth. "It won't come to that. We won't let it."

Julia looked into his eyes, wishing she could draw from his reservoir of confidence. But the unsettling image of that luxurious, sprawling model suburb was imprinted into her mind. And the haunting echo of James' cold, calculating laugh still rang in her ears—so sure he had the votes, so certain he could secure the road access. With a heavy heart, she took another bite of the cake, but its sweetness twisted into ash on her tongue.

"I hope you're right," she said.

She reached into her coat pocket and pulled out the crumpled flyer she'd found on the village green, hoping the short notice of Jessie's resourcefulness wouldn't deter the people of Peridale from turning up from the grand unveiling.

Barker noticed the flyer and said, "We'll fight this. Everyone will."

Julia met Barker's eyes, and for a moment, she allowed herself to believe that they could change the course of the future. But it wasn't up to them. The committee held the keys, and the society half had made their intentions clear to Julia tonight. Peter had said the wrong people had the power, and she knew now he was referring to his peers. With Peter's guidance, James Jacobson had written the recipe for their future. Tomorrow, the people of Peridale would get their first taste.

As much as Julia liked to think she knew her fellow villagers' tastebuds, she had no idea how the day was going to unfold.

13

*J*ulia awoke with a start to the crack of nearby fireworks—5:32 a.m. and still dark at the edges of the curtain. Olivia wailed from her nursery, jarred awake by the noise. Rubbing the sleep from her eyes, Julia realised it was November 5th, the morning after Barker's birthday. Bonfire Night.

She'd forgotten all about the annual village bonfire. The café would be busy tonight as families stopped by for hot chocolates and cinder toffee after watching the fireworks. But before that came the unveiling at the village hall. Julia's stomach twisted in knots. After the grim model village makeover she'd discovered the previous night, facing reality in broad daylight filled her with dread.

Donning her dressing gown, Julia hurried to the nursery. Barker was already there, comforting a tearful Olivia.

"Shhh, it's okay."

Julia cradled Olivia, holding her close and kissing the top of her head until her cries softened to hiccups.

"Who sets off fireworks this early?" Barker remarked.

Julia offered a weak smile. "I can take it from here if you want to catch some more sleep. I'm wide awake."

"And leave you to face the day alone? Not a chance," Barker said, giving her shoulder a supportive squeeze. "I'll put the kettle on."

Julia sighed, shifting Olivia in her arms. "Make mine a coffee this morning. *Strong* coffee."

Going through the motions of her morning routine a few hours earlier than usual, Julia braced herself for the long, trying day ahead. She'd tossed and turned all night, haunted by nightmares of wandering deep in a maze of identical houses, every turn leading her to another row stretching out as far as she could see.

Hours later, with Olivia at her nursery play day, the café hummed as the lunchtime crowd poured in. But the atmosphere was different; it wasn't the usual blend of clinking cutlery and casual chatter about the upcoming bonfire. Today, urgent whispers focused solely on one topic: the mysterious flyer.

While Sue managed the counter, Julia had been stuck by the window, watching the village green filling with murmuring onlookers on their way to the village hall.

At quarter past one, she spotted the man of the hour, James Jacobson, exiting Richie's, grinning and waving as if he were a much-loved local. The sight unsettled Julia as much as seeing the 'James Jacobson invites you...' branded on the Halloween invitation. Perhaps he'd been priming the village for this moment, softening them up for his big revelation.

The crowd parted around him until he reached the small group of protesters blocking the church gates, led by Dot, Ethel, and Percy. They had a stand-off, Dot and Ethel's finger wagging in his face as they told him what for, but he only put up with it for a humouring moment. He sauntered around them and continued to the hall, and Dot and her new group went back to stuffing flyers in the hands of anyone who'd take them.

Trailing at a distance, Jessie trained her camera on him. Julia exchanged glances with Barker, who lingered near the hall's side entrance, watching the unfolding spectacle.

From the warmth of her café, Julia observed the

scene with a sense of numb disbelief. She'd hoped the familiar routine of the morning would distract her until the time came, but she felt detached, unable to slip into her regular café cheeriness.

Leaving the window, she dragged herself back to work, scooping up empty cups on her way to the counter.

"Cheer up, love," her dad said when she passed his table, flipping through a brochure filled with antiques. "It might not be so bad. Could be nice to have some new faces around."

Katie pouted her lips at him. "But it won't be the same village, will it, Brian? If Julia's right about the size of those houses, it'll be like having the Wellingtons running around the place again."

"But you *are* a Wellington," Amy Clark pointed out.

"A Wellington-*South*," she corrected, "which makes me qualified to say I'm much happier living out of that bubble. I grew up thinking we were the most important people in Peridale because we had the biggest house."

"And that's how you treated it," Amy grumbled.

"And that's not right," Katie said.

Brian shrugged and flipped the page. "People will adjust. They always do."

In a corner, Neil stared into his tea, his face as pale

as milk. Since Julia had filled him in about the scale of James' plans, he'd been even quieter than normal.

At her usual table, deep in thought, Evelyn swirled the dregs of her tea. "I don't have a good feeling about any of this. If that's what's becoming of our little rural corner, I might consider selling the B&B."

"Oh, Evelyn," Julia said, sighing. "Would you really?"

"I enjoy my quiet life here far too much," she said, reaching for her crystal necklaces with a sigh. "Peridale might not be perfect, but we have a real community here."

"I'll be able to play organ to bigger crowds at the church," Amy said, almost to herself this time. "They're just houses."

Veronica, who'd ventured out of the office for a rare café appearance, cleared her throat. "Luxury houses that'll inflate property values and prices. Look at the domino effect that happened with Fern Moore when the developers started sniffing around. Now multiply that by ten. You won't recognise this place in a few short years if this goes ahead."

Amy started to respond, but Julia interrupted, "Veronica's right. The essence of Peridale will fade, maybe not immediately, but eventually."

"Well, you all talk as if James has already won," Amy retorted. "Have a little faith."

Brian rustled his brochure in agreement. "Exactly. Plans change all the time."

But given how far James and Greg had come with their plans, she thought otherwise.

As speculative chatter swirled around her, Julia retreated to the kitchen. She began rinsing dishes, struggling to quell the rising dread. Sue stood beside her with a tea towel, nibbling her bottom lip. She opened her mouth to speak, hesitated, and closed it again.

"You haven't said much about all of this," Julia finally asked. "What's your perspective?"

"Julia, I... I need to tell you something," she whispered, glancing over her shoulder. "But I'm afraid of how you'll react."

Twisting the tap to stem the water flow, Julia flicked the soap suds from her fingers and turned to meet her sister's eyes. Sue had looked worried all morning, but Julia had put it down to Neil's conflict of interest.

"Sue, you know you can tell me anything," Julia assured her. "Anytime. About anything."

"I know." More lip nibbling. "I've done something that—"

Before Sue could get her words out, the kitchen door burst open. Sue ducked away, turning to dry the dishes, leaving Julia to part the beads. With one last concerned look at her sister, she poked her head back into the café.

"It's starting," Jessie panted. "Half an hour early."

"Typical!" Veronica cried, the first to follow Jessie out. "More underhand tactics."

Julia's heart skipped a beat. Gripping the counter, she took several deep breaths as the café emptied. Sue came up behind her and patted her back before joining the flow. The last to leave, Julia locked up and followed them out.

Adrenaline propelled Julia across the village green, but anxiety tightened her chest with each step. Upon reaching the village hall, she squeezed into the crowded space as the flow continued around her. She noted planning committee members—Prunella, Richard, Martin, and Alice—taking seats at the front. Alice was the only one looking around at the spectacle. She caught Julia's eyes before looking away in a flash.

James held centre stage, chest puffed out, chin raised. Given the lack of advertising, he must not have expected an audience, but his barely contained smirk let everyone know he was pleased to have one.

She found Barker in the crowd and joined him at the back of the room. He gave her hand a reassuring squeeze, and she squeezed back.

This was really happening.

And all Julia could do was join her fellow villagers in watching and waiting.

When the chatter began to settle, James approached the microphone, its shrill feedback making the crowd wince. He grinned, giving it a few booming taps.

When he spoke, his voice was as smooth and rich as ever.

"Welcome, friends," he began, as if they were gathered for a congenial poetry reading. "Quite the turnout. It's fantastic to see how many of you share enthusiasm for our village's future."

Julia's hand tightened around Barker's. From her vantage point at the back, she could see the shifty sideways glances of the sceptics and an equal number of smiling faces settling in for his speech.

"I'm here today to discuss an exciting development that could revitalise our beloved community." The crowd buzzed with excited whispers. James let them build for a moment before raising his hands, calling for silence. "As many of you know, I've taken a great interest in Peridale since returning to the place of my birth. I have revitalised your local library, and looking out, I see many of the faces of those who attended my party there." He paused as though weighing up if he should remind them how the party ended. Clearing his throat, he continued, "I transformed a dilapidated manor from a home for the few into apartments for the many. A charming village like Peridale deserves that kind of investment. Wouldn't you all agree?"

There was a rumble of agreement from the nodding heads. Dot, who'd snagged seats with Ethel and Percy at the front, snorted a laugh.

"I'm glad we're all on the same page," James said, loosening up a little. "But you didn't just come here to hear me talk, did you? Your time is valuable, so should I get on with it?"

His sudden casualness brought some laughter, and with a click of his fingers, the same men in council-branded shirts appeared on stage and grabbed the velvet's edges. They looked at James for approval. Rather than give the nod straight away, he looked out at the crowd as people shuffled to the edge of their seats. Julia clenched so hard to Barker's hand, she must have been cutting off the circulation.

When the moment had been stretched to a nail-biting peak, James gave the nod. They whipped off the velvet cloth with a theatrical flourish to reveal the model.

"May I present to you... Phase One of the *Howarth Estate!*"

Despite their Cotswold stone disguises, the enormous houses, packed together in neat rows, bore no resemblance to Julia's beloved village.

"Phase one?" Barker muttered. "Should we say something?"

Julia surveyed the interested faces around them as they rose from their seats to get the best view of the tilted display. "I'm not sure it'll make a difference right now."

"Designed in collaboration with the Peridale Preservation Society," James continued, bowing slightly to the councillors on the front row. "As you can see, much care and consideration has gone into ensuring the Howarth Estate respects the appearance of your local landscape. Unlike *other* recent developments in neighbouring villages, Howarth Estate will be built from locally sourced golden Cotswold stone."

More nodding heads of approval.

"Named after Duncan Howarth, a visionary son of Peridale whose dreams of an industrial future were tragically cut short, this estate will bring two hundred new homes to the area," he asserted. "As someone born only a stone's throw from where we stand now, I am honoured to take up the torch Duncan left behind and lead this village into a new age of prosperity!"

Unable to bear another moment of his twisted narrative, Julia turned away, repulsed. His hollow promises made her feel sick; she had to escape.

Dot couldn't stand it either; she stormed the stage with a megaphone.

"Don't believe this crook's lies!" she shouted. "If this monstrosity is so marvellous, why all the secrecy? Why is this the first we're hearing about it?"

Security guards who'd blended into the crowd hopped onto the stage and dragged Dot off. James didn't flinch an inch.

Ethel was next, storming the stage to kick over the 'Howarth Estate' sign. Security seized her even quicker, dragging her off in the same direction as Julia's gran. Percy ascended the steps and kicked the table leg. The model wobbled before he limped back down before the security could get to him.

Unperturbed, James invited the crowd to examine the model. Villagers surged forward, captivated by the miniatures, and the hall continued to fill with more from outside.

"Please, stick around for our special guest speaker," he called, checking his watch. "There'll be time to answer the many questions I'm sure you have about this exciting opportunity at the end."

But Julia had heard enough. Slipping through the crowd, she left the village hall and didn't stop until she was on the green. She inhaled a deep lungful of the crisp afternoon air, still suffocating from James' syrupy spin.

"You should have heard him last night," she said as Barker caught up with her. "He was a man unmasked. He's peddling a fantasy, and people are falling for it."

"It's new and shiny," Barker assured her. "Some people might need time to see through it, but Julia..." Clutching her hand, he pulled her closer. "Don't look now, but I believe we were followed out of the village hall."

A chill unrelated to the autumn wind swept over Julia. She resisted the urge to turn around, staring ahead at her lit-up and locked café.

"Black suit?" Julia asked.

Barker nodded, and as tense as she felt, vindication washed over her. She hadn't imagined the man following Alice out of the library. And Peter hadn't been paranoid; he hadn't been wrong about anything he'd said.

"What do we do?" Julia asked.

"We take a very convoluted path home," he said. "If they follow us, we'll know we've been marked."

They walked towards Richie's and down the alley as inconspicuously as possible. They circled the bar, nodding to Richie as he stacked barrels by the back door. He shot them curious glances but returned their nod before looking down the alley as soft footsteps stalked their trail.

"Ten paces behind from the sounds of it," Barker whispered. "They're making no effort to be subtle about this."

Back at the edge of the village, Julia looked at her café and hesitated.

"Let's split up," she whispered.

"That's the worst plan I've ever heard."

"Don't you want to know which of us he's following?" She let go of her hand. "It's broad daylight and there are people all around. Who ever he follows, try to lose him, and then we'll meet in your office."

"Julia, I—"

Head down, Julia set off across the green, her steps deliberate as she navigated the stream flowing in the direction of the village hall. Slipping through the wrought-iron church gates, she entered St. Peter's. The air inside was icy, the scent of old wood and incense heavy. Father David was a solitary figure in the vestry, lost in study. At the altar, Julia paused, her ears picking up the hushed echo of cautious footsteps. Pushing through the door at the rear, she emerged into the graveyard.

In the adjacent field, a group tossed scrap wood from the back of a van onto the unlit bonfire, the clatter punctuating the stillness. Digging her hands into her coat pockets, Julia went to the only grave she frequented. Nestled in the shadow of Howarth Forest, she felt the chill of her mother's gravestone beneath her fingertips. Crouching, she cleared the weeds sprouting around the withered yellow chrysanthemums. For a moment, she felt safe.

Peering around the edge of the gravestone, she spotted the man in the dark suit. He was weaving through the headstones, his eyes scanning each one systematically as he closed the distance. She peeked at the forest's edge over her shoulder, weighing the risk of losing him in the dense trees. There was no way he knew the forest better than her. It wasn't a risk she was willing to take. If he got too close, the bonfire builders were only a leap over a wall away.

She glanced around once more, finding no trace of the suited man. Had he given up? Just as she straightened up, so did he, appearing several rows away. His eyes met hers, unflinching. His face held no expression, his stance as still as the surrounding gravestones.

He didn't care that she was looking right at him.

A chilling realisation settled over her as she thought about Jessie's article. He wasn't trying to 'catch' her, he wanted her to know she was being followed.

She stepped towards the man, and he mirrored her, retreating a step back. She took two. He took two. They continued this eerie dance until they neared the church gates. His eyes never left her, his lack of expression never changed. Sliding her hand into her coat pocket, she gripped her phone and lifted it. He pivoted and melded into the crowd, disappearing before she could capture his image.

Not that it would help.

The man with the shaved head and plain features could have been anyone, but he wasn't just anyone. He had to be a member of the Cotswold Crew. She wondered how long he'd been following her, but this must have been his first day.

A harassment campaign wouldn't work if she didn't know she was being harassed.

Peter had warned her, and now she understood why.

There were people who'd stop at nothing to get their way. The mutilated 1840s plan might have been revealed, so where did Julia fit into it?

∼

Jessie fought her way out of the village hall, elbowing through the villagers, desperate to catch a glimpse of James' new toy. She'd been suppressing the urge to grab the microphone and yell, "How many of you can afford these luxury homes?" Instead, she pocketed her fury, saving it for her next scalding article in *The Peridale Post*.

Breaking out into the fresh air, Jessie wondered where her parents had gone. They'd vanished into the crowd soon after Dot and Ethel had been marched off the stage. Jessie had admired their nerve, but she'd watched their cries fall on deaf ears. It was going to take more than geriatric screaming to make a difference. She checked around the side of the village hall for her parents, but she saw something better.

Greg Morgan paced in the shadow of a large oak tree, dressed in a rumpled suit. He clutched notecards in one trembling hand, muttering under his breath.

Jessie altered her course, curiosity overcoming caution. She hadn't seen Greg in the flesh since publicly confronting him at the hospital press conference weeks ago. He looked thinner and older than she remembered, with dark circles smudged under his eyes. But he had at least tried to clean up, shaving the unkempt beard.

"...and that is why I stand here today," she heard him mumble as she moved closer. "We must embrace visionaries committed to reviving—no, could be perceived as an insult—damn speechwriters." He produced a pen and made a quick amendment. "*Regenerating* left behind..."

He looked up as he tucked the pen away. A flicker of panic crossed his features.

"Can I help you?" he asked with false pleasantness as she approached.

"Hasn't been that long, has it, Greg?" she said, joining him in the shadow. "Jessie, from *The Post*?"

"*The Post*?" He shrugged, focused on his cards. "There are many *Posts*."

"*The Peridale Post*."

"A fine publication. Have we met?"

She'd have thought he'd bumped his head if he weren't trying to avoid looking directly at her.

"Twice," she pushed on. "At your library press conference and then at the hospital when you were there to open that new ward?"

Greg's throat bobbed like he was swallowing sand. "Hmm. I don't recall."

Of course. Jessie had confronted him with the allegations of hiring the Cotswold Crew in front of reporters from every paper in the area. She'd expected to see it splashed across every front page the following week, but *The Peridale Post*'s 'Unnamed Politician' headline had stood alone.

"You must have a busy schedule being an MP," Jessie said, sarcasm dripping from each word. "Looks like you've had a nice break from all the issues facing our local area, given that you haven't been seen in public for a while. Have a pleasant little holiday?"

Greg stood taller. "Even politicians need the occasional respite to unwind and... reflect."

"By 'reflect' I assume you mean 'hide out in one of your pal's luxury flats until the heat dies down?'" Jessie couldn't resist finding his discomfort satisfying. "Well, I'm glad to see you looking so rested. That beard didn't suit you."

His eyes narrowed to slits. "I'd like to get back to preparing my speech, if you don't mind."

Jessie stood her ground. "Don't let me stop your important rehearsing, Mr Morgan. Although, public speaking shouldn't be too challenging for someone like you. You have lots of experience at these sorts of gigs. Paid quite well for it, too."

Greg's face paled, and his eyes twitched as if he were about to explode. But he seemed to remember they were out in broad daylight, only paces from a hall packed with witnesses. He was biting his tongue, but the question he wanted to ask was written all over his sweaty face: how do you know how I accept my bribe money?

"I'm a simple rural politician trying to make a positive difference in my community," he said, turning to leave. "Now, please excuse me. I need to review these notes before addressing the good people of

Peridale. Wouldn't want to let them down." Peering over his shoulder, he added, "Oh, and Jenny? Send my love to my sister. I hope she's having fun playing journalist."

Greg walked into the hall, his entrance met with polite applause. Her article had been the talk of the village, but people had memories as short as Greg pretended to have. And even if he couldn't remember her name, he wouldn't be able to forget it one day. She'd make sure of it.

Fighting back the urge to crash his speech, Jessie left the church grounds and scanned the green for any sight of her parents. The café lights were on, but the place was unusually still. Maybe they were in the office? Before she could check, Veronica slipped past Jessie's yellow car parked in the alley and waved to her.

"There you are," Veronica panted. "I've been looking everywhere for you. Crisis at the office. Another leak."

"Radiator?"

"Council."

Before Jessie could reply, Veronica set off at a pace shy of a sprint. Jogging to catch up, Jessie debated sharing details of her unsettling encounter with Greg. By the time they reached Mulberry Lane, she decided against it. His parting words loomed like an ominous threat. She understood his influence, but did it extend to the paper's higher-ups?

In the cold office, Veronica dropped behind her computer and gestured for Jessie to join her. She wheeled over as the emails refreshed on the screen.

"The attachment was too small to read on my phone," Veronica said, rotating around a satsuma as the loading wheel spun. "Their emails normally come through blank, leaving us to guess the context. This one has a message. I think I know who our inside contact is."

Jessie leaned in to read the email.

From: Anon

To: To Whom It May Interest

Subject: My Last Stand

Attachment: LetterScan.jpg

If you're receiving this email, the plans have been unveiled, meaning I couldn't stop them. I'm either imprisoned for taking matters into my own hands, or they've neutralised me. You've achieved remarkable things with the information I've provided up until now. I regret I can't offer more.

I hope you can find what I could not.

Good luck.

"Our mole must have been Peter," Veronica said, hands shaking in disbelief as she double-clicked the attachment. "He's been sending us the plans, reports, and everything in between. I wouldn't be surprised if he were the one sending Johnny all of Greg's statements before me. He must've scheduled the last few emails in advance. We've lost our inside source."

"And Peter lost his life. He must have sensed something was going to happen to him. Let's see what he chose as his 'Last Stand.'" Jessie nudged the mouse. "Crossing my fingers for a signed confession from Greg Morgan."

With a double-click, an image sprang onto the screen: a yellowed fragment of a time-worn letter. Jessie couldn't decipher the swirly handwriting faded by time, yet Veronica's lips traced the words as she read to herself.

"'Rest assured, I am aware that my time on this mortal coil is woefully limited,'" she began, her accent adopting a more refined tone. "'Do not pity me, for I have reconciled myself with the inevitable embrace of the world beyond. I am prepared for what awaits me. I look forward to reuniting with my love. However, while I remain on this plane, I require your assistance one final time. Though our village's inhabitants may view me with contempt, let it be known that when time has tempered their rancour and future scholars record the histories of our time, I implore that my confession herein contained be displayed alongside my portrait. I extend my most heartfelt thanks for your companionship during these challenging months.'" She swivelled to face Jessie. "It's signed 'D.H.'. These must be Duncan Howarth's final wishes. You asked for a confession…"

Jessie scrolled further down. "'Herein contained?' Where is it?"

"That's all there is."

"And who did he send the letter to?"

"The top looks like it was ripped off."

Pushing back into her chair, Jessie stared at the letter. She had no idea what to make of it. "Why would Peter want us to see this? How does a letter from a man who's been dead for donkey's years help us here and now? It's a dead end."

Veronica read over the letter again. No new revelations seemed to come to light.

"Peter wanted us to glean something from this," Veronica insisted. "We need to figure out the context. Perhaps your mum and dad can shed some light? They're investigating Peter's murder."

"They're knee deep in the looming Jacobson Armageddon," Jessie replied, exasperated. "I can show them, but we need to write up what happened at the village hall. The plans are out. The people are in the dark about how we got to this point. It's time to let James and Greg know there are people who will stand in their way."

"Oh, they'll know people *will* stand in their way," Veronica said, opening a new document. "What they've proved thus far is they don't think anyone *can*. I'll get started. Get their take on this letter. It's important, even if we don't know why yet. He saved it for his last message for a reason. We're flying solo now, Jessie."

With the photograph saved on her phone, Jessie dashed from Mulberry Lane back to the village green. Cheers spilled through the village hall's open doors. A cluster of people outside shook their heads near Dot and Ethel, who wielded megaphones, but the crowd's enthusiasm was undiminished. Jessie blocked out the noise. She had another mission at hand.

She pivoted towards the closed café, but they might be hiding in the kitchen. Her eye caught her yellow Mini Cooper. The bonnet was up. A man in a suit was delving into the car's engine. Sprinting towards him, she yanked him back by his jacket, half-expecting to see James or Greg. Instead, she found another familiar face.

"You," she muttered.

He must have recognised her, but his face didn't show it; it didn't show much. Without a word, he sauntered down the alley, dusting off his palms. Cool, calm, collected. Just another assignment for a Cotswold Crew member.

They didn't have names.

They had numbers.

"Send my regards to your boss, Six," Jessie shouted after him. "I trust he's enjoying his stint as a politician while it lasts."

But regardless of her bravado, she was back in that abandoned barn during the Knight case, staring into the dark abyss of the well. Six's knife glinted in the moonlight as he marched her to the fall that should have killed her. She could smell the moss as the farm building creaked around her. Desperation washed over her afresh. She'd escaped by the skin of her teeth. Perhaps she'd still be at the bottom of that well if Six had carried out his orders. She'd convinced herself that the ordeal had been worth it. She'd managed to escape with a map of their hiding places. Arrests had followed, but clearly not enough.

Six didn't glance back as he strode across the field. Jessie had the nerve, but she wouldn't follow him; the well had taught her a lesson about recklessness. Instead, she clung to the fact she'd caught him in the act, avoiding a nasty surprise behind the wheel.

She must have rattled Greg to the core earlier.

Message understood, but it changed nothing.

Crouching, she assessed the glistening liquid pooling in the cracks of the cobblestones under her Mini. Given the puddle's size, Six had cut something important.

"Everything alright?"

Jessie swivelled to find Richie scanning the scene, a cigarette dangling from his lip.

"I quit years ago," he said, snuffing the cigarette under his boot. "Stressful day. Car trouble?"

"I'm no mechanic, but I reckon my brakes have just been cut."

Joining her beside the immobilised Mini, Richie dipped his finger in the puddle and rubbed it between his thumb and forefinger with a sniff.

"Don't know why I did that," he said with a cheeky smile. "I know as much about cars as I do about healthy relationships with parental figures. Come with me. You could use a drink, and I know a guy who can help."

Drained by the aftermath of the confrontation, Jessie lacked the energy to turn down Richie's offer. She followed him into the empty bar and slid onto a barstool. He fetched two tumblers and a bottle of top-shelf Irish whiskey.

"I know you're partial to espresso martinis, but this should do the trick." He poured a generous measure into each glass and slid one towards her. "I'm sorry I didn't intervene. I saw him. Assumed he was a mechanic."

Despite everything, a faint smile tugged at the corners of Jessie's mouth. She accepted the tumbler and took a sip. The whiskey scorched a path down her throat, its lingering warmth calming her jangled nerves.

"Thanks," she said, wiping her mouth with the back of her hand. "What a day."

"I know a guy who owns a garage nearby. I'll give him a call." He slid the full bottle to her and said, "Help yourself."

While she waited, Jessie ignored the bottle, wanting to keep a clear head. She checked her phone to look at the picture of the letter again. Five unread messages from Dante blinked on the screen. She should reply, but she couldn't summon the mental energy. How could she begin to explain the day? Her relationship with Dante felt too new to burden him with the chaos.

Not that she would describe their handful of dates and near-kisses as a 'relationship.' She'd been sure he'd been about to kiss her again last night after they'd finished with their flyer-canvassing. And they hadn't been interrupted by children in Halloween costumes. Jessie had pulled away, unable to let herself cross that line. She wasn't sure why, but she was terrified of letting Dante go too far behind her high walls.

Jessie finished the first pour of whiskey, willing her thoughts to calm.

"All sorted," Richie said as he returned. "My mate will be here within the hour. Well, I say 'mate'. Two dates, but it's always handy to have a mechanic in your phonebook." Leaning across the bar, he flashed a mischievous smile. "So, this brake-cutter? Not a friend of yours, I'm guessing."

"Cotswold Crew," she said. "Hired by your dad's friend, Greg."

Richie's lips tightened, pulling downward as his eyes clouded over with a heaviness that spoke volumes. Shocked, but not surprised.

"You must have seen old Greggy more than most lately?" Circling her glass with a finger, Jessie studied his reaction. "You have one of the penthouses at Wellington Heights."

"I've seen too much of him," he muttered with an irritated sigh. "He's been sleeping in my guest bedroom."

"You're kidding…"

He pushed away from the bar and leaned against the back, folding his arms tight across his chest. "My dad owns the penthouse. He owns the building. He owns this bar." His eyes glazed over, as though one step from adding 'he owns me' too. "I wish he'd stayed away."

"You must have overheard a lot," she said.

"Not really. I stay out of their way. Been working every hour in here, so I don't have to keep seeing Greg wandering around in his underwear."

"Gross." Jessie shuddered at the thought as she showed Richie the letter. "Seen this before? A mystery letter from your dad's apparent hero, Duncan Howarth. About some confession and a portrait. Any idea what it could be?"

Jessie studied Richie as he scanned the letter, the first of the evening's fireworks popping off in the background. Without zooming in on the faint writing, there was no chance he could read it, but his eyes scanned anyway. Had he seen it before? He shrugged, reluctant to unburden himself. She couldn't blame him for grappling with conflicted loyalties. As strained as Richie's relationship with James was, he was connected by blood.

"Dunno," he said, running a cloth around in

circles on the clean bar. "I'll give my mechanic another—"

"Look, I know you're in a tricky spot with your dad," Jessie said, meeting his drifting eyes. "Maybe you don't want to pick sides. But remember, you always have a choice. Even if it's not easy. Even if it feels like he owns you."

Richie held her gaze with a squint, and she couldn't read what he was thinking. His lips parted and closed an instant later when the door swung open. Two builders swaggered in, making a beeline for the bar.

"Back to work," he said, drumming the bar with his palms. "What'll it be, fellas? Hard work or hardly working?"

Richie whipped the bottle of whiskey away and returned it to the top shelf before moving to the other end of the bar. Jessie lingered while he poured pints for the blurry blokes, but Jessie might as well have not been there. The moment had passed.

"Don't worry about paying them," Richie called after her, pushing the first frothy pint across the bar. "I'll sort it."

Richie's money was James' money, and James' money had lined Greg's pockets to pay off the men in black suits.

"Thanks, but I'll handle it."

Zipping her jacket, she headed out into the darkening night. Across the green, the crowd dispersed from the hall. No more cheers or camera flashes. James' triumphant dog-and-pony show had ended, at least for today. Many of the crowd stayed within the church grounds, cutting across the graveyard to hop the wall to the bonfire. As the fireworks crackled above, Jessie wondered if her parents had taken Olivia to see the fireworks for some normalcy. She sent the picture of the letter to her mum and dad separately before climbing the stairs to her flat, not in the mood for another crowd.

Sinister roots tied Peridale's past to its unsure future, and the committee meeting was in exactly one week. She needed to decode Duncan Howarth's cryptic letter. As Veronica had said, Peter's timing wasn't random.

It *had* to mean something.

14

Julia paced the café kitchen, phone pressed to her ear as she left yet another message with the council planning department. "Hello, it's Julia South-Brown. *Again*. I'm calling about the proposed Howarth Estate development and your refusal to provide details on..."

With a frustrated huff, she ended the call. Three days had passed since James' big unveiling, and she was still being stonewalled at every official turn.

"Any luck?" Jessie asked, glancing up from her laptop.

"Answering machine."

"I keep getting the same email responses too," Jessie said, slamming the laptop shut. "They've logged my complaint, and nothing has been confirmed until the council vote next week."

"We have to keep trying," Julia insisted.

The café door opened, and Neil walked in, carrying something wrapped in brown paper under his arm. Struck by inspiration, Julia studied her brother-in-law. His past with James and his social influence in the library should have made him the perfect advocate. But from his sheepish smile, she knew she couldn't expect too much. Barker looked up from his conversation with DI Moyes in the corner and watched Neil's path to the counter.

"Good to see you, Neil," she began, offering him a smile. His distracted stare didn't notice. "I know you and James have become... friendly. But we're trying to raise awareness about the realities of his planned development before the committee meeting at the end of this week."

"Shoddy builders, fake eco-claims, gang harassment, bribes..." Jessie listed off. "And the rest."

Neil's polite smile faded, and he busied himself scanning the cake cabinets.

"You know I can't get involved with this," Neil finally said, facing her. "I wouldn't be where I am without him. I can't jeopardise my career over some protest that won't change anything." Leaning in, he whispered, "I have a family to provide for, Julia. Your nieces. Your sister."

"How can you say that?" Jessie cut in. "You, of all people, must see what's at stake here. Phase one, Neil. One of how many?"

"I'm sorry, but I must remain neutral," he said. "I was only passing through. I wanted to give you this." He placed the wrapped item on the counter, backing away. "I thought you might like this to cheer you up... Sue mentioned how upset... I'm sorry, I need to go."

He hurried out without another word.

"Well, that was useless," Jessie fumed. "He's stuck under James' thumb."

Julia sighed, stung by Neil's refusal to help. She had hoped he would stand with her along with the rest of the villagers waking up to the realities of what James' changes would mean, but she refused to concede defeat before the battle had begun. Even if people within her family didn't believe anything could be done, she couldn't think like that. She looked down at what he had brought: an apology gift for his guilty conscience. She ripped off the paper to reveal the back of something in a frame. Flipping it over, her hands began to shake as her imagination ran away with her.

It wasn't the painting—wishful thinking. Why would Neil have the lost portrait of Duncan Howarth?

What he'd given her was older. She smiled down at a copy of the eighteenth-century sketch of her café, though it didn't stir the same reaction as when she'd seen it for the first time in the history book.

"No way," Jessie said, joining her at the counter. "Is that our café?"

"Circa 1786. The Shepherd's Rest."

Julia could hear the cheerful murmur of the patrons inside, smell the ale and the horses tethered out front. She imagined the artist sitting in the middle of the village green, their pencil primed over the page as they captured the slice of history—an ordinary day like any other, no doubt. She longed for an ordinary day.

The uniformed officers stationed outside hadn't left her or Jessie's shadow since the stalking and brake-cutting incidents—after Jessie finally told them and reported it the next day. Neither had spent a moment alone, yet Julia had been jumping at shadows. Every day since Peter's visit, she crept closer to his temperament than her own. She couldn't believe she'd thought the offer of a cup of tea would have calmed him down.

DI Moyes sent her a sympathetic smile. She'd been talking with Barker for almost an hour, but their conversation seemed to be wrapping up. Finally draining the last cold dregs of her coffee, Moyes brought the empty mug to the counter.

"Could I get one more for the road?" she asked. "Your pumpkin spice blend is really growing on me."

"On the house."

As the espresso dripped, Moyes leaned against the counter. "Look, Julia, I know you want to get to the bottom of what happened to Peter, but things are more complicated than any of us could have predicted. I think it's time for you to step back. Leave the official investigating to us professionals. Perhaps you and Barker could get away for a while."

"Go on holiday?" Julia arched a brow as she steamed milk. "It's not the right time."

"It's precisely the right time," Moyes urged.

"It's not just Peter's murder. Something needs to be done about the Howarth Estate before the committee. I won't watch that from afar. I can't."

Moyes let out a resigned sigh. "I understand. I really do. Now that I live here, I get why you love this place."

"Have you found any more gang members?" Jessie asked, spraying the display cabinet with window cleaner. "Six? The rest?"

"We're doing everything we can to sniff them out," Moyes said, her sigh giving away that no arrests had been made. "We *will* establish concrete ties to

Morgan, but they're too practiced at covering their tracks."

"And you'll find Peter's murderer too?" Julia popped the lid on the finished drink and slid it across the counter to Moyes. "That still matters."

"Of course, but I have to be honest. I'm losing hope that we'll find Peter's murderer. Some cases go unsolved. Maybe this is one of them." Fingers wrapping around the cup, Moyes exhaled through her nostrils. "And I know that's frustrating. I've worked on cold cases for long enough. Maybe we'll find the clues we need one day."

"Rubbish," Jessie muttered. "You're saying we wait ten years for someone to let slip what happened? Peter deserves better."

"A crowded party, everyone in disguises, a maze with a thousand hiding places?" Moyes stated, as though she'd gone over the list a thousand times. "It was always going to be tricky—maybe even impossible."

"I can't believe in 'impossible' right now," Julia insisted, though doubt needled at her. She retrieved the picture she'd printed of the scanned letter. Over the past few days, Julia had scrutinised every faded word until they were seared into her brain. "Peter sent this to the council. That's Duncan Howarth's handwriting. We've cross-referenced it with other samples of his writing. It's legitimate, and it proves the lost portrait of Duncan Howarth isn't a myth."

"Julia, I'm not sure what—"

"Peter was obsessed with finding this portrait," Julia continued. "He saw this painting the day he died. He was offered it by a man—a man I believe to be James Jacobson. I heard it, and I know it's important." Her desperation echoed back at her around the quiet café. "I know it, Laura."

Moyes sighed. "I'll look into it more. I'm not saying you're wrong, but without the physical painting, how are we ever going to know what it means, if it means anything?"

She took a slow sip of the latte, glancing back at the officers by the door.

"You sure about that holiday?"

Julia didn't need to think about it. "Maybe when it's over."

"Don't say I didn't try." Moyes gave her a sad half-smile. "Since you're determined, I'll share my latest scoop so you don't waste time on a dead-end. Martin Green didn't kill Peter. His alibi checked out. He was only at the library to show his face. He threw his own party at his giant eco-house, and he was there long before Peter was killed and long after."

"One down," Jessie said, giving the glass one last polish. "And the rest?"

"Can't confirm whether Prunella was home alone feeding her cats, or if Alice seemed to have gone for an early night. As for Richard..." She arched a brow. "Let's just say, with his criminal history and ties to Greg Morgan going back to Henderson Place, my money's on him."

"What about the change of clothes at the party?" Barker asked, joining them.

"It wasn't blood," Moyes confirmed. "Sometimes a spilt drink is a spilt drink, but remember when I said he wasn't shy about letting people rent out his old farm to store their stuff? I did some digging. He has as many connections to the Crew as Greg. Stolen cars, weapons, and the rest. Stay safe, and if you turn around and don't see those officers, call me. Thanks for the coffee."

With a parting nod, Moyes headed for the door. The officers nodded but stayed planted outside the window. Anything for an ordinary day.

"What now?" she asked.

"We talk about the elephant in the room," Jessie said, an edge to her voice. "Howarth Estate doesn't have road access yet. You never told me what happened when you talked to Shilpa about James' offer to buy the post office. Am I going to need to find a new flat?"

Eager to discuss anything but that looming elephant, Julia shook her head.

"I've tried a couple of times, but she hasn't been in the post office. Jayesh says she still has a cold."

"Or she's at home planning how she'll spend her millions once the sale goes through," Jessie countered, heading for the door. "Dot told me he made her an offer last summer, and she turned it down. Maybe this was his plan all along; he was just waiting for the stars to align. I'll go and wring the truth out of Jayesh."

Before Julia could dissuade her, the door closed behind Jessie.

"I'm not so sure Shilpa would sell to James now," Julia said to Barker. "Not after everything." But doubt tinged her words. If the offer were substantial enough, would Shilpa refuse a second time? "Would she?"

"I wish I could say, love." He held her hands across the counter. "Let's focus on what we can do. I share your hunch about that painting. Its secrets could be the key to stopping James' plans and solving his murder. How?" Kissing her hands, he shrugged. "I don't know. But Peter has got us this far, and he wasn't wrong about anything else."

"If only he hadn't been so scared to open up," she said, almost visualising Peter scrambling around for his paperwork over Barker's shoulder. "I think James has the painting. If Peter thought Vincent Wellington once had it, then it's safe to assume Vincent had it. Maybe James thought it would sway his vote?"

Jessie returned, slamming the door a bit too hard.

"Shilpa doesn't have a cold," she announced, pushing Moyes' abandoned chair under the table with a huff. "Jayesh said she's at home, out of her mind about some 'decision.' He doesn't know what, and I didn't tell him. She's really considering it. How many days?"

"At least since the party," Julia replied. "Shilpa said she had something to tell me, and I never got back to her. I should have talked to her then." Clenching her eyes, Julia shook her head. There was no turning back. "Jessie, what's your angle on finding this painting?"

"We have a Duncan Howarth expert running a tiny museum around the corner, don't we?" Jessie said. "Alice knows more than she's letting on, and I think she might be the weak link. I may be able to get through to her. Mind if I finish early?"

"It's Monday. You weren't even on the rota."

"I know," she said with a shrug. "Didn't want to leave you stewing on your own today."

After packing up her things, Jessie set off for Alice's hidden museum, leaving Julia and Barker alone in the café. Maybe it was the November weather turning colder day by day, but since James' announcement, the village had felt abandoned. Even on Saturday, she'd been able to send Sue home at lunchtime.

"I should talk to Prunella again," she said, redirecting her focus where it could make a difference. "Prunella is a retired art history lecturer. Now that I have proof there was a portrait, she can't claim it was a myth. She must know something."

"And I'll get back on James' tail," Barker added, checking his watch before glancing at the officers who were chatting outside the window. "After the café closes. For now, you're not leaving my sight, and there's no argument about it."

Julia nodded, in no mood to argue. For once, she didn't want to be alone in the café with the shadows, her thoughts, and the road-access elephant. As scared as she was that Shilpa might accept James' offer, she was more worried about what would happen if she didn't. There were only so many routes to that field, and after George Knight and Shilpa, Julia knew she had to be next.

15

Jessie quickened her pace as she hurried down Mulberry Lane, noticing that every second shop was closed. She hoped Alice was brave enough to open her hidden museum, even on a dead day like Monday. She waved to Brian outside the Antique Barn; there was no time to stop and chat. Once he got going about chairs and wardrobes, he wouldn't stop, and her mum had already exhausted his knowledge of the Duncan Howarth portrait. Rounding the corner, she breathed a sigh of relief at the sight of the museum's lights illuminating the gloomy back end of the street.

Inside the narrow space, Alice stood behind the counter, counting out piles of money. One of the debt collectors who'd accosted her was back, counting the money after her with a pleased grin. He'd done his job, and Alice must be about to do hers at the committee meeting.

Jessie didn't doubt that the money changing hands could only have come from one place. Sealing the thousands in a clear envelope, the debt collector tipped his head and left. Jessie cleared her throat, and Alice flinched. She had been so engrossed in counting the money that she hadn't noticed Jessie creep in.

Alice shoved another pile of money under a book as she plastered on a smile. "You startled me. What brings you by again so soon? Caught the history bug?"

"Generous donation?" Jessie kept her voice even. "Or did James cough up the funds to pay off your debts? How much does a thumbs-up at the committee meeting cost from you? I'm sure you're all on a sliding scale."

Alice's already fair complexion turned a ghostly shade of grey. "I..." she croaked before her shoulders slumped. "Please, you must understand. My museum —my dream—was sinking. The bills were piling up. I tried to refuse his offer, I promise. But then the debts kept mounting, and the letters kept coming, and then they started knocking at the door..."

She trailed off miserably. Jessie felt a flicker of sympathy. Katie and Brian had gone through something similar, and James had been the one to rescue them by buying the manor. But this wasn't one building being turned into a few apartments. She couldn't back down.

"A bribe is a bribe. You're selling out the heritage you claim to care about."

Alice looked stricken. She sank down onto a stool behind the counter, staring blankly ahead. Jessie pressed on. "What would Peter say to you if he were here now?"

"Oh, don't." Her bottom lip wobbled. "He'd tell me I'd sold my soul. And he'd be right. I can't deny it. But... I didn't feel I had a choice."

"You always have a choice. You could have chosen a better location." Alice was on the verge of tears, and Jessie didn't want to pile on anymore. "At least tell me why Peter was so obsessed with Howarth's portrait. I know it exists, so don't deny it."

"It does exist," she admitted in a whisper. "I saw it. Only once."

"*What?*"

"My grandparents ran a museum in that abandoned art gallery. It was quite popular—more popular than this dump." She glared around the place. "I wish I could have taken over, but they died when I was young. I did look at the rent for that building, but I just couldn't afford it. It was there that I saw the painting. I caught only a brief glimpse. I shouldn't have been there, but I was so curious..." Her face lit up as she wandered back down her winding memory lane. "They had a box I was told to never open, never touch, never think about and never, ever tell anyone about. But what happens when you tell a child not to do something?" She chuckled, and Jessie couldn't help but join in. "It's *all* I thought about. I thought they had an Egyptian mummy, or maybe royal jewels. When I heard that a man was coming to buy 'the box,' I made sure to be there. I hid myself away, and after years of wondering, I watched my grandpa unlock the chest and pull out a painting." Leaning in, she whispered, "And I'm no art expert, but even as a child, I didn't think it was a very good painting. When the man they sold it to took it away, the mystery died for me."

"Was that man Vincent Wellington?"

"Yes, how did you—ah, yes, you're related. It was Vincent. I heard my grandpa say they'd been given the painting to keep hidden away. Vincent promised it would never see the light of day, offered them £100,000, and locked it up at the manor. I didn't think about it for many years until Peter brought it up to me when I joined the society. He wouldn't shut up about it, to be honest. I made the mistake of telling him I'd seen it and that I knew Vincent had it. He went and harassed the man when he was in his nineties, but Vincent didn't give it up. He kept his promise."

"Why did they promise to keep it hidden away?"

"I don't know," she admitted, and Jessie believed her. "But Peter became convinced that the lost painting was the key to altering Duncan's unpleasant legacy. He said he'd found proof it contained some revelation that would…" She searched for the word, "redeem Duncan and, by extension, redeem Peridale from what he saw as its decay in the name of development."

"Redeem him how?" Jessie showed Alice the picture of the letter, and her eyes bulged as she realised what it was. "Know anything about Duncan's confession?"

"Where did you get this? I… I've never seen this letter."

"Peter sent it to the newspaper before he died."

"Do you have the original?"

"Just a copy."

"Shame. It would be quite the find for my museum. With Howarth Estate coming, there's going to be a renewed interest in Duncan's story. Perhaps that'll be what my museum needs?" She looked around again, although she didn't seem hopeful. "I'm sorry, but I'm afraid that's all I know."

"How did the painting end up with your grandparents?"

"Like I said, they wouldn't talk to me about it. They don't know I saw it." Alice's fingers teased the edge of the notes sticking out from under the book. "Whatever happens next, I want you to know that my love for this village and its history are sincere. Peridale is my home, and I only want what's best for it. I can only hope my decision hasn't jeopardised its future too much."

"The vote hasn't happened yet," Jessie urged. "But I hope so too. Take care, Alice."

Stepping back into the gathering dusk, Jessie felt as if she'd found a unicorn—talking to someone who'd seen the painting. She'd confirmed it had been owned by Vincent, so James must have it. But if it contained secrets that could change his plans, he was never going to give it up. She wouldn't be surprised if he'd followed in Banksy's footsteps and shredded the thing.

About to type out a message to update her mum, Jessie spied a familiar silhouette lingering behind Brian's barn at the end of the lane. Six. And although he glanced at her, he resumed staring at Alice's museum. His presence here could only mean Greg was keeping close tabs on Alice as well. Bribe or not, they couldn't have trusted her enough to take their eyes off her. On the other side of the street, the officer who'd followed Jessie was on his phone. She cleared her throat and waved to him, pointing to the barn. The officer approached, but Six had already slipped into the shadows.

"What is it?" PC Puglisi asked. "Want me to buy you a coffee to warm you up? I could think of other ways."

"You're so gross." Jessie rolled her eyes; she hadn't even realised her protection was *that* police officer. "You just missed your chance for a promotion, Pug. Tell your boss Alice is being tracked."

Leaving Puglisi scrabbling for his radio outside Vicky's Van, Jessie joined Veronica, who was scribbling in the office. She looked up, pushing her large glasses up her nose.

"How did it go with Alice? Learn anything useful?"

"Admitted the bribe," she said, dropping into her swivel chair. "She saw the mythical painting, confirmed Vincent stashed it away, and Six is following her too."

"Stretched thin," Veronica pointed out. "One Crew member stalking three people? Can't be that many left. Anything else happened to you since your brakes?"

"Not yet."

"It's taking everything for me not to go and cut

Greg's brakes." Veronica tossed a dart at the board. It missed, clattering down the back of the radiator. "He could have killed you, and guess where he was today? Hugging old people at the nursing home."

"Scare tactics followed by a photo op. Classic Greg." Jessie stretched down the back of the icy radiator for the stray dart. "I wouldn't be surprised if he waited until he saw me to start playing mechanic. Those rumours about Greg having his predecessor's brakes cut to clear the way for the election seem less absurd now."

"You're right. We're closing in on him. I can feel it. We just need that concrete slab of proof he won't be able to wiggle out from under—him and James."

Still feeling around behind the radiator, Jessie's hands wrapped around a wire. "A marriage made in hell."

"Now we know where Greg is staying, maybe there's a way—"

Jessie lifted her finger to her lips, signalling for Veronica to be silent. Her eyes narrowed, focused on what she had discovered. With a cautious, deliberate tug, she pulled free a tiny microphone attached to a battery pack. The room seemed to close in on them, each second stretching longer than the last as she walked over and dropped the device onto Veronica's desk with a soft thud.

They both stared at it in disbelief. The silence was deafening, broken only by the low gurgling of the broken radiator.

"Oh, you..." Veronica's lips curled into a snarl as she leaned into the fluffy end of the microphone. "If you can hear me, little brother, you might want to hold off buying your Christmas presents. I promise you'll be behind bars before the first snowfall." Closing her eyes, she exhaled. "For Peter, for Peridale, and for Sebastian."

Veronica stabbed a dart through the battery pack, and her energy seemed to vanish. Jessie scraped the bits into the bin, wondering who Sebastian was. She was sure she'd heard the name before, but she wasn't going to push Veronica if she didn't open up. But she did have one burning question.

"Where did you find that plumber?"

"I'm an idiot," she said, turning in her chair and peering through the permanent pink glow at the window. "I saw a plumbing van across the street. I thought I was being proactive, and he was cheap."

"He could have at least fixed the radiator if he was going to bug us," Jessie said, eliciting a smile from Veronica. "We don't know who killed Peter, and we don't know how we're going to stop the committee meeting. But I think I know a way into Greg's flat."

"No breaking in. We can't afford any slip-ups."

"Don't worry," Jessie said, yanking open the back door. "I know his roommate."

～

After tossing back a shot of espresso and closing the café, Julia set off for Prunella Thompson's countryside cottage. She needed to uncover whatever Prunella knew about the elusive Howarth portrait.

Rapping on the oak door, Julia braced herself for more question-dodging. Heavy footsteps approached before the door creaked open. Prunella's smile was strained, but she didn't shut the door in Julia's face, given how Julia's one and only society meeting had gone.

"Julia. What an unexpected pleasure."

"I'm sure." The time for a civilised conversation had passed. "I have some new questions regarding Duncan Howarth and his lost portrait."

Prunella tensed. "I've told you, I don't know anything about it."

"With all due respect, I don't believe you. I've seen a letter written by Howarth confirming the portrait exists."

"I see." Prunella cleared her throat with a rattly cough. "You've had a wasted journey because I don't have the faintest idea what you're talking about."

"I think you do." She narrowed her eyes. "I know you do. Howarth mentioned a confession tied to his portrait. What was he confessing?"

Prunella glanced back into the cottage before stepping outside, pulling the door almost closed behind her. "Listen, you're chasing ghosts. Howarth is long dead. Nothing can change that now."

Julia pressed further. "You come from a line of painters and you taught art history. You must know who painted it." Taking a stab in the dark, Julia asked, "Did Catherine Thompson paint it? Because if she did, finding the painting could restore her legacy after you tarnished it with your fake university reports."

"How dare you!" Prunella stiffened, her jaw clenching. "My paper had a few errors. Nothing more. Those students who accused me had a personal vendetta." She took a breath. "I understand you want to stop the development, but preservation and progress *can* coexist. It's a field, Julia. One little field. Why fight it?"

"Phase one, you mean. What's next, Prunella? Phase two? Phase ten?"

Prunella hesitated. "I don't know the full scope. But soon, I won't be here to see it play out." She lifted her chin. "An opportunity has arisen for me to ascend from local politics. To follow in Greg's footsteps, you might say."

Dread tingled down Julia's spine. Greg and Prunella rubbing shoulders in Westminster together? A troubling prospect.

"Are you sure those are footsteps you want to follow in?"

"As usual, you continue to prove you don't know what you're talking about." Her scrutinising gaze swept Julia up and down before she stepped back inside. "I really must be going. Do take care."

The door slammed in Julia's face, and she hadn't gained a single answer. Maybe she could have played the polite dance Prunella was quick at, but she was sure she'd have ended up with the same result after a longer conversation and a cup of tea in her lavish home.

"Yes, the usual stuff," she heard Prunella say on the other side of the door. "More questions about that blasted painting. Don't worry, I didn't tell her anything. But you know she won't stop digging, and she must be getting close. You know her reputation. Do something because I've put too much on the line for this project."

Julia's blood turned to ice, but at last they agreed about something. She'd come too far to stop digging now. If she was getting close, the truth must have been right under her nose.

Back at her car, Julia froze. The man who'd

followed her—the man Jessie had called Six—leaned against a black car with tinted windows. He was blocking the road, and behind him on the other side of the junction, the officer tasked with following her was still there, glued to his phone behind the wheel.

"You've been requested," he said, opening the door like a chauffeur. "Get in."

"And if I don't?"

"Get in."

His hand went into his pocket. Was there a knife in there? A gun? Or more mind games? Julia wasn't sure she wanted to find out. Looking off to the police car one last time, she rolled her eyes at the sight of the officer laughing at his screen.

Keeping her chin high, Julia slid into the back seat. The door slammed behind her with grim finality, and Six climbed behind the wheel. As scared as she was, she knew she should have been more scared as they drove past the police car. He watched them pass, then went back to his phone.

If Julia had been requested, she was on her way to meet one of two men, and she had a lot to say to both of them.

The bar door swung shut behind Jessie as her eyes adjusted to the dim interior. She spotted Richie behind the bar, chatting up the mechanic who'd fixed Jessie's car. He'd assured her it was fixed, but she hadn't dared get behind the wheel. For a Monday, there were enough people mingling to make it feel crowded. She'd hoped to get Richie alone, unsure of how long it would take to convince him of her plan.

Weaving through the crowd, she claimed the bar stool nearest Richie and tapped her nails on the sticky wood. His bright laughter carried over the music as the mechanic whispered something in his ear, while a group of young women tried to get his attention by waving cocktail menus. Jessie sat rigid. She couldn't afford to lose her nerve.

"Always a pleasure," Richie said, slipping away long enough to notice Jessie. "The usual?"

"Excuse me!" one of the girls cried, scowling at Jessie. "We were here first."

Jessie jerked her head for him to skip her. She was fine to wait. While the girls shouted their endless cocktail orders at him, Jessie went over the plan in her head. Convince Richie to take her home. Convince Richie to leave her alone long enough to dig around Greg's room. Somehow, not get caught and snag the evidence she needed to put an end to Greg's schemes. She glanced at the mechanic, whose eyes hadn't left

Richie. Maybe she wouldn't be the one going home with him tonight, but a Plan B presented itself to her.

A glint of silver caught her eye—a bundle of keys by the till. Jessie's breath stalled. She didn't know if Greg would be at the flat now, but Richie definitely wasn't.

After a trip to the bathroom, she returned and sat on the stool nearest the till. The cloth he was always wiping with was there. She grabbed it and dropped it over the keys. Watching Richie as he impressed the group with his cocktail-shaking skills, she scooped the keys up in a silent grasp.

She shot her focus back to Richie's hands as he poured a bright pink drink into a cosmopolitan glass. The mechanic still hadn't taken his eyes off him. Now that Jessie was looking around, all eyes were on Richie. There was no denying he was handsome—and sweet. And she was stealing from him. Jessie wiped her clammy palms on her jeans, willing her nerves to steady.

The moment Richie turned to retrieve the coffee liqueur, Jessie made her move. She lifted the cloth and scanned the keys. They came in all shapes and sizes, and some were labelled things like "Bar Front" and "Bar Cellar," but only one had a "W.H." engraving. In one smooth motion, she slipped the key off the ring and tucked it into her pocket. Bundling the keys back in the cloth, she reached across as though looking at the bottles behind the bar and nudged the keys back where she'd found them.

They hit the side of the till with a metal clank. She froze, certain Richie had heard the noise over the ambient din, but he was too busy mouthing something at the mechanic while he strained another cocktail. She folded the cloth and sat back down.

"Be right with you, Jessie," he called. "Espresso martini?"

Jessie managed a tight smile. "Another time. Just remembered I promised to feed my mum's cat. You working late tonight?"

"Till midnight."

"I might see you later."

She slid off the stool and hurried outside as the streetlamps flickered to life, her pulse roaring in her ears. Safety seemed miles away until she turned the corner and leaned against the cold brick wall, gasping for air. Before she could doubt her impulsive mistake, she cooked up the new plan.

Go to Wellington Heights. Hope Greg was preoccupied. Find crucial evidence.

Her phone vibrated in her pocket.

Had Richie noticed already?

VERONICA

SHOCKING NEWS!!! James has agreed to the interview. TONIGHT. His place. He's giving you twenty minutes. I promised him the questions were light, so you might only end up with five.

JESSIE

I don't think I'm ready…

VERONICA

Four days left, Jessie. Give him what for.

The stolen key scorched against her thigh in her pocket. She wasn't sure what she'd done, but she'd already done it. No turning back now, but it had to wait. If talking to Alice about the painting had been her first big scoop of the day, snagging an interview with James was the second.

New plan. Interview James. Then go to Wellington Heights for her third scoop. A scoop big enough to expose the slimy politician and bring his house of cards crashing down before the committee meeting.

∼

The black car slowed to a crawl outside a ramshackle cottage, nestled in a remote pocket of an overgrown meadow. Ivy and moss crawled over the crumbling stone walls, which slumped with a sad, forgotten air. Six demanded she leave her phone on the back seat, his hand back in his pocket. She fished it out and left it on the leather before stepping from the car. She followed Six into the cottage; the thick scent of musty decay wafted around her. Each cautious footfall released clouds of dust from the rotting floorboards.

The interior fared no better than the exterior. Mould bloomed across the peeling floral wallpaper in ominous, dark patches. Brittle leaves and dirt crunched underfoot, blown in by broken glass and drafts. The skeletal rafters creaked overhead, devoid of any insulation. Shafts of fading light cut through swirling dust, illuminating cobwebs trailing from every surface.

At the far end of the main room, beside a soot-choked fireplace, Greg Morgan reclined in a moth-eaten armchair. He rose with an oily grin that turned Julia's stomach.

"Ah, Julia. So pleased you could make it."

"I didn't have much choice."

"Oh, nonsense." His polished shoes clicked on the debris-strewn floor as he approached. "Please, have a seat."

Julia perched on the edge of a rickety wooden chair positioned in the middle of the room. Six walked behind her, pulling a length of rope from his pocket. Her heart raced, but she kept her head held high.

"What are you doing?" Greg chuckled, shaking his hands. Julia turned to glare at Six. Had he been about to tie her to the chair? "That's not necessary, Six. Let's keep this civilised. We're not animals, are we?" The hypocrisy of his words in this lawless setting almost made Julia laugh out loud. "Water? It's sparkling."

Greg offered her a glass bottle as though they were business partners at a board meeting, rather than captor and captive. She refused with a shake of her head. Shrugging, Greg took a long swig himself before pulling up a chair. Unbuttoning his jacket, he seated himself, crossing his legs in a slow, measured movement.

"What do you think of the place?" he asked, tossing his hands out. "Needs a bit of work, but I think I'll have it on the market soon." He chuckled to himself. "You've caused quite the headache, you know. You and your family and your incessant digging." Any humour faded from his face. "Dig. Dig. Dig. Digging as if you're digging a grave."

Six was leaning against the fireplace, one hand in his pocket. She noticed a shovel leaning against the wall in the corner.

"Was it necessary to call the council three times a day for the last three days?" He tilted his head. "So much disruption, and you'll keep causing it, won't you? You just can't help yourself."

Julia met his smug gaze and offered him a smile.

"Neither can you."

"I'm just a local lad trying to make a difference," he said, chuckling as if she'd told a fine joke. "And you're a local woman. A woman who runs a café and can't quite mind her own business. Dig. Dig. Dig."

This time, Greg glanced at the shovel.

"Listen, I'm not an unreasonable man," he said, opening his palms. "I'll make this easy for you. I'm prepared to offer you a generous compensation package to smooth things over. Stop whatever silly little protests you're planning. No fuss, no muss. Just step aside and let progress march onward, as it should. There's no need for you to be so anti-development. It's so... old fashioned."

Julia set her jaw, looking Greg dead in the eyes, but she said nothing. She crossed her legs, matching his posture, and tilted her head at him as he had done to her. His suave mask slipped; his dark eyes narrowed.

"I'd choose my next words very carefully if I were you, Julia."

Six resumed his stance behind her and rested his heavy hand on her shoulder, pressing her down into the creaky chair. She focused on slowing her hammering heart, refusing to show an ounce of fear to these bullies. Lifting her hands, she glanced at her nails.

Greg leaned on the edge of his chair, legs spread wide, head low. "Let me make this simple, Julia. You have two options. Take my generous offer, or my associates and I will make your life very difficult. If you refuse to sign a non-disclosure agreement and back down, I can't guarantee your safety."

A dark chuckle escaped Julia's lips, devoid of humour. With surprising force, she shook off the thick fingers crushing her shoulder and rose to her feet. Greg also rose, so they were eye to eye. Up close, she saw a hint of Veronica in his dark eyes. Where had their lives diverged so drastically?

"Mr Morgan, you don't intimidate me," she stated clearly, smoothing the creases in her dress. "Go ahead. Threaten me, intimidate me, even try to kill me if you must. You seem to think you can get away with anything you please, but like you said, my family can't seem to stop digging. Dig. Dig. Dig." She let her eyes linger on the shovel. "Do your worst, Mr Morgan. It'll be the last thing you do."

It was Greg's turn for prolonged silence. His eyes, which had sparkled with malevolent glee, lost their lustre. The slick grin that had spread across his lips moments before morphed into a tight line. It was as if a spell had been broken, and for the first time, he truly saw Julia—not as a pawn in his deranged game, but as a formidable opponent.

"No deal," Julia said, taking a step towards Greg. Like her dance with Six in the graveyard, he stepped back. "I think we're done here."

Julia turned on her heels and walked to the door. She waited for the axe in her back, the bullet in her arm, the knife in her side. Nothing. She opened the door and stepped outside; the cool night air had never felt more refreshing.

"That precious family of yours?" Greg called. "You don't know them as well as you think. One of them has already been bought."

Outside, Julia's composure cracked. Breath left her lungs in a ragged gasp. Her hands trembled as she snatched her phone from the back seat of the car. Setting off into the unknown, she tried to slow her pounding heart and calm her swimming head.

From the moment she'd climbed into the car, she'd known she would walk away unscathed. James had warned Greg about using the Crew. He wasn't going to do anything else that would put his career in jeopardy. And could they really be called a 'crew' anymore? She had a feeling they might have been down to their last desperate member.

Greg had wanted to scare her, and he had, but she

knew she'd scared him more. She hadn't crumbled, and he hadn't known what to do with that.

Cresting a hill, Julia caught sight of something familiar. Between trees bare of their leaves, the monolithic sandstone exterior of Wellington Heights drew her in. She'd never been happier to see the old building, and a feeling of safety washed over her.

And with it came the echo of Greg's parting words.

"One of them has already been bought."

She really hoped it was another of his empty threats.

16

Julia trudged through the village as the night wore on. She needed somewhere to collect her rattled thoughts and regain her strength before returning home. Up ahead, she spotted a warm glow pooling from the windows of her gran's cottage. Perfect. Julia sped up, ignoring her aching feet.

She let herself in. "It's only me, Gran."

"Julia?" Dot emerged from the dining room, the dogs scampering at her heels. "You look like you've been dragged through a hedge backwards!"

Too drained to explain, Julia sighed and slipped off her muddy shoes. The scent of stew and wood smoke washed over her as she leaned against the floral wallpaper. For a moment, she let her eyes drift shut, some of the tension releasing from her shoulders.

Dot reappeared, holding a bowl of steaming stew. "Here, eat this. You really have never looked worse. What happened?"

"Long walk."

She accepted the beef stew, picking up on raised voices drifting from the dining room. Curious, she wandered over to investigate while Dot fussed over the dogs as they fought for her attention.

Julia was surprised to find Amy, Shilpa, and Evelyn gathered around the long table, cluttered with art supplies. Posters bearing slogans lay half-finished alongside hand-drawn signs piled high. At the chalkboard, Percy and their unlikely new ally, Ethel, were drafting protest strategies. Petitions. Marches. Sit-ins. Boycotts. Social media. Sabotage. They weren't leaving a stone unturned. Greg had been a fool to think throwing money at her would stop the disruption. The cart had left the station, and Julia wasn't even in the driving seat.

"Welcome to the war room," Dot said, following her in. "And this is just the start. Ethel's been putting out the call all day. There won't be room to move before we know it."

Julia hoped so.

"What can I do?"

"Come help me with this sign," Shilpa said, patting the chair next to her.

Shilpa was using a chunky pen, writing 'Village Not For Sale' on a placard. Evelyn's said 'Green Not Grey', and Amy, who must have had a change of heart after seeing the plans, had written 'Keep Our Village, Village-Sized!' Julia grabbed a pen and a blank piece of card and without thinking, channelled something Greg had said to her.

'We're Not Anti-Development, We're Pro-Community.'

"That'll look good on a t-shirt," Shilpa said, handing Julia a second blank piece of card. Leaning in, she whispered, "I've been wanting to talk to you since the party. The day before, James made me another offer to buy my building. An exorbitant amount of money to pave over the post office for a road."

Julia didn't tell Shilpa she already knew.

"And did you..."

Shilpa shook her head. "I considered it. Oh, I considered it. I could retire three times over with what he proposed. But how could I live with myself if I let that man walk all over us again? I've worked in that post office my whole adult life. If I ever decide to sell it, it'll be for the right reasons."

"Good for you," Dot said, butting in to fill Shilpa's

teacup. "Oh, it's good to be back, isn't it? Keep churning these signs out, ladies. We need as many as we can hand out at the vote on Friday. This is like the old days."

"The *new* days," Ethel corrected. "Stop faffing around with tea and get to work, Dorothy. Friday will be here before we know it."

"Need I remind you whose house you're in, Ethel?"

"How could I forget?" Ethel looked around with a wrinkled nose. "And if you're insisting on procrastinating with tea, at least give me a top up."

Dot continued with the teapot, and Shilpa leaned in again.

"He'll likely come for your café next," she whispered. "He didn't hide that he's determined to get what he wants."

Julia's phone vibrated in her pocket.

> **BARKER**
> Don't forget, housewarming in half an hour. Did Prunella give up the ghost?

> **JULIA**
> Not quite. Lots to tell you though. You sure this party is a good idea?

> **BARKER**
> No, but it's an opportunity to see what he has to say for himself.

Julia groaned. She'd forgotten about their

neighbour's party. The thought of plastering on a fake smile and making nice with James after the day she'd endured made her want to crawl straight into bed. But Barker was right—this was an opportunity to glean more information.

After finishing her stew, Julia ran herself a bath upstairs, and the hot water helped thaw her chilled bones and weary mind. By the time she'd towelled off and rummaged through her gran's eclectic wardrobe, Julia felt almost human again. She chose a dress with a vintage floral print that reminded her of the wallpaper downstairs. After wrestling her damp curls into a twist, she assessed herself in the mirror. Presentable enough to attend a party hosted by her nemesis.

Descending the creaky stairs in a pair of her gran's heels, she found the makeshift workshop even more chaotic. Crumpled posters littered the floor alongside empty cups and glasses. Evelyn snored in a corner armchair while Dot and Ethel sniped at each other over the best rhymes for their protest chants.

"I haven't worn that one since your sister's wedding," Dot said as she inspected her outfit, clucking in approval. "You look smashing, dear. Give that snake a piece of your mind, and a piece of mine."

After bidding everyone goodnight, Julia slipped out into the night, nerves and anticipation warring within her. Despite her exhaustion, she was grateful for the reunion with her gran and the other women. Kindred spirits banding together to protect their village, sandwiched in the middle of meetings with the two men working together to destroy it. The perfect reminder of what they were fighting for.

Community.

And it was time to take to the fight to James' home.

17

*J*essie's nerves mounted with each step that brought her closer to the modern bungalow. She paused at the front door to steady herself, rubbing her clammy palms against her faded jeans. She shivered, doubting her plan to confront James alone. Before she could change her mind, she gave three sharp knocks. The sound seemed to echo inside the cavernous house. Footsteps approached, and the door swung inward.

Impeccably dressed as always, James filled the doorway, regarding Jessie with an indecipherable smile.

"You must be Jessika from *The Post*?" he confirmed. "Please, come in."

Jessie bristled at the use of her full name, but

forced a polite smile. She never went by Jessika, but maybe that would help her slip into the role of someone who knew what they were doing. She'd done her research, but she'd never conducted an interview for the paper alone. Somehow, she was more comfortable stealing keys.

Inside, the cold white walls and marble floors exuded an austere, modern feel. He led her down a long hallway into a huge sitting room, glowing with flickering firelight. Jessie perched uneasily on the edge of a leather sofa while James settled casually into an armchair. The open firepit in the middle of the room separated them, the heat of the flames twisting his smarmy features.

Richie had inherited his father's good looks, but that was about it.

Jessie fumbled for her recorder, nerves making her hands unsteady. "Get it together," she told herself. With a deep breath, she hit record and placed it on a small table.

"Thank you for agreeing to this interview, Mr Jacobson," she began, hoping her voice sounded steadier than she felt. "I know you value your privacy, so I appreciate you taking the time."

"Of course. I want to foster an open dialogue with the people of Peridale. Feel free to ask me anything. Can I get you a drink?"

"If you're happy to, I'd rather jump right into it," she said, and he nodded, checking his watch. "I want to start at the beginning."

She pulled out the grainy photograph she'd printed from his website—young James on the swing set in Fern Moore. His smile faltered at the sight of it. She placed it next to the recorder, and he could barely bring himself to look at it.

"You grew up on the Fern Moore housing estate. What was that experience like as a child?"

"Difficult," he said without missing a beat. "My mother was... a troubled woman. She struggled to care for me. We had nothing except for the clothes on our backs, and as you can see, they didn't fit very well." He leaned forward and plucked up the photo. "I knew from an early age I wanted a better life. The boy in this picture wasn't all too happy."

Jessie took a moment to regroup after James' revelations about his difficult childhood. She hadn't expected him to be so open with her first question. It almost made him seem human.

"That sounds tough," she said, injecting some empathy into her tone. "It's impressive you were able to build such a successful career coming from those circumstances."

James nodded, seeming to relax now that they'd moved past the tricky personal territory.

"Growing up in the shadow of a picture-perfect village like Peridale lit a fire under me," he confessed. "I knew from a young age that I wanted—needed—more out of life than what Fern Moore had to offer. The desire to prove myself was a strong motivator. What I really want people to realise is… I'm just like them. This place is as much home to me as to them."

Jessie could hear the spin, not bothering to mention that he'd spent most of his life living away from the village and Fern Moore. London, mostly, according to his website.

"I can understand that motivation," Jessie said, wanting to seem like she was on his side. She decided to switch gears. "At the village hall, you mentioned being inspired by Duncan Howarth and his big ambitions for Peridale. Can you expand on that?"

James brightened, sitting up straighter. "Ah yes, discovering Duncan Howarth's story was a pivotal moment for me. There I was, a boy from the rougher end of town, with big dreams of my own. My mum brought me a book she'd taken from work. A history book, and there was a chapter about Howarth. He had a vision that was decades ahead of his time. He could see, even then, what Peridale needed to thrive. More industry, more housing, more commerce. The village resisted such notions back then, of course. Preferred to keep things quaint. Small. Quiet."

Jessie had travelled the world, and quaint and quiet were two of her favourite things, but she didn't want to interrupt. She nodded for him to continue.

"But Howarth didn't let the limitations of the era stop him," he continued. "He kept pushing for Peridale to evolve, even in the face of hostility from those afraid of change. I admired that greatly. It inspired me not to listen when people said my ambitions were unrealistic or unwanted."

"You had the idea of Howarth Estate as a child?"

Laughing, he shook his head. "My ambitions were smaller, but to those around me, they seemed huge. I simply wanted to get out. I didn't plan beyond that. No, my idea for the Howarth Estate came when I spent some time in the village last year. That field caught my eye, and I realised the council was open to negotiating. When I understood what I saw that day could be possible, there was no other name that would fit. I intend to lead Peridale towards the prosperity Howarth envisioned."

Jessie suppressed a cynical reaction, keeping her expression neutral. "Some argue that progress doesn't have to come at the expense of two hundred new houses in the middle of a small, rural village. What would you say to people with that perspective?"

James waved a dismissive hand. "Everything has its time. The rustic dreams of the past must evolve. If

Howarth Estate had been built in the 1840s, people would be fighting to preserve it today. In a century, people will be fighting to preserve what I'm about to build. People, especially rural folk, are sticklers for change. I challenge them to embrace it."

"And if they don't want to embrace it?"

"Then they will remain stuck in the past." He fixed Jessie with an intense stare. "Take your mother's café, for example. Charming, yes, but tell me it's turning an adequate profit? I've run some hypothetical numbers, and they could be better. More people means more business."

"The café does just fine." She wondered if 'Jessika' had any cover at all. She should have known that even if they'd never met, he might know who she was. She needed to steer the conversation back on track. "Okay, so Duncan Howarth inspired your outlook. But there's still confusion around your numerous development proposals for the field. If honouring Howarth's legacy was your aim all along, why not reveal that vision from the start?"

James sighed. "I have been accused of secrecy, and perhaps there is some truth to that. I worried that publicly announcing my plans prematurely would ignite too much opposition. So, I explored different options, keeping the details private until I felt sure I had the right approach." Spreading his hands, he added, "I know that bred mistrust and suspicion. In retrospect, I could have been more transparent. But believe me, my vision has always been consistent—honouring Howarth by bringing new life to Peridale through sustainable, sensitive development. I want to get it right."

Jessie bit her tongue, scepticisms mounting. She decided to voice it diplomatically. "Some feel things have moved too quickly, without enough community feedback. Only a very small public meeting, no advertising, or notifications. Does that concern you at all?"

James shook his head. "At a certain point, we must stop debating and start building. That time is now. The people of Peridale want new housing and amenities. If you read the council's new report, 'Preserving Tradition, Embracing Progress,' you'll know that most people are embracing the future."

He checked his watch, and Jessie realised her time was running short. Every answer had been a perfectly worded spin.

"Just one more thing about Duncan Howarth," she hedged. "*The Post* has good reason to believe you possess a lost portrait of Howarth. A portrait that interested Peter McBride, who died at your party. Any comment on that?"

James' polite expression hardened. "No comment."

"You were seen talking to Peter in your son's bar before that party, and soon after, he claimed to have seen the painting. Any comment?"

"No comment." He stood up. "Now, unless you have more questions, I believe our time is up."

She held his icy stare, undeterred. Her instincts screamed that James was hiding something about the painting. She decided to change course, saving her most crucial question for the last.

"There is one more topic I'd like your comment on, and I do have evidence for this one," Jessie continued, steel in her tone. "Multiple inside sources have confirmed that you and disgraced local politician, Greg Morgan, have offered bribes in exchange for securing a favourable outcome at the upcoming committee."

"Those are rather serious allegations."

"Yes, they are," Jessie said, picking up the voice recorder and holding it out to him. "Care to respond to the people of Peridale?"

Jessie watched James closely, searching for expressions of guilt or denial. But his face remained an unreadable mask.

"I believe we're finished here," he stated.

Jessie grabbed her bag before James ushered her down the hall. "Are you sure you have no comment?"

"No comment," he said when she was on the doorstep. "And take your time to think about what you choose to send to print. You wouldn't want to make any unwise decisions."

James shut the door, and Jessie allowed herself a moment to steady her adrenaline. Like Greg, James' evasive non-answers spoke louder than any of his print-ready statements.

As Jessie hurried down the lane, her mind raced with all she had learned. James' inspirational tale about Duncan Howarth now seemed like a thinly veiled con for his true profit-driven motivations. And his refusal to address the bribery allegations all but confirmed their legitimacy.

She rested her hand on the stolen key in her pocket. Dumb idea. She'd give it back tomorrow.

Tonight, all she wanted was to collapse into bed and shut out the world for a few hours. At her flat door, she fumbled for her keys, cursing under her breath when they slipped through her numb fingers and clattered to the ground. As she crouched to retrieve them, a shadow moved towards her from the direction of the field. She barrelled back, falling on her backside.

"Sorry, I didn't mean to scare you," came a familiar voice. "I keep doing that."

Jessie squinted into the dark at Dante. Ignoring his outstretched hand, she righted herself and picked up her keys. His posture was open, shoulders relaxed, but the fidgeting of his fingers betrayed his nervousness.

"Maybe that's because you keep sneaking up on me."

"I don't mean to. I just... never know what to say when I see you." Even in the darkness, she could make out his sheepish smile. "I was just passing by and thought I'd... say 'hi'?"

"At this time?"

Dante held up his hands. "Okay, you caught me. I wanted to see you." His expression turned serious. "You haven't been replying to my texts, and I was worried. Is everything good?"

"Long day. Long few days. You should probably go home. It's late."

"I know, but I just... I haven't been able to stop thinking about you." His voice dropped lower. "Ever since we almost..."

He trailed off, but Jessie knew what he meant. That electrifying almost-kiss in the haunted maze still lingered when the case wasn't clouding her thoughts. Things between them had shifted after that charged moment. She'd felt the difference in their interactions, though neither had acknowledged it outright. The sensible part of her brain urged her to say goodnight and retreat into the safety of solitude. But deeper down, something tugged at her —an emotion she hadn't felt in a while: trust. Maybe it was the honesty in Dante's eyes, or perhaps her own tiredness stripping away her usual defences, but she yearned to let her guard down and invite him in.

Dante seemed to sense her inner turmoil. He took a half-step back, giving her space.

"Sorry, I'm probably being way too forward," he said. "I'm not meaning to pressure you into anything, Jessie. I just can't stop thinking about... us." He gestured between them. "Whatever this is turning into."

"Us?" Jessie repeated with a soft, doubtful laugh. "We're two journalists who keep overlapping."

"Why do you do that?"

"Do what?"

"What you're doing right now." He searched for the words, and she gave him the space to process his frustration. "That day in the bar when I was out of it after we saw Peter's body. You told me to drop the mask. So, drop the mask."

Jessie looked away. She tried to retreat behind her walls, but they felt as flimsy as tissue paper in this moment. Drawing a shaky breath, she said, "Dante, I... I..."

"I like you, Jessie. I *really* like you."

"You don't even know me."

"You're stubborn, hot-headed, impulsive," he said, that smile that made her melt perking up his cheeks. "You're... brave. You impress me every time I'm near you, and I don't think you're ever trying to. You have conviction about the things you care about. When you drop those walls, and you talk about your life, the things you've been through, you're never bitter about it. You could be. You should be. And I just... like being around you." His voice drifted off, and he looked as if he were regretting opening his mouth—and his heart. "Tell me to go, and I'll go, but I want to know I'm not imagining that you're into me too. Because I don't think I got here on my own."

Her thoughts raced. The sensible part of her screamed caution, but another voice, softer but more insistent, whispered that maybe, just maybe, it was time to take a risk that wasn't for a story for the paper.

Before she could second-guess herself, propelled by a newfound clarity, she closed the distance between them and pressed her lips to Dante's. He tensed in surprise before wrapping his arms around her, returning the kiss as she pushed him against the post office wall.

Jessie's ever-churning thoughts finally stilled, and for a blissful moment, the chaos stopped swirling. When they eventually drew apart, Jessie felt self-conscious. Her cheeks flushed hot despite the night's chill, and she couldn't look at him.

Clearing his throat and running a hand through his hair, he said, "Well, that was..."

"Nice," Jessie offered, glancing up at him. "You're right. You didn't get there on your own."

An awkward silence stretched between them. Jessie scuffed her boot against the ground, wanting to regret how she'd just complicated things. But she couldn't bring herself to regret it. He was a good kisser —a *really* good kisser. She hadn't known him for long, but she already cared a lot about Dante, and he saw through her in a way not many had. A relationship would only become a distraction, but maybe that was just what she needed.

"Fancy going on a date?" she asked.

"Name the time and place, and I'll be there."

"Right now." She retrieved the key from her pocket and held it up between them. "Wellington Heights. Greg Morgan's bedroom."

"How did you get that?"

"By being impulsive." Tossing the key, she caught it in her palm and clenched her fist around it. Backing down the alley, she flashed him a grin. "You coming?"

Running his tongue across his lip, he caught up with her, and before she could question if she wanted to, she wrapped her hand around his.

"I missed something off that list," he whispered into her ear, his warm breath tingling down her spine. "You're trouble."

18

Barker stood at the streamlined, contemporary sink in James' opulent bathroom, scrubbing his hands with a cedarwood-scented soap. The sink was nothing more than a hole in barely concave polished concrete, and the soap squirted out from a machine he only had to wave under. He stared at his reflection in the expansive backlit mirror as the soap bubbled between his fingers. Even in the bright lights, the dark circles under his eyes were evident. This exhausting case was taking its toll, and he still hadn't started his next book. Maybe tomorrow.

He sighed and turned off the tap and found the fluffiest hand towel he'd ever touched, monogrammed with the same 'JJ' from the wax seal. He took his time, not wanting to rush back to the 'party.'

When they'd arrived, Barker had been dumbfounded to find they were the only guests at James' housewarming. He'd expected the place to be packed with the elite and influential from across the Cotswolds, all eager to rub shoulders with the wealthy developer. Instead, they were met with a lavish but empty house, and James playing the role of gracious host.

Barker stepped out into the gleaming corridor, doubling back as he passed by an office with the door ajar. He paused, glancing inside. The space was all geometric lines and minimalism, much like the rest of the home's cold decor. But what drew his gaze was the large architectural model displayed prominently in the centre of the room.

Unable to resist, Barker slipped inside and moved closer. It was another scale model of the planned Howarth Estate development. But something was off. Leaning down, Barker realised with a jolt that this model was different from the one publicly unveiled days ago. The houses sprawled further and wider, many more than two hundred at a glance.

He straightened, scowling. Was it an earlier draft, or plans for the future phases? He studied the walls lined with modern art, searching for any sign of a safe where the elusive Howarth portrait might be secreted away. But nothing jumped out. Not wanting to leave Julia alone for too long, he left the office after another scan and retraced his steps. Barker might have lived on the land when he'd first moved to the village, but the inside of James' sprawling bungalow shared nothing in common with that long-gone cottage.

In the theater-sized living area sporting a television bigger than any Barker had seen, he found Julia perched stiffly on a leather sofa, nursing her first glass of champagne. James sat across from her in an armchair, holding court like a king before his subjects, the indoor firepit separating them. An untouched spread of hors d'oeuvres occupied a sleek table in front of floor-to-ceiling windows, offering uninterrupted views of the dark countryside.

Seeing Barker return, Julia shot him a tight smile. He could tell she was struggling to remain civil around their infuriating host. Barker couldn't blame her. His own politeness was hanging on by a fraying thread.

He circled past the buffet and swiped a cracker topped with something fancy and fishy. He resumed his seat next to Julia, and James raised a curious brow at Barker's obvious lack of manners, using his hands rather than the little forks.

"Caviar," James said. "Ever tried it?"

"No," Barker spat it into a napkin and bunched it up. "And I won't be again."

"How disappointing. It's the good stuff. Cost a fortune."

Barker looked around and wondered how the caviar differed from anything else.

"I must say, this is quite the intimate affair," Barker remarked. "Will more guests be arriving?"

James smiled thinly. "No, I believe this might be it for attendees. Perhaps my invitation didn't successfully convey that outsiders would be welcome."

Julia set down her untouched flute of champagne. "Can you blame people for declining?"

"Now, now." James held up a diplomatic hand. "I was rather hoping we could move past old conflicts this evening. Consider tonight an opportunity for a fresh start."

Barker crossed his arms, leaning back against the cushions. "A fresh start requires trust on both sides. You'll understand why that might be difficult for us. You could have told us what you were planning a long time ago, but you didn't."

For a moment, his polished veneer seemed to crack, revealing a flicker of loneliness in his calculated gaze.

"You're quite right, of course," he conceded with a

heavy sigh. "When I returned to Peridale the first time, you two were the only ones who offered me friendship. I haven't forgotten that, believe me. I always knew my return would ruffle some feathers, but I did hope you'd stand by my side. We went through a lot, after all." He rose and moved to the window overlooking the pitch-black field, hands clasped behind his back. "Do you remember that day we went to Fern Moore together, Julia? It was your encouragement that first inspired me to invest there. To try to lift up the place that shaped me, rather than turning my back on it."

Julia's expression remained guarded, though Barker noted a softening in her eyes. He knew that visit had meant something to her at the time. She'd thought she'd made a difference. James turned back to them, a faraway look on his face.

"You told me I should buy the row of shops. Fix them up and make them better. Give back. Isn't that what I'm trying to do here? Take an abandoned field and build something of value?"

Barker wanted to cling to his mistrust of the man. But in this unguarded moment, he recognised the lonely boy from the grainy photograph peering out from behind the polish.

Still, he had to keep sight of the truth.

"Look me in the eye right now and tell me this isn't

about the money," Barker challenged. "That your only aim is improving people's lives, not lining your pockets."

James opened his mouth but faltered. At last, he dropped his eyes, a guilty expression flickering across his face.

"Thought so," Barker said. "Don't pretend your motivations are pure philanthropy. We know you too well for that."

James turned away, a scowl marring his refined features. All hints of vulnerability had vanished. He downed the rest of his champagne before slamming the empty flute onto a side table.

"So much for a civilised evening," he muttered. "I should have known neither of you would have the dignity to accept what you can't change. But, if that's how you wish to be, very well. Let's skip straight to business, shall we?"

Reaching into his suit pocket, he retrieved a check and held it out to Julia. She eyed it warily until James gave it an impatient shake. With extreme reluctance, she accepted the slip of paper.

"A gesture of good faith." James moved to an ornate alcohol cabinet and refilled his glass. "Write down any amount you wish, and I'll pay it. Within reason, of course."

"Twice in one day," Julia said under her breath. "And what do you get out of this?"

James turned, regarding her as one might a stubborn child. "It's for your café, naturally. I'm prepared to offer you an extremely generous sum."

"My business isn't for sale, James."

"I only want the bricks and mortar." James moved to a panel on the wall and pressed something that made the giant flat-screen TV switch on. It displayed architectural renders of the planned Howarth Estate development.

Only this version was even larger and more overwhelming than the one unveiled days ago. Hundreds more luxury houses crammed together on much denser plots. The sweeping aerial view made Julia suck in a shocked breath.

The digital camera swept past St. Peter's Church and the village green. But the familiar green was gone, replaced by a paved roundabout with no grass in sight. Julia stared at the screen, speechless, and Barker felt his own gut twist at the cold, sterile vista. The rendering took them down a main access road leading to the gates of the new estate. Row upon row of mini mansions sprawled as far as the eye could see. And nowhere to be seen was the café.

Barker watched his wife. He could tell she was trying not to show a reaction; he could read the distress in her eyes. He moved closer and grabbed her knee tight.

"Perhaps I could build an even grander café for you within the new development?" James suggested. "There's ample commercial space planned. I could even evict my son from the bar and sign the lease over to you instead, if you'd prefer? Barely a change for you. Or maybe you could move to Mulberry Lane? You'd get much more foot traffic there, I'm sure. Right now, your café just happens to be in the perfect position for my new road."

Barker could stay silent no longer. "Just like the library had the perfect light for a restaurant."

James waved a dismissive hand, refusing to acknowledge the reminder. His eyes stayed fixed on Julia. "Come now, be reasonable. Don't let sentimentality cloud a smart business decision. It's just a café, Julia."

Barker longed to whisk her away from this manipulative ambush. But he knew Julia needed to stand her ground herself, for her own sake.

"I believe I've made you several very generous offers," James said, his voice softening as he slid a pen into her frozen grip. "All you have to do, Julia, is name your price."

19

"It's not too late to turn back," Jessie said as the silhouette of Wellington Heights came into view. "We'd be breaking the law."

"Where's your sense of adventure?"

At the front door, Jessie loosened her intertwined fingers from Dante's and slid the stolen key into the lock. It clicked open with a single twist, and they slipped inside the polished lobby, their footsteps echoing on the marble floors as she took the familiar route to the sweeping staircase.

The penthouse was only accessible from a lift on the second floor, built in what she was sure used to be a cleaning cupboard. She used the key again to activate it, and before long, they were gliding up to the top floor. Of the three penthouses to choose from, she found the match for the key on the second attempt.

Exchanging tense looks, Jessie and Dante stepped across the threshold into the lion's den. The expansive penthouse was shrouded in shadow, illuminated only by the kitchen's under-cabinet strip lighting. The place reeked of wealth, and something else; unwashed clothes.

"Looks like there's a home office," Dante whispered. "I'll start in there."

"I'll look for his bedroom."

In Greg's small, chaotic home office, Dante began rifling through the heaps of paperwork and file boxes. Meanwhile, Jessie crept down the hall to the bedroom, bracing herself for the possibility that Greg could be tucked up in bed for an early night. He wasn't.

Unlike the rest of the apartment, Greg's bedroom looked like some of the bad hostels Jessie had stayed in while travelling—the bed was unmade, and clothes lay strewn across the floor alongside dirty plates and cups. In public, Greg strived for an illusion of perfection that was nowhere to be seen behind closed doors.

Kneeling, Jessie searched under the bed and inspected the closet but found nothing of note among the mess. She moved on to the en-suite bathroom, flicking on the lights. The gleaming marble space was at least clean, though just as vacant of clues.

Moving onto the bedside table, she opened the bottom drawer. It was filled to the brim with money, as messy as his sock drawer. She imagined him diving in and pulling out fistfuls of the cash whenever he needed a fresh bribe. She was tempted to take a few fistfuls herself, but the money was as tainted as the man keeping it in his bedside table.

She moved up a drawer, and her heart fluttered at something more shocking than a drawer filled with money.

Greg Morgan, MP slept with a gun within reaching distance.

~

Unmoving on the plush leather sofa, Julia was still transfixed by the blank cheque in her trembling hands. The dark ink of James' signature taunted her, daring her to fill the empty box. With a few strokes of the pen, she'd never have to worry about money again. The sagging roof and drafty windows of their cottage could be repaired. She could take time off to be with Olivia. She could give her daughter all the little luxuries she never had growing up.

Julia nearly laughed out loud at the direction of

her thoughts. Since when had she ever cared about money and extravagance? But something about holding the cheque made fantasies dance through her mind, accompanied by a creeping temptation she'd never experienced before.

She stared at the empty box until the lines blurred, a war waging within her.

"Be sensible," the practical voice urged her to take the money and run. "Use it for good while you can. What's the café, really, but old bricks and beams? Just a building."

But her heart rebelled at the cold reasoning.

The café wasn't merely four walls to her. It was as much a part of her as her family or her heartbeat. And as much a part of the village as the trees and fields. It had stood since 1786, and she wouldn't let it fall on her watch.

She clenched her eyes, willing the turbulent thoughts to quiet. She focused on steadying her breath, finding her centre. This was a test, she realised. And whatever decision she made in this moment would define the person she was—the person she would become.

"Not even for your daughter's future?" James whispered. "Not even for Olivia?"

The sound of her daughter's name leaving his mouth ignited Julia's resilience. The person she wanted to become was someone who could show her daughter that she could stand up for what she believed in. She tore the cheque down the middle—then again, and again, until only confetti remained. She let the pieces flutter into the firepit, releasing the breath she'd been holding as she watched the shreds char to dust. Centred once more, she opened her eyes. The first offer of the day in the rundown cottage had been much easier to turn down.

"Well, isn't that a pity?" James said, filling his glass yet again. "I think you'll live to regret your foolish decision."

"Likewise," she said.

"No matter." He tossed the drink back. "There are many roads to the same destination that don't require your involvement."

"I think we've outstayed our welcome," Julia said, standing with Barker. "You have a lovely home, James." She paused, looking back at him with open defiance. "I'll see you at the council meeting. I suspect you'll have many more angry constituents to deal with then."

Without waiting for his reaction, Julia marched into the night, Barker close behind. As they walked up the lane beneath the emerging stars, she looped her arm through his. The casual touch comforted her rattled nerves.

Glancing back, she saw James' silhouette in the doorway, watching them depart. Though too far to make out his expression, she could feel his lingering glare between her shoulder blades until they turned a corner out of sight.

Only once his house had vanished around the bend, the dizzying fog of possibilities cleared. No wonder Shilpa had taken days to decide. No wonder so many were inspired to do the worst things for a slice of the pie. But she hadn't just turned down his money. She'd chosen to stand against a ruthless opponent who could ruin their lives on a whim.

And she'd done it twice in one day.

As though sensing her dread, Barker wrapped a steadying arm around her shoulders and pressed a kiss to her temple. "That took real courage. I thought you were considering it."

"Just for a second," she admitted, "I think I was."

As they approached their cottage, Julia paused to take in the sight of the humble dwelling, with its uneven stones and slightly overgrown garden. After the cold opulence of James' grand house, their home looked smaller and shabbier than ever. Yet a feeling of warmth spread through her chest. This cottage held a lifetime of memories that money couldn't replace—just like her café.

Inside, they found Neil in the sitting room reading

a picture book to a sleepy-eyed Olivia and the twins. He looked up with a frown. "You're back early. Is everything okay?"

Before Julia could respond, Olivia broke into a huge smile and came toddling over on unsteady legs. "Mama!"

Julia's heart melted. She swept her daughter into her arms. Mowgli wound around her feet, meowing until she bent to scratch under his chin. The cat purred, and Julia felt the last of the tension leave her shoulders. She was home.

She found Sue washing up in the kitchen. Grabbing the tea towel to dry, Julia recounted everything that had happened at James' housewarming, including the blank cheque.

Sue blinked in astonishment. She seemed troubled, swirling a sponge around on a plate in a repetitive circle until Julia reached out and touched her arm.

"Is everything okay, Sue?"

With a heavy sigh, Sue sank onto a stool at the breakfast bar. "I have a confession to make, Julia. I wish I'd been brave like you were tonight, but I just wasn't strong enough to turn down James."

Greg's words rang out in her ears. She hadn't given it much thought; she had hoped it had been to plant seeds of distrust in her mind, but her sister was the last person she'd expect to take a bribe from James.

"What do you mean, Sue?"

Sue twisted a napkin in her hands, knotting it around her fingers in tight loops. "I've been trying to find the right way to tell you this for weeks now. Months, even. James gave us money too—a *lot* of money."

"A... bribe?"

"No, no. It was for our new house," Sue confessed, tears glistening in her eyes. "Last year, Neil and I could see the writing on the wall. We'd never be able to afford a nice place of our own on our salaries at the time. The library had been struggling for years, and I wasn't being paid anywhere near enough as a nurse. We couldn't get approved for a mortgage, and all we could think about was getting the girls out of our old cottage and into a proper home." She took a shaky breath. "Then James showed up for a meeting at the library, and he overheard us talking. He made it sound so simple, so perfect. Like it was nothing. A done deal before we'd had time to think about it. He paid for the mortgage, and all we have to do is pay him back."

"Oh, Sue." Julia breathed, her heart aching for her sister. "How much does he have you on the hook for?"

"Almost one hundred thousand pounds," Sue

whispered. "And we're just about making the payments. That house is a death trap. Something new breaks every week, and it's draining us. We're trapped there—trapped by what we owe him. That's why I didn't want to join the bandwagon. I was scared he'd make things harder for us. I'm so ashamed I didn't tell you sooner. I just couldn't admit how stupid we'd been in trusting that man."

They held onto each other for a long moment before Julia pulled back, keeping her hands on Sue's shoulders. "We're going to figure this out, okay? You're not in this alone."

Sue managed a watery smile. "I'm not sure how to figure it out."

"No, me neither," Julia admitted. "But we will."

They turned to see Neil and Barker standing in the doorway, sharing the same solemn expressions. Neil held his hand out, and Barker shook it.

"I'm sorry I didn't listen to your concerns sooner, Barker. You were right to be suspicious of James' intentions from the start. I let myself get blinded by all his talk of investing more and more in the library. But after the village hall, it hit me that this isn't just about us—it's about the whole village we care about."

Julia gave Neil's arm an appreciative squeeze, heartened to have him as an ally again instead of polite opposition. She saw the same relief shining on

Sue's face. She'd moved into Henderson Place at the beginning of the year, before she'd started working at the café, so Julia could only imagine the weight her sister had been carrying whenever James' name cropped up in another scandal. No wonder she'd sat on the fence.

She didn't know how to ease that burden, and after seeing the chilling vision of her café erased from the village, she didn't know how to stop him, either. The battle lines were drawn, and James wasn't going to give up without a fight.

But neither would Julia.

∼

Jessie sat on the edge of Greg's bed, unable to tear her eyes away from the gun staring at her from the bedside drawer.

Dante entered the room and sighed. "I've been through everything in here and only found boring financial statements. Greg knows how to cover his tracks."

"Not all of them," Jessie nodded at the gun. "Look what I uncovered."

Dante's eyes widened as he joined her on the bed. "I know Greg is twisted, but keeping a gun so close? Who's he scared is coming for him?"

Jessie shivered. "Just imagine who he's used this on already... or who he might use it on if we don't stop him."

At that moment, they froze at the sound of a key turning in the front door lock. Exchanging panicked looks, Jessie closed the drawer before they hid inside the spacious walk-in wardrobe. Crouched together in the dark, Jessie clasped her hand over her panting mouth as the steps grew closer. Through a crack in the wardrobe door, she glimpsed Greg enter, yawning as he shuffled over to his desk.

Her relief at not being discovered lasted only a second before he was joined by a hulking man with a shaved head and pit bull features—Six. Jessie's insides twisted. They were trapped.

Oblivious to his stowaway guests, Greg dropped onto the edge of his bed. "Whiskey?"

Six declined with a grunt. "You asked for an update."

"Very well, let's get on with it then." Greg leaned back, propping his feet up. "Tell me what my friends in Peridale have been up to lately."

In the shadows of the closet, Jessie tensed. She fumbled for her phone and set it to record. Maybe Greg would incriminate himself.

"Activities have been scaled back on your instructions," Six reported.

"Yes, best to let them look over their shoulders for now. But stay vigilant." He swirled his whiskey pensively before his features hardened, and it took Jessie a moment to realise he meant her family. "You saw how Julia was with us earlier. That woman is *not* to be underestimated, but there's a new problem requiring our attention—a thorn that needs urgent removal. You recall that trashy newspaper causing all the trouble last month?"

Six gave a single nod.

"Veronica Hilt." Greg spat the name like venom. "She won't stop her foolish crusade against me. She found the wire you planted in your plumber disguise. It's time to shut her infernal operation down for good. The methods are up to your discretion. But the directive is clear—silence her. *Permanently.*"

Jessie clenched her fists. Beside her, Dante laid a calming hand on her leg.

Oblivious to their presence, Greg continued plotting his sister's demise mere feet away, and Six nodded, unfazed by the callous orders.

"It will be done."

"Excellent!" Greg announced. "You've served me well, Six. I'll see you're rewarded should I find myself in a position of greater influence soon." He raised his whiskey in a mocking toast. "To removing thorns from my side."

Jessie trembled, barely holding herself back from bursting out to confront Greg face-to-face. She had to get this evidence to the police; Veronica's life depended on it. Beside her, Dante rubbed gentle circles on her back, offering wordless comfort until the conversation finally lulled.

After what felt like an eternity, Six grunted his goodbyes and lumbered out. Greg lingered on the bed a while longer, swirling his drink round and round before dragging himself away. They listened to his footsteps cross the room and disappear into the en suite bathroom, leaving a trail of clothes behind him.

Running water filled the air as Greg stepped into the shower. Seizing the opportunity, Jessie and Dante slipped out of the wardrobe and tiptoed out of the bedroom. They crossed the penthouse, and the front door came within touching distance.

On the other side, more keys slotted into the lock.

Dante yanked Jessie into the shadows behind a marble column. They peered out as the door swung inward and Richie shuffled inside. He looked more drained than Jessie had ever seen him. He plodded along, throwing his coat down on the back of a chair before resting his head on the kitchen island. Dante tried to pull Jessie out with him, but she shook her head, stepping out from their hiding spot.

"Richie?" she called softly.

He whirled around, surprise melting into anger as he spotted her. "Jessie... What... What the hell are you doing in my flat?"

"Richie, I can explain." Jessie stepped forward, hands raised in apology. "I'm sorry. We shouldn't have broken in. But we had to find evidence against your dad and Greg."

Richie ran a hand over his face, looking more deflated than furious now. "Unbelievable. *You* stole my key, didn't you? I had to go crawling to my dad to get the spare. I thought I could trust you."

Guilt gnawed at Jessie. She dropped her gaze. "I betrayed your trust, but the stakes are so high. I panicked and made a reckless choice."

Richie sighed, sinking into the sofa. "It's not the strangest thing that's happened all day. People have already started boycotting the bar because of my dad. At this rate, I'll be out of business soon. This isn't even my apartment anyway. Not really. Maybe I deserve it."

"No, you don't," Jessie insisted, sitting beside him. "You're nothing like your father. I meant what I said before. If you ever want to stand against him, we'd welcome your help. The offer still stands."

Richie lifted his head. "You know what? I might take you up on that. He only uses me anyway—for an ego boost when it suits him or for a hug when it makes him look paternal in front of the cameras. I'm done being a prop in his scheming. If he wants a hug, he can get one from his bank manager."

Jessie knew what it felt like to be used by someone who was meant to protect you, but she'd never had to endure it for too long with any of her foster parents. Richie had a life sentence when it came to James Jacobson.

"Wait here a second," he said. "There's something I think you should see."

He disappeared down the hall into his bedroom, leaving Jessie and Dante to exchange puzzled looks. A minute later, Richie returned holding a large, rectangular object wrapped in white fabric. He set it down gently before them.

"My dad asked me to keep this here for him. But I think it's time I return it to who it really belongs to..."

With great care, Richie peeled back the sheet. A portrait of a dour-looking man stared back at them, his stern appearance captured in unflattering detail.

"Is that..." Dante breathed.

"The long-lost painting of Duncan Howarth," Jessie said, unable to believe her eyes. "It never left the manor, did it?"

"Said he found it in some secret safe behind a wall in the basement. I don't know why my dad wants to keep it hidden," Richie said, "but if this could help stop him in his tracks, maybe some good can come of it."

Jessie couldn't believe their luck. After all their searching, and who knows how many years Peter had spent looking, the portrait had been under their noses in the manor the entire time. Peter would have wept tears of joy if he could see his white whale finally unearthed. Leaning closer, she searched for the mysterious confession Howarth had mentioned, but the image yielded no hidden clues that she could see.

"No artist signature," Dante observed.

"Can I take this to show my parents?" Jessie asked. "They might be able to make more sense of it."

Richie hesitated, uncertainty clouding his face. Jessie knew she was asking a lot—requesting he turn completely against his father in this way. But they were so close to unravelling the portrait's secrets. At last, Richie nodded, relinquishing the painting into her care.

"I'll be glad to see the back of the ugly thing. I can feel him watching me when I sleep, and wasn't a looker, was he? Just... put it to good use."

"I promise." Jessie squeezed his hand. Together, they wrapped the portrait snugly before passing it to Dante for safekeeping.

Bidding Richie farewell, Jessie and Dante hurried

out into the night, electrified by their monumental discovery.

"You found the smoking gun and a *literal* gun," Dante marvelled as they half-jogged down the wet streets, the painting between held them. "I know I said you were trouble, but this could blow everything wide open."

20

The day before the pivotal planning committee meeting, Julia and Barker gathered in the basement office under the café to collate their investigation findings. Julia tacked handwritten notes onto the green investigation board while Barker paced, piecing together their tangled threads aloud.

"Alright, let's go over what we know," Barker began. "Someone murdered Peter McBride at James' Halloween party. Peter visited you the day before, frantic to share information but too afraid to fully open up. He mentioned being hounded by men in black suits, which we now know were the Cotswold Crew, doing Greg Morgan's dirty work."

Julia nodded, pinning up the bearded photo of Greg. "Right. Peter was fixated on finding a lost portrait of Duncan Howarth, convinced it held some revelation that could stop the development plans. Do you really think Jessie has the painting?"

"She wouldn't make that up," Barker said, checking his watch. "She'll be here soon. James hid it at the manor, so it must mean something."

"And don't forget the bribery," Julia added. "Jessie all but proved that James and Greg are paying off the Preservation Society members to sway that planning committee vote, and Peter was the only one with a clean record."

Stepping back, she assessed the pictures of Prunella, Martin, Richard, and Alice already on the board. Red strings connected them to the picture of Peter in the middle. Martin and James had been crossed out, which left them with three likely suspects.

"Corruption, bribery, and secrets." Barker scratched at his stubble. "Prunella appears the most ruthless in my eyes. But any of them could have motives."

"We're still missing a piece. The why. Why is this painting the last puzzle piece?"

At that moment, Jessie finally joined them, slightly

Pumpkins and Peril

out of breath as she lugged the painting wrapped in a sheet down the stairs with Veronica's help. They set the large rectangular object on the desk, neither of them needing to say a word. With great care, Jessie peeled back the covering to reveal the portrait.

The stern face of Duncan Howarth glared at them through the years, dark eyes narrow and unsmiling. Dressed in an intricate suit with layers and ruffles that hadn't been fashionable in Julia's lifetime, he almost looked like he was in a Halloween costume. Behind him, sprawling green fields stretched out into the distance, a single factory with a looming chimney pumping thick smoke into the blue sky.

"Okay," Barker said, the one to break the silence. "We have it. Now we need to figure out why it's important that we have it."

"If only Peter was here," Julia said, sure he'd see what they couldn't. "Does anyone else think it's a little…"

"Rubbish?" Veronica filled in the blank. "I didn't want to say it."

Julia agreed, and she didn't know how Veronica was so calm. After listening to the voice recording Jessie had captured hidden in Greg's wardrobe, she was surprised Veronica hadn't taken the first ticket out of Peridale. Moyes had wanted Julia to do the same, and maybe she would have if the order for her 'silence' had come from her brother.

"How are you feeling?" Julia asked.

"Oh, I'm not worried," Veronica answered, twitching her black glasses with a shaky touch. Julia had never seen her in plain black glasses before. "Gregory is nothing more than a thug with a fragile ego. He doesn't scare me."

"I've seen what the Cotswold Crew can do," Barker countered. "You should take him seriously."

"Something tells me there isn't a united crew anymore," Jessie said. "Anyone else seen anyone other than Six?" They all shook their heads. "We never knew how many members there were. Maybe after all the arrests... he's the last of them."

"Still," Barker said, exhaling. "One ruthless gang member is still one too many for my liking."

"Don't worry, Dad, Veronica isn't leaving my side." Jessie wrapped an arm around Veronica, patting her shoulder. "I'll handcuff her to me if I need to."

"'Cowards die many times before their deaths. The valiant never taste of death but once,'" Veronica recited.

"Julius Caesar?" Barker asked.

"Act Two, Scene Two." Tossing her hands up, she cried, "Finally, someone of culture."

Despite her breezy denials, the editor did seem

shaken—and nobody could blame her—but at least she was taking it in her stride. The police had the voice file, so perhaps they'd found their proof. Julia hoped so.

"Do you think Greg could be behind Peter's murder?" Julia posed. "He has the connections."

Jessie considered this. "He's corrupted enough, but the Crew's methods are more subtle, aren't they?" She shot Veronica a pointed look. "They like to make things look like accidents. House fires, faulty brakes... What do you think, Veronica?"

Veronica hummed, lost in thought.

While they continued debating suspects, Julia found herself drawn into a staring match with the dour face of Duncan Howarth. She hadn't known what to expect, but she'd expected something of quality. His oil paint features were amateurish at best, with no skill or fine detail that she could see. One of his eyes seemed off-kilter, giving him a somewhat cockeyed appearance, and his nose looked too high and short on his face.

What was it about this mediocre portrait that had inspired such obsession and secrecy? Peter had been adamant that it held vital revelations, but staring into Howarth's mismatched eyes, Julia questioned whether its significance had been exaggerated.

She pulled out her phone and sent a text to her

father. If he couldn't solve the riddle of the painting, he'd at least want to see it. Almost as soon as the text sent, hurried footsteps descended the stairs, followed by Brian's astonished gasp.

"I cannot believe my eyes. You found it!" He approached the painting like Indiana Jones, beholding a sacred treasure. Katie trailed behind, wide-eyed. "The lost portrait of Duncan Howarth... it's real."

"Oh," Katie muttered. "It's... ugly."

Brian scrutinised the painting, his finger tapping on his chin. "I wish I could disagree, but it is rather terrible work. The proportions are dreadful. Maybe it was hidden away as not to offend our eyes."

"Do you see any secrets?" Julia asked hopefully.

"Hmm." Brian retrieved a satchel from his jacket pocket and unravelled it on the desk. With his magnifying glass and other antiquing tools, he went nose to nose with Duncan. "It seems like an ordinary painting to me. Let me just..." He turned off the lamp, casting the windowless office in total darkness. He pulled out a small torch and illuminated the canvas with a blue light. "Well, it was worth a shot. There's nothing."

Veronica peered closer. "Perhaps it needs restoration to reveal what lies beneath? Like the Mona Lisa?"

Brian considered this, holding the canvas up and viewed the paint surface from the side. "There's no evidence of extensive over-painting or attempts to conceal previous layers. The craftsmanship is consistent, albeit unskilled."

"So much for lost masterpiece," Katie sighed. "I can't believe Father kept this eyesore hidden away all those years."

"Maybe he knew it held some secret?" Julia countered.

Katie tilted her head. "Or maybe he just wanted to hoard a rare treasure for himself, even if it was rubbish."

That did sound more like Vincent Wellington, but it didn't explain the secrecy surrounding the portrait. Julia willed the wonky-eyed, stern-faced Howarth to give up his secrets.

"Where did James find it?" Katie asked.

"Secret safe behind a wall in the basement," Jessie said.

"I knew it!" Katie hissed, clicking her fingers. "I told you we should have taken a sledgehammer to the place, Brian! Finding that safe could have saved us. If we'd found this painting and sold it when we still owned it... we could have avoided selling to James. He'd never have bought the manor. We'd still be there, and he'd have steered clear of Peridale."

"Do you still want to be at the manor, my love?" Brian said.

"Oh, heavens no." Katie shuddered. "It's just that thing, isn't it? The caterpillar effect. You step on a caterpillar, and then next thing you know... World War Three. So many wrong turns."

Julia exchanged glances with everyone in the room, and though everyone seemed to want to correct Katie, none did. She was close enough.

Leaning closer, Brian exclaimed, "Wait, there's writing here." He flipped the frame to unfasten the back with his tools. "It's partially obscured, but I believe..."

With great care, Brian and Barker removed the canvas from the frame. Julia held her breath as her father pulled out a different torch to shine in the corner of the canvas.

"It's a signature," Brian announced. "The artist who painted this was... Catherine Thompson? Never heard of her."

"I have," Julia said, squinting at the corner of the painting. "She painted landscapes. Why did Prunella pretend this didn't exist?"

Brian tilted his head, holding the painting at arm's length. "Now that you've said that, the background does show real promise."

"Brian, stand still," Katie cried, waving her

hands. She'd noticed something on the back of the painting. "There's something stuck on the back of the canvas."

They all gathered around for a closer look. It looked like a piece of blank paper. Brian examined the yellowed envelope, inhaling deeply. "Hmm. Rabbit skin glue, and it's long since dried out. Should come off cleanly."

With great care and a scalpel, he pried the paper from the canvas. Julia held her breath, and she was sure everyone else had too. Surely this had to be what Peter wanted them to uncover.

The paper came clean, and Brian turned it over. It was an envelope. A sealed envelope addressed: 'To the People of Peridale.'

"We shouldn't open this," Brian said with an uneasy laugh. "I have some expert friends who can come in and—"

"There isn't time," Jessie said, snatching the letter opener off Barker's desk. Before anyone could object, she slit open the envelope and pulled out the contents. "It's addressed to us. We are the people of Peridale. It just got lost in the post for a few hundred years."

"Oh, dear." Brian crumpled into the desk chair as Jessie unfolded a letter like it was nothing more than a utility bill. "I suddenly feel quite faint."

"Jessie's right. This letter was meant for us," Katie insisted. "We should read it."

Jessie handed Julia the yellowed page covered in elaborate cursive writing. The paper was thick and textured, the cursive impossible to read.

As though sensing her difficulty, Veronica took the letter instead, and Julia watched as she silently read, eyes scanning back and forth. Gradually, Veronica's expression shifted from concentration to shock. She lifted her gaze, eyes blazing behind her glasses.

"Well? What does it say?" Julia pressed.

A grin stretched across Veronica's face. "It's Duncan Howarth's lost confession, just as Peter suspected. This could change everything."

~

That night, after tucking a sleepy Olivia into her cot, Barker retreated to the bedroom. Julia was reading a typed-out copy of Duncan Howarth's revelatory confession again on the edge of the bed, as though she were committing every shocking word to memory. She glanced up as he slid under the covers beside her.

"Someone needs to read this at the committee meeting tomorrow," she declared. "The truth about Howarth's last wishes needs to be heard by everyone."

"Who do you think it should be?"

Julia considered for a moment. "Maybe my gran? She's never shy about public speaking."

"I have a feeling this won't go over well if it's blared through a megaphone." Barker shuffled to the edge of the bed, resting his chin on Julia's shoulder. "I think it should be you."

Julia folded the letter with a sigh.

"I had a feeling you were going to say that."

"People will listen to you," he assured her. "This letter undermines James' entire narrative."

"But do you think it will be enough to sway the vote?"

"I hope so."

"Only time will tell." Crawling to the top of the bed, Julia joined him under the duvet, and they cosied up. "But first, I'm going to make sure there's one fewer committee member to worry about. I think I know who killed Peter."

Barker agreed, but they'd spent the day exhausting their theories. He cuddled in closer, and Mowgli curled up between them, the comforting rumble of his purr filling the quiet. Outside, the air had a bite to it; the first frosts of winter weren't far away.

For Barker, it was one of those disarmingly simple moments that brought life into sharp focus. Tomorrow promised to be a decisive day for Peridale, one that could reshape the very fabric of their community.

But tonight, he set those concerns aside in the quiet gathering of strength before the fight that awaited them. In that ordinary moment that felt anything but, Barker thought that he could have stayed there forever.

21

The morning of the planning committee meeting dawned bright and crisp. A crowd had already gathered outside the village hall, their spirited chatter filling the green. Handmade signs bobbed in the air, the slogans crafted in Dot's dining room on display.

At the heart of it all stood Dot and Ethel, straight-backed and square-shouldered, flanked by their fellow silver-haired comrades. Megaphones in hand, they orchestrated the demonstration with military precision. Amy, Evelyn, and Shilpa made up their faithful lieutenants, corralling the rabble-rousers into formation.

Jessie darted through the energised crowd, handing out flyers hot off the press. These detailed the corruption plaguing the planning committee, though she had omitted Alice's name at the last minute. Jessie seemed to hope that their museum manager would see sense and vote with her conscience.

Julia watched the spectacle unfold with a mix of pride and optimism. The sheer numbers flocking to protest spoke to the village's spirit of solidarity. Peridale was wide awake, and this time, the people would not be silenced.

"Would you look at the turnout?" Barker remarked as another busload of pensioners disembarked, each being handed a placard from Dot and Ethel. "I haven't seen this much excitement since the Queen popped by the library for story time."

Julia laughed. "Let's hope this has a happier ending than your staring contest with the corgi."

She gave his hand an affectionate squeeze. Despite everything, she felt a glimmer of hope. With Duncan Howarth's shocking confession soon to be exposed, perhaps the sordid secrets of the past could pave the way for a brighter future.

"Julia, Barker, over here!" called a familiar voice. They turned to see her father jogging over, waving a newspaper. "Thought you ought to see this. The lad in the shop said I was the first to buy a copy. It'll be all over the village by noon."

He showed them the front page, emblazoned with the headline: 'Murder and Corruption—The Ghosts Haunting Howarth Estate.' Beneath it ran a scathing exposé on the development scheme, covering everything from Peter's suspicious demise to the committee's rampant bribery.

"Jessie and Veronica have outdone themselves this time," Julia said, watching them as they handed out flyer after flyer.

"Let's hope it makes a difference," Barker said, his smile fading. "James always seems to evade consequences."

As if on cue, his black car pulled up across the road. The crowd booed as James stepped out, his smug grin unfazed by the hostile reception. Flanked by an entourage of security, he strode straight past the angry mob towards the doors.

"Come to step over us peasants, have you?" Dot called through her megaphone. "You will hear what we have to say!"

James tipped his head and disappeared inside, leaving the venomous chants echoing after him.

"And so it begins," Julia said, kissing Barker on the cheek as she pulled out her car keys. "I'll be back soon. This shouldn't take too long."

While protests raged outside the village hall in preparation for the meeting's start, Barker slipped away to meet DI Moyes for an urgent pint at The Plough pub. He found her seated at the bar, staring moodily into her glass.

"Afternoon, Detective," he greeted, taking the stool beside her. "You're looking rather down. Have they stopped stocking your favourite flavoured vape cartridges?"

Moyes responded with only a faint twitch of her lips. "No rest for the wicked. But I'll take any excuse to skive off from paperwork right now." She nodded at the bartender. "Get this man whatever he fancies."

Once Barker had a pint in hand, Moyes fixed him with a solemn look. "I asked you here because we've had a significant development in the McBride case."

Barker sat up straighter. "Go on."

"A new witness has come forward."

"Who?"

"Roxy."

"Your girlfriend saw something? Why didn't she say so before?"

Moyes nodded. "She didn't think anything of it until she was, let's say, reviewing case notes in the bath last night."

Despite the circumstances, Barker suppressed a smile at the mental image.

"Not exactly the material I'd recommend for nighttime reading. Don't let the superintendent find out," he winked. "Julia was always reading mine. Couldn't keep her away. So, what did Roxy see?"

Moyes lowered her voice, leaning in close. "She read Julia's statement about the woman in the witch hat at the Halloween party. We both saw that woman talking to Peter in the courtyard, but we didn't see her face. I stayed outside for the fresh air, but Roxy went in to refill the punch. She said she saw that witch going into the maze with Peter. Any idea who that witch was?"

Barker's pint froze halfway to his lips. "Julia thinks it was Prunella."

"Did she get a clear look at this woman's face?"

"No, but Prunella confirmed it was her when Julia confronted her."

Sighing, Moyes said, "Why didn't she tell me that? Now that she was seen going into the maze with Peter, I'd bet my badge that pompous old battle-axe is behind this. She's been a nightmare to interview."

"Lines up with what Julia thinks, then," Barker said, rubbing his chin. "She thinks this all goes back to Catherine Thompson, the ancestral painter."

"And where is your charming wife?"

Barker stopped rubbing his chin and sprang off

the bar stool, waving for Moyes to follow him. "Oh, I'm an idiot."

"Yes, you are. But why?"

"Because Julia just told me she'd be right back," he said, pulling open the pub door. "I was so distracted watching the protest, I didn't think to ask where she was going."

"You think she's gone to confront Prunella?"

Barker arched a brow at Moyes, prompting her to throw her arms into her coat. "Good point. Of course she has. If we get there in time, today might end up being the best day of my career. Two arrests in one day."

"Two? Who's the first?"

A sly grin spread as she unlocked her car with a click of the key. "Neither has happened yet, but after your daughter's latest statement, let's just say we've nailed the rotten scoundrel at last. The raid is scheduled for tonight."

"Who's being raided?"

"Isn't it obvious?" She winked. "Something tells me you won't want to miss it, but first..." She patted down her pockets. "I left my vape in the pub. Let me just—"

"Moyes!" Barker cried, jumping into the passenger seat. "Car. Now."

Pumpkins and Peril

∽

Jessie lingered by the village hall door, scanning the chanting crowd for any sign of her mum. The ever-growing protest raged on, placards and banners bobbing above the sea of people. Thanks to Dot and Ethel's campaigning and the paper's quick turnaround with their latest headline, hundreds had shown up to voice their opposition. But Julia was nowhere to be seen among the familiar faces.

With a worried glance at her watch, Jessie ducked inside. The packed hall starkly contrasted the eager atmosphere of James's earlier unveiling. There were no smiles; the chatter was dull, and Jessie couldn't wait for it to start. Folding chairs had been brought in to accommodate the observers, with twice as many people standing around the edges.

At the front, the planning committee members sat at a long table facing the incensed audience. James sat at the end, regarding the uproar with an indifferent smile. Beside him, the chairman banged a gavel.

"If we could all take our seats," he called over the din, "we'll begin."

Jessie slid into the empty chair Veronica was guarding near the front. The editor sat with her shoulders squared, observing the chaos as if she were watching a live performance from the Globe.

Leaning in close, Jessie asked, "Have you seen my mum anywhere?"

"Not since this morning."

Jessie bit her lip, scanning the crowd again. Julia couldn't miss this; it was too important. She sent her another text message, the previous three still unread. She couldn't shake the uneasy feeling that something had gone wrong.

At the committee table, the chairman continued his futile pleas amidst angry heckling from all sides. James reclined with his fingers steepled, wearing a patient expression as if waiting out a harmless tantrum.

Beside him, Richard seemed sweatier than usual, dabbing his brow every few seconds. Martin kept his head down, jotting notes. And Alice stared at her hands, unable to meet the room's condemnatory glares. The only absent member was Prunella, whom Jessie expected to fly in any minute. They hadn't put out a space for Peter, but he should have been up there too.

"She faked that 'Preserving Tradition, Embracing Progress' report too," Veronica whispered, nodding at Prunella's empty chair. "I called the council to ask about their sources and whom they sampled, and they said I'd need to talk with the Councillor for Heritage and Culture, who spearheaded the report. That's Prunella."

"Seems she didn't learn her lesson in 1999."

Veronica craned her neck at the uneasy crowd. "She must have known an unbiased report would never have given her the needed results. She tried to fake her ancestor's legacy. Maybe this was her way of faking hers."

After several more minutes of fruitless gavel-banging, the chairman finally gave in and let the objectors shout themselves hoarse. Gradually, the outcries tapered off into resentful grumbling.

The chairman, Mr Wilson, stepped up to the central podium, facing the restless attendees with several clearings of his throat.

"We have gathered today to vote on the proposed development of the Howarth Estate site," he began in a nasal tone that grated. "There are eight voting members present, so in the event of a tie, I will cast the deciding vote as chairman." He gestured to two mousy individuals stationed at smaller tables. "Miss Jones and Mr Davies will be taking minutes as our secretaries. The proposal we will be considering is the development of fifteen acres of unused greenfield into a new housing estate by Jacobson Developments. This will create two hundred new homes for the local area. We will begin with opening statements from each committee member. Then we will hear objections from attendees, followed by a final statement from the developer, Mr Jacobson." He cleared his throat again. "Now, let us commence with councillor statements, starting with Mr Martin Green, our Area of Outstanding Natural Beauty representative."

After several more minutes of fruitless gavel-banging, the chairman finally gave in and let the objectors shout themselves hoarse. Gradually, the outcries tapered off into resentful grumbling.

The chairman, Mr Wilson, stepped up to the central podium and faced the restless attendees. Clearing his throat multiple times, he began, "We have gathered today to vote on the proposed development of the Howarth Estate site. Eight voting members are present, so in the event of a tie, I will cast the deciding vote as chairman." He gestured to two mousy individuals stationed at smaller tables. "Miss Jones and Mr Davies will be taking minutes as our secretaries. The proposal we will be considering is the development of fifteen acres of unused greenfield into a new housing estate by Jacobson Developments. This will create two hundred new homes for the local area. We will begin with opening statements from each committee member. Then we will hear objections from attendees, followed by a final statement from the developer, Mr Jacobson." He cleared his throat again.

"Now, let us commence with councillor statements, starting with Mr Martin Green, our Area of Outstanding Natural Beauty representative."

All eyes shifted to Martin as he slowly stood, shuffling papers before launching into his prepared remarks in support of the controversial Howarth Estate plans.

"While I appreciate the concerns raised," he started, a tremor in his voice, "repurposing this long-vacant greenfield site aligns with my sustainability principles. The developer has demonstrated a willingness to implement eco-friendly building practices."

"This man wouldn't know what sustainable was if it bit him in the backside!" Dot heckled into her megaphone. "Ask him how big his house is!"

"One more time," the chairman barked, "and you will be removed."

James smirked, nodding for Martin to continue.

"Further, the project will fund much-needed upgrades, like flood resilience. With collaboration, we can shape an environmentally conscious addition to Peridale that balances development and conservation while still maintaining the surrounding natural beauty."

Martin sat to tepid applause and grumbling.

Richard rose next, gripping both sides of the

podium. "I stand by my position. Peridale needs more affordable housing stock, and this project will provide it via the agreed-upon quota of lower-priced units."

"But they're *not* affordable!" Dot cried. "They're *enormous!*"

"Have this woman removed," the chairman ordered.

For the second time that week, Dot was marched out of the village hall by security, and this time, the crowd was on her side. Their boos rattled Richard, who squirmed as if he wanted to be anywhere else.

"While none of us want change," he continued, sticking to his prepared lines, "some compromise is required for progress. Working together, I'm confident we can ensure the new Howarth Estate integrates harmoniously, meeting the needs of all Peridale residents—both current and future."

Richard retook his seat amidst a renewed uproar, mopping his damp forehead with a handkerchief. His arguments failed to temper the crackling outrage in the room.

Jessie glared at the committee members. Did they realise they were selling out their own community? That every word from their mouths only stoked the fire growing in the hall? She shook her head, checking her phone. Still no response from her mum.

"Alice?" the chairman asked.

"I..." Staring at her notes, Alice didn't move. "I have nothing to add."

James shifted in his seat. It wasn't an argument against, but it wasn't another voice for the development either. Jessie flashed her a smile, and Alice returned it with a wobble.

"Any statements from the objectors will now commence," the chairman said, rubbing his forehead. "Something tells me we'll be here all day."

"Jessie, go." Veronica pushed Jessie out of her chair. "Before the noise."

"What? We never—"

"Podium!" Veronica's teeth were gritted as she eyed the people forming an orderly line. "You know what to say. Just imagine everyone naked."

Jessie felt sick to her stomach. Public speaking had never been her thing. But one glance at James' gloating expression strengthened her nerve. She pictured her mum's face, imagining Julia's outrage if she were here. Jessie slipped behind the podium with unsteady legs and adjusted the microphone with a quivering grip. The chairman gave her a wary nod.

Drawing a deep breath, Jessie began, "I'd like to raise... erm... urgent concerns about a lack of due process and... bias regarding this planning committee." Murmurs rippled through the seated observers. Jessie coughed, willing her voice to steady.

She looked out at the crowd for her mum. She still wasn't there, but she locked eyes with Dante. He gave a nod that she knew meant 'you've got this,' and she took another breath. "There is substantial evidence that certain members have had their votes influenced through bribery and coercion." She turned her gaze to the committee table. "Specifically, Martin, Richard, Alice, and..." She faltered as her eyes landed once more on Prunella's vacant seat. Pressing on, she continued, "Prunella Thompson. Their ability to vote on this matter fairly has been compromised."

The chairman held up a hand, his impatience straining his polite tone. "Those are significant accusations, young lady. Do you have tangible proof to submit to the council?"

"I do. My—our local paper has run multiple stories exposing the allegations. Copies are available by the door."

"Ah yes, I am familiar with your little paper's proclivity for sensationalism." The chairman peered down his nose. "Unless you have hard evidence to present now, we must move on."

Flushed, Jessie persisted, "The corruption runs to the top of this project. James Jacobson and Greg Morgan are both implicated—"

"That's quite enough," the chairman interjected. "If you have criminal allegations, I suggest submitting them to the proper authorities for investigation. Now, please retake your seat so we can proceed with the vote."

"But you must see how compromised this whole process is?" Jessie insisted, finding her voice more with each word. "James and Greg have these members in their pocket. How can the vote be considered fair or valid? How can…"

Jessie's voice drifted away, not just from her throat, but from the microphone. They'd cut her off.

"You pig," Jessie called at him. "How much did they slip into your pockets too?"

"Young lady, I will remind you only once more that you are dangerously close to disrupting an official council meeting. The planning committee was selected through approved channels. Unless you have irrefutable evidence of illegal activity concerning the voting members, we will move forward as scheduled. Please vacate the podium." Jessie clung on as security crept in from the corners of the room. "Vacate."

Jessie returned to her seat amidst murmurs from the crowd. Some voices called for her to keep arguing, while others insisted things move ahead. Veronica offered an encouraging pat on the back.

"I'm sorry, Jessie," Veronica said. "That was always going to happen. You spoke the truth, even if they refuse to hear it. The people will believe you. Now the choice is theirs what they do with it."

They exchanged solemn looks as a man with fading red hair shuffled to the podium.

"My name is George Knight," he began, "and that man there," he paused, pointing at James, "used his influential friend, our local MP, Greg Morgan, to harass my family..." He stared around the room. "To burn down our home... All for poxy road access. Now, if you'd all get comfortable. I have twenty-seven pages of evidence to read through."

As George Knight began to speak, boring the audience into submission, Jessie was sure it wouldn't make a difference if he had twenty-seven thousand pages of evidence at this point. In this room, the truth didn't seem to matter.

Their last hope was Duncan Howarth's confession.

What was taking her mum so long?

22

Julia raced along the winding country lane, her heart pounding as Prunella Thompson's cottage came into view. She had to reach the planning committee meeting before the crucial vote, but first, she had an urgent stop to make.

Tyres spraying gravel, Julia pulled up outside the quaint cottage. Through the lace curtains, she could see Prunella hurrying about in the sitting room, muttering to herself as she gathered papers into her purse.

Julia knocked sharply on the oak door. Moments later, it swung open.

"Julia?" Prunella's eyes bulged at the sight of her

unexpected visitor. "What on earth are you doing here? I'm running dreadfully late."

"This will only take a moment," Julia said. "May I come in?"

Before Prunella could object, Julia stepped inside. She set the wrapped canvas she had been cradling down on an antique side table.

Prunella eyed it warily. "What's this about?"

By way of reply, Julia unwrapped the painting from its cloth. Prunella's jaw dropped at the sight of the dour face glaring up at them.

"It... it can't be," Prunella whispered. "The lost portrait of Duncan Howarth..."

Julia watched as emotions warred across the older woman's face—shock, awe, euphoria. Prunella reached out a trembling hand to touch the cracked oil paint.

"But how?" Prunella asked. "Where did you get this?"

"James Jacobson had it hidden away all this time. You lied about this painting," Julia said. "You knew it existed. Your own ancestor painted it."

Prunella flinched at the accusation. She turned, defiance flashing across her features before they crumpled into remorse.

"You're right," she admitted. "Catherine Thompson was my great-great-grandmother. Her letters were passed down through generations of our family. She grew close to Duncan near the end, against the wishes of the village. Catherine's offer came during one of her painting excursions into Howarth Forest. She would often go there seeking inspiration for her landscapes."

Prunella's gaze took on a faraway look. "I can just imagine her venturing deeper than usual and stumbling upon the elusive man himself, wandering among the trees. Judging by her letters, she wasn't a woman who was afraid of speaking her mind. I imagine she was the one to strike up the conversation with Duncan. When Catherine learned Howarth had no portrait or photographs to leave behind, she made the offer. Portraiture wasn't her speciality, but she wished to grant him a legacy. She, no doubt, oversold her skills, but it wasn't as if people were lining up."

Julia could envision the scene. "It was kind of her to make such a gesture, even knowing it would anger the villagers."

Prunella nodded. "Too kind, according to her descendants. Catherine developed a true friendship with Howarth in his final year. She looked past his sins to find the humanity within. But when he died soon after, Catherine faced scorn for aligning with the man who'd nearly destroyed their home. People felt she'd betrayed them. She tried to have the painting shown, but there was little interest."

"So, how did it become a 'lost treasure'?"

Prunella traced a finger over the stern portrait. "Catherine's children were ashamed that our family's name would be forever tied to Howarth's. So, once she died, they hid away her painting and letters. Any legacy she might have had was snuffed out when she died. I've collected many of her landscapes over the years." She glanced around the room at the painting-lined walls. "Never cost much. Nobody cared enough about her work to give it value."

"That's why you faked those papers?"

Sighing, she nodded. "I know it was a foolish mistake. I over-egged the pudding, so to speak. I just wanted people to respect her name, and by extension... me. My family never let the bitterness fade. Generation after generation passed on the story of Catherine's betrayal. I was tired of carrying that burden. I knew from her letters that she was a kind, intelligent, caring woman who deserved a legacy. I hoped to make things right somehow by finding this lost portrait. I was all for Peter finding it until..."

"Until?" Julia prompted. "You realised the 'confession' could mean something?"

"Oh, it was always going to mean something. I assumed my family destroyed the 'confession,' not wanting Howarth to have redemption, but Peter theorised that if they'd gone to such lengths to hide the portrait, perhaps..." Prunella picked up the painting with great care and turned it over. "It was never confirmed, but Peter thought the two would have been hidden together."

Howarth's letter burned a hole in Julia's pocket, but she had more to learn before she shared her final treasure.

"How did Peter know about this confession if it was such a family secret?" she asked.

"Peter would often visit for tea and go through my collections. I have quite the historical hoard here, and nothing fascinated him more than Duncan's letters to Catherine. Once Peter read Duncan's final letter to Catherine asking her to display his confession, he became obsessed. He believed the people had a right to know Duncan had a side that history had no record of." In a whisper, she confessed, "I never dreamed we would actually uncover the lost portrait."

"James offered this to Peter, didn't he?" Julia guessed. "As a bribe for his vote."

Prunella tensed. "I couldn't say."

"I think you could," Julia pressed. "But Peter had too much integrity. He refused to be bought."

Prunella turned away. Julia felt sure she was right. And Prunella knew more than she'd admitted so far, and the time had come for the truth to emerge. Julia withdrew the precious envelope containing Duncan Howarth's lost confession.

"There's just one little problem," Julia revealed, handing it over. "Peter was right. The confession was hidden with the painting."

Prunella took the envelope with trembling fingers, shaking her head in disbelief. She read the faded script inside, and Julia studied her closely. Tears glistened in the corners of her eyes. Blinking, she didn't move to stop them rolling down her cheeks. The prickly politeness Prunella had painted as her mask was no more.

"After all these years," she murmured. "The confession still exists. Catherine really did change his heart in the end."

Julia sensed the pivotal moment was upon them.

She sighed.

Maybe they had been 'old friends,' but Prunella had been blinded by all that glittered like too many before her.

"Given that you'd read the rest of Duncan's letters to Catherine, you must have known what this letter would confess," Julia said, returning the letter to its envelope. "You must have known that if Peter found it, and exposed the truth from within the committee, it might have put a stop to Howarth Estate getting this far." With a heavy sigh, Julia returned the letter to its envelope. "Prunella, I need you to tell me everything you know. I know you killed Peter."

Prunella dropped onto the antique sofa, and Julia joined her as she wrung her hands, seeming to wrestle with herself before the words tumbled out.

"I tried to dissuade him. But he was convinced he could rewrite history if he found the portrait. He read Duncan's final letter around the time the society first formed. He believed it would be insurance against future misguided developments. After Jacobson turned up to one of our meetings to find someone who could consult on his new house, nothing was the same again."

"Ironic," Julia said, "that the man he wanted to use the confession against had the confession all along."

"I don't think James knew." She frowned into the distance. "But I knew. We couldn't go back once James and Greg had tempted us all with promises of money and power. Martin was up to his eyeballs in debt from loans, Alice from her failing museum. Richard didn't need a reason to accept cold, hard cash, and I..." Closing her eyes, she lowered her head. "Greg promised that he'd help me advance my career in politics. All we had to do was not object to the plans. But Peter resisted, and the longer he resisted, the more dangerous he became. James and Greg thought if they found what he wanted, they could tempt him. Everyone has a price, but not Peter. He knew time was running out. He was going to expose the whole rotten plan."

"So, you put a stop to him," Julia said. "You stabbed your friend in the back."

"All I could see was scandal!" she cried defensively. "My career, my reputation, everything I'd worked for suddenly at risk... I'd gone too far along with things. My past mistakes, my present mistakes, all on show for the world to see. The plan had to succeed. He'd ruin the lives of every society member if he had to."

Julia couldn't find any words.

"Don't you see why I had to stop him?" she cried. "With my sights set on Parliament, I couldn't afford that kind of exposure. When James' final bribe of the painting failed, I realised Peter left me no choice. If that wouldn't work—"

"An axe would?"

"A moment of impulse." Her shoulders slumped. "Peter was so eager, convinced I'd have a change of heart because Catherine's painting had resurfaced."

"So, you took the axe from the stump and followed him into the maze?" Julia said, and Prunella closed her eyes to the memory. "He was found lying on a book, open on a page about Catherine."

"He wanted to convince me that Duncan wasn't

the only one we could write the history books on. That Catherine's footnote could become a whole page. My forged reports could come true." She looked away, sniffing back tears. "I told him the confession must stay hidden, at least until after the committee vote, but he intended to rip apart every James Jacobson property until he found it. But I knew, even without the confession, he'd have ignored the non-disclosure agreement, eventually. He couldn't afford the legal trouble, but there'd come a moment when he'd snap. He was already leaking to the newspaper. Trying to warn you." She shot Julia a cold stare out of the corner of her eyes. "I pulled out the axe. I only meant to scare him into backing down. But even then, he told me he'd never stop. Before I knew it, I'd... I'd..."

"You killed him."

She hid her face in shaking hands. "That brave, foolish man. He didn't deserve such a fate. I've never known regret like this."

Though Julia had expected this admission, hearing the truth from Prunella's own lips still sent a chill down her spine. This refined, ruthless woman had murdered a man out of desperation and pride.

"I know saying sorry cannot undo what I've done," Prunella whispered. "I will answer for my crime. But please, you must believe me—I never wished Peter harm. I only wanted to protect what I'd worked so hard for." She lifted her eyes, remorse swirling in their depths. "Ambition can make monsters of us all."

Rising solemnly, Julia moved to the window and peered out at the police car skidding to a halt outside. DI Moyes' electric car joined it a moment later, and she jumped out with Barker.

Julia turned back to Prunella. "Peter spent years searching for the truth about Duncan Howarth. Don't you think it's time the whole truth came out?"

Prunella lifted her chin, resignation settling across her features. She must have known this reckoning would come, eventually.

"I'll accept the consequences for my actions," she stated. "But that painting, as terrible as it is, deserves to be seen. It's hidden in the shadows for long enough. Promise you'll make sure that happens?"

"You have my word that I'll try," Julia assured her. "But the painting belongs to James. I'm technically harbouring stolen goods right now."

"Far too much belongs to James," she said, grabbing her coat. "Perhaps you can hide it a little longer. I'm afraid I underestimated you, Julia. I didn't think Peter stood a chance to halt the wheels of Jacobson's progress... but you?" She took one last look at the portrait as the police officers burst down the hallway. "I don't think James has any idea what he's got himself into."

Pumpkins and Peril

After Prunella had been led away, Julia returned the painting to its protective wrapping. The portrait had sparked obsession and murder. Yet, like Duncan Howarth, maybe it could still be redeemed.

Well, not the painting.

That really was bad.

But the confession?

"Nice of you to slip away like that!" Barker cried, his anger melting in their hug.

"I'm fine, Barker. And I'm sorry. I just wanted to level with her, once and for all. I had a feeling the painting would break down her walls."

"And she confessed?"

"She painted quite the picture." Pulling away from the hug, she set off to her car. "Come on. We can't miss this meeting."

23

At the entrance to the village hall, Julia paused to catch her breath. The raucous energy vibrated through the air, even through the closed double doors. Drawing herself tall, Julia pushed through into the noise.

She searched the familiar faces of the standing spectators pressed shoulder-to-shoulder along the walls. Towards the front, she spotted Jessie and Veronica in the third row, their expressions switching from concern to relief at the sight of her.

With an apologetic glance, Julia wound through the narrow aisle left between rows of creaky folding chairs. She headed for the vacant spot Veronica guarded beside her like a faithful sentry.

"Where have you been?" Jessie whispered as Julia slid into place. "We were so worried. It's almost over."

"Long story," Julia murmured back. "I'll explain later."

James noticed Julia's arrival and greeted her with a slippery smile that made her skin itch. She held his cold gaze, refusing to show the weakness he craved.

Beside her, Veronica leaned in. "They're nearly finished with statements. Only James left."

"And now," the chairman said, "it's time for Mr Jacobson to present his plan before the final vote."

James rose smoothly from his seat, straightening his sleek tie. With an earnest gaze, he addressed the restless crowd.

"My esteemed friends, this is a momentous day for our beloved village. After months of hard work and dedication to create the best possible future for Peridale, the time has come to vote on our transformative plan."

He pressed a hand over his heart. "I know there has been opposition from a vocal minority. Change is often met with skepticism at first. But rest assured, our vision will lift up Peridale to the prosperity and prestige it has long deserved."

With a dismissive wave, he continued, "Do not believe the fear-mongering rumours being spread.

This sustainable, state-of-the-art development will provide everything our community needs - luxury housing, shops, restaurants, entertainment. It is thoughtfully designed to preserve our heritage while propelling us into the future."

James leaned forward, tone urgent. "The misguided few clinging to outdated notions of tradition are missing the incredible opportunity before us. Peridale has stagnated for too long, falling behind while other villages modernise. We owe it to our children not to deprive them of progress."

He shook his head sadly. "What kind of future are the naysayers fighting for? One of decay and lost potential? Of boarded-up shops and crumbling infrastructure? That is the inevitable fate if we refuse this gift of renewal."

With arms spread wide, James implored passionately, "My friends, be on the right side of history today. Duncan Howarth—Peridale's visionary son—would be smiling down on you all. His bold spirit compels us forward. Will you answer the call and secure a bright destiny? The choice is yours."

Thumping a fist over his heart, he concluded, "I urge you to open your minds and vote 'yes' with me. Together, we will lead Peridale out of the past and into a new golden age of prosperity!"

James retook his seat to scattered applause, visibly pleased with his rousing speech. He made eye contact with Julia, as if daring her to counter his grandiose promises.

"If there are no further questions, we will now proceed with the vote," Mr Wilson announced, mopping his brow with a handkerchief.

The onlookers responded with another round of boos and jeers. James smiled wider.

Beside Julia, Jessie shook with frustration. "Do you have the letter?"

All statements had been made, all arguments heard. The planning committee held Peridale's fate in their hands now. But as the gavel banged again, Julia felt her anger and helplessness morph into resolve. She rose from her seat before she could second-guess herself.

"Excuse me, I'd like to speak," she called out, her voice ringing clear above the noise.

The room quieted in surprise. The chairman frowned, caught off guard. "I'm afraid the time for public comments is past, Ms—"

"Mrs. South-Brown," she said. "Julia South-Brown. I own the café that will be cast in the shadow of Mr Jacobson's development if his plans are allowed to go ahead." Locking eyes with James, she said, "A café I never intend to sell."

"Is there a point to this, Mrs South-Brown?" the chairman urged. "Like I said, the time for—"

"The time for James to stop using Duncan Howarth's name and legacy as his smokescreen has come to an end." Julia reached into her pocket and pulled out the letter. The original letter. She knew it by memory now, but the people needed to see the original. She held it out, showed it around, and said, "This letter contains—"

"With all due respect, Chairman," James cried, half-rising from his seat, "we cannot allow this disruption—"

A chorus of boos drowned out his objections.

"Let her speak!" someone shouted.

"Yeah, we want to hear what she has to say!"

Sweating, the chairman held up placating hands until the clamour ebbed.

With a stern look at Julia, he said, "You may speak. But make it quick."

Pulse racing, Julia strode down the centre aisle toward the dais. She looked at the podium, wondering if that was where everyone else had spoken, but she wanted to stay where she was. Among her community. This was her chance to change their fate.

Drawing a steeling breath, Julia turned to address the crowd. "You all believe James Jacobson is fulfilling Duncan Howarth's legacy with this development. But I have here Howarth's final words." She held up the letter again. "His confession."

"Without delay, Mrs South-Brown."

"Yes, Chairman." Closing her eyes for a moment, Julia held out the letter, and began, "My Dearest Villagers, As I lay here ravaged by consumption in the final days of my life, I feel compelled to unburden my conscience and confess the grave errors I committed against you all."

She paused, and she could have heard a pin drop.

"When I first arrived in Peridale, I saw only open fields ripe for industry and houses begging to be demolished in the name of progress," she continued, reading in slow and measured breaths. "In my arrogance, I sought to transform this beloved village into a bustling industrial centre, heedless of your lives or livelihoods. I claimed an altruistic motive, insisting my bold vision would bring prosperity for all. But in truth, my aims were selfish."

She looked at James as he stared at her with dagger eyes.

"I sought only to enrich myself, uncaring of how my schemes impacted your families or your future. In my blind ambition, I conspired to destroy all that you held dear, from felling ancient forests to dismantling homes and buildings steeped in history. Worst of all, I sought to silence dissenters who opposed my plans. I spread vicious lies and made vile threats. And when those failed, I resorted to violence. As I prepare to leave this world, I confess it all. I allowed greed to corrupt my spirit and poison my thoughts toward you, my fellow villagers. In these final moments, clarity has come to me. I see now that I should have walked with you, not over you. My vision for Peridale was tragically misguided. I should have listened, adapted, and compromised, instead of imposing my will like a tyrant. I hope as you hear my name in future generations, you will remember this confession. Remember that though I brought harm, what I built can be un-built. Though I showed hatred, what I destroyed can be restored. Cherish your homes and shops, your forests, and fields. Protect your village; preserve its charm. And when ambitious men seek to overwrite history, stand together as I should have stood with you."

Julia closed the letter, bowing her head.

After a moment, she lifted her gaze with a defiant stare, only looking at her fellow villagers. "These are the words of the man whose 'vision' James claims to be fulfilling. That's all I have to say."

Julia returned to stand by Jessie and Veronica's seats. There was no applause, no cheers, no boos, just a stunned silence. Martin looked on the verge of throwing up, tugging at his collar as if it choked him, no doubt thinking about losing his new home. Richard's stony expression had faded into uncertainty, perhaps already seeing future bribes trickling away. Alice was the only member of the committee who looked relieved.

"These documents require further verification," the chairman declared, his sharp tone brooking no dissent. "Until substantiated, they are irrelevant to this hearing."

"Irrelevant?" Jessie cried in disbelief. "You all swore to uphold the village's heritage and values. Howarth confessed his plans would have ruined Peridale."

"And yet here we still stand, centuries on," Martin retorted, some colour returning to his cheeks. "I move that we proceed with the vote?"

Desperate, Julia turned to Alice. The conflict was plain on her kind face, but she remained silent as if forbidden to speak. With a sinking heart, Julia watched Martin's motion proceed to a vote.

One by one, the committee members cast their ballots, voices devoid of emotion. Martin and Richard voted 'yes,' Alice and two others voted 'no,' and when it came to the final three councillors, they nodded their 'yes' votes in quick succession, unable to look anywhere but the floor.

The crowd erupted in outrage as the tally was announced.

But the deed was already done.

"The motion to approve the Howarth Estate development passes," declared the chairman with a tap of the gavel. "This committee is over."

24

The mood was sombre as Jessie, Julia, Barker, and Veronica congregated outside Wellington Heights later that night. Despite the committee's crushing decision, a glimmer of hope remained—the imminent arrest of the man behind the scenes.

They stood huddled in the shadows, watching as DI Moyes and her team silently surrounded the block. With military precision, the officers stormed the building and ascended toward the penthouse apartment.

Moments later, a commotion erupted from inside. Shouting echoed down, followed by pounding footsteps. Jessie lifted her camera, poised to document the downfall of their nemesis.

With a bang, the front doors flew open. Flanked by officers, a handcuffed Greg Morgan was frog-marched out wearing nothing but boxer shorts and a murderous scowl. His usual slicked-back hair stood at all angles.

Flashbulbs popped as Greg was led past the onlookers. Despite the indignity, his eyes blazed with defiance.

"You'll regret this!" he bellowed at Moyes. "I'll have your badge for unlawful arrest!"

Jessie stepped forward, snapping photos of Greg's unravelling. She hoped the image of him defeated and exposed would splash across the front pages of every paper around.

"No comment for your constituents?" she taunted.

Greg's lip curled, but before he could respond, Veronica strode up to him. The siblings regarded one another coldly.

"I told you I'd see you behind bars before the first snowfall, brother," Veronica said. "You should have fled the country when you had the chance."

With a guttural roar, Greg lunged against his restraints. The officers yanked him back as he strained toward Veronica like a rabid animal.

"This isn't over!" he seethed, flecks of spittle flying. "You have nothing on me. No evidence. No witnesses. This won't stick!"

His manic laughter followed Veronica as Greg was forced into the back of a squad car. She watched impassively until the door slammed shut, muffling his deranged cackling.

Moyes approached, shaking her head. "No sign of the gun."

"What?" Jessie's heart sank. "It was right there."

"He must have ditched it. Let's pray we've still got enough to make the charges stick."

"We have my testimony about the recording," Jessie insisted, though doubt needled her. "And all of our records."

Just then, Richie emerged from the building looking dazed. Catching Jessie's eye, he flashed a thumbs up. "Thanks again for taking out the trash. I owe you all a round if I still have a bar to open tomorrow."

Despite everything, Jessie managed a faint smile. At least some good had come from this ordeal.

As Richie wandered off, Jessie turned to Veronica. "Do you feel vindicated now that Greg's been arrested?"

Veronica considered this before shaking her head. "I'll feel vindicated when the judge's gavel falls and my brother is sentenced for his crimes. Until then, we still have work to do. I see now that Greg was just the errand boy. The true threat remains." Veronica's eyes hardened with renewed conviction. "James won't stop simply because the pawn has fallen. We need to checkmate the king before he deals more damage."

Straightening her spine, Jessie nodded. Greg might have been in handcuffs, but with the finest lawyers and James' endless supply of money, he'd be as slippery as ever. They still had a lot of work to do, and Jessie had a burning question.

"When we found that bag," she started, "you mentioned Sebastian. I didn't connect the dots at first, but you mentioned him before when you first told me Greg was your brother. You said he was your older brother?"

Veronica confirmed with a nod, but she didn't offer anything else.

"What happened to him?"

"He died," she said, sniffing back tears. "A long time ago. A story for another day." Turning, she nodded to the lane as the police car vanished with Greg. "Looks like we're done here. Take the night off."

Jessie turned to see Dante walking up the lane. She didn't try to stop her smile from spreading.

"Did I miss it?" he asked.

"You did," she said, looping her fingers between his. "But you're just in time to take me for that drink."

Seizing the fine weather the next morning, Barker bundled Olivia into her pram and set out along the winding lane behind Julia's café. The fresh air and exercise would do them both good after the stresses of recent days.

As they strolled past James' bungalow, Barker turned down the front path. After James' brazen scheming, he deserved to squirm. Perhaps today, Barker could appeal to the lonely boy who'd once swung sadly on the rusty Fern Moore playground. Make him see sense before he wrought more damage. It was a long shot, but Barker had to try.

He rapped his knuckles against the front door. Footsteps approached, and the door swung open. James' look of surprise swiftly morphed into a patronising smile.

"To what do I owe the pleasure?"

Ignoring the sarcastic tone, Barker met his eyes. "I'm here to give you a chance, James. An opportunity to walk away from this madness with dignity intact."

James smirked. "And why would I want to do that?"

"Because deep down, some humanity lingers in you still." Barker glanced pointedly at Olivia. "That's why I've brought my daughter today. To remind you that lives hang in the balance. Her future—all our futures."

He took a step closer, lowering his voice. "You don't have to let greed consume you. It's not too late to change course and do what's right."

For a moment, James' arrogant mask seemed to crack. Conflict flickered across his face as his eyes dropped to Olivia. She burbled up at him, innocent and oblivious.

But just as quickly, his jaw tightened, and his eyes glazed over. "I think you should be on your way. Wouldn't want to miss story time."

He moved to shut the door, but Barker wedged his foot in. "I haven't given up on you yet. The boy from Fern Moore—"

James cut him off with a caustic laugh. "There's no 'boy' left in me. There's only what you see before you." He wrenched the door open wider. "But since you're so keen, let me show you something."

Warily, Barker followed James down the hall to a home office. The space was dominated by an enormous architectural model. James hit a switch, and tiny lights illuminated rows of boxy houses sprawling as far as the eye could see.

"Behold, Phase Two," James declared, spreading his hands. "Two hundred more luxury family homes, built to elevate our modest village into a world-class satellite town."

He jabbed a finger at a familiar rectangle of green

at the centre. "Once we pave over that dreary village green, this will be the most sought-after postcode in the Cotswolds."

Barker's heart sank. The charming village he loved was nowhere to be seen beneath this sterile sprawl of cookie-cutter mansions.

James continued gloating, drunk on his demented vision. "See the new road plan? Cuts right through that ugly forest, so we can clear those old trees away. And that crumbling Gothic house comes down too."

With a sneer, he added, "Perhaps the Farley family farm as well? I'm sure they can be persuaded to sell off their pastures for the right price."

Barker willed himself to stay calm. He had to keep trying, for Olivia's sake.

"This isn't what Duncan Howarth wanted," he implored, meeting James' impervious stare. "His confession proves that he regretted what he tried to do to Peridale. You're only fulfilling your own greed."

James barked a derisive laugh. "Come now. You didn't really think I cared about resurrecting that old crackpot's legacy? The people needed a heroic narrative to latch onto. So I gave them one."

He clapped Barker on the shoulder with condescending familiarity. "People cling to stories. They distrust facts. Leverage that, and you can mould them like putty. Howarth, his blasted confession, it was all set dressing."

James smiled coldly. "Now, if you'll excuse me, I have calls to make. I suggest you get back to writing mystery novels. Your last book was rather subpar."

With that parting jab, he withdrew his hand and turned his back on Barker. A clear dismissal.

Jaw clenched, Barker left without another word. He'd allowed himself to hope that some fragment of conscience lingered inside James, but it was clear now that appealing to his humanity was futile. James cared only for expanding his empire, heedless of the wreckage left in his wake.

James could sneer all he wanted, but he didn't know this village—not like Julia and Barker did. He had no idea what he was up against.

25

Julia gazed out the café window as the season's first snowflakes drifted down. The quaint village green looked even more picturesque dusted in white. She sighed, wishing she could enjoy the peaceful sight instead of dreading what the coming months might bring.

With James' schemes still looming, it was hard to feel festive. But she wouldn't give up hope. And today, she would take solace in small rituals.

Humming under her breath, Julia moved a stepladder over and climbed up with a hammer and picture nails. It was time for some new—or rather, old—pictures to join the wall. The Shepherd's Rest from centuries past, along with a sepia photograph of the 1800s tearoom that would have stood during Duncan's time. She'd even dug out a picture of the toy shop and the market hall from her gran's photo boxes.

Julia wished she'd made more effort to appreciate more of the village's rich history before it was under threat. But she could still honour it now through preserving memories. Each print she hung was a silent act of resistance, proving life had flourished here long before James Jacobson arrived, and it would continue to.

The bell above the door jingled, and Julia turned to see a delivery man stomping snow off his boots. He held a beautiful bouquet of winter flowers.

"Special delivery for Mrs South-Brown?"

Puzzled but pleased, she signed for the arrangement and inhaled the fresh scent. She hadn't ordered flowers herself, and she wondered if they were from Barker. A small piece of paper tucked in the greenery caught her eye. Unfolding it, she read the message:

'Keep holding out for Peridale and for Peter's legacy - Alice.'

Julia's throat tightened. After Prunella's arrest, Martin, Richard, and Alice resigned from the council and the Preservation Society. Julia didn't know where Martin and Richard had gone off to, but Alice had closed her little museum. Maybe she'd left the village altogether.

She was disappointed Alice had given up, but she understood it took courage to admit mistakes. Sending these flowers was Alice's way of making amends. Their fragrant petals gave Julia strength. She wouldn't give up. For Peter, and for everyone else depending on her to keep the path that field blocked, she would keep holding out.

After finding a vase and arranging the bouquet on the counter, Julia locked the café for the day and bundled up against the swirling snow and headed out with no destination in mind. At Jessie's flat, her stepdaughter emerged also dressed for the weather. Before Julia could react, Jessie lobbed a powdery snowball at her shoulder.

"I surrender!" Julia laughed, brushing snow off her coat. "To what do I owe the ambush?"

"Dot's orders," Jessie replied with a grin. "We've been summoned. She was quite insistent that you come too."

Arm in arm, they strolled down the lane to Dot's cottage. Inside, warmth and clamour greeted them. Julia froze in astonishment at the crowd packing the house. So many familiar faces—not just family, but villagers Julia had known for years.

"Here's our guest of honour!" Dot hurried over, presenting Julia like the prize turkey. "We've put the call out, and people heard. I wanted to bring together as many people I could whose lives you've touched."

"Your speech inspired a lot of people to dig into our history," Percy pointed out. "You help so many people in little ways without expecting anything in return."

"It's time we showed our thanks," Dot said. "And if anyone is going to lead this charge against James, it's you, Julia."

Overwhelmed, Julia's gaze roamed the room. Denise from the farm gave her a little wave. Malcolm from the gardening club smiled and saluted. George Knight and his children lifted their mugs in a toast. And so many more. People she saw all the time in her café, others she hadn't seen for months, even years. Villagers whose paths she'd only fleetingly crossed. They'd all showed up.

"I... I'm not sure I deserve such praise," Julia stuttered. "Just did what anyone would do."

"No, you go above and beyond." Hilda from the food bank patted Julia's hand. "When Ronnie died, murdered in one of James' schemes, you didn't rest until things were put right. Your kindness helped me survive my grief."

More stories followed of Julia reaching out, having a listening ear, and being an advocate during difficult times. Even the simple things like being there for a cup of tea, a delicious cake, and a chat. She dabbed at her eyes, moved beyond words. She really had made a difference in small ways, even when the bigger picture seemed bleak.

"If James has his eyes on your café, we won't let that happen," Shilpa said.

"Never," Amy added.

"I sense victory is within our grasp," Evelyn offered, draping a crystal necklace around Julia's neck. "I foresee a brighter new year without Mr Jacobson looming over us."

Her family stood clustered nearby, her sources of daily strength. Sue's shoulder to lean on, Neil's quiet solidarity, Brian's beaming pride, Katie's unconventional wisdom, Dot and Percy's fighting spirits, Jessie's fire, and Barker's unconditional love. Even Olivia's wild-eyed wonder. With these people around her, she could endure anything.

Julia accepted Olivia from Barker's arms, holding her daughter close. She babbled happily, oblivious to adult worries as she captured the room's attention. Olivia had no idea what uncertainties lay ahead, or how many were willing to battle to protect the village Olivia would grow up in.

"So, Julia…" Dot met her gaze. "What do we do next? How can we help?"

The room fell silent, waiting for her response.

Julia stood tall, her resolve renewed. "We keep fighting any way we can," she declared. "For as long as it takes."

A chorus of cheers resounded. Julia smiled through her tears.

Julia locked eyes with the wonky stare of Duncan Howarth's portrait, hiding in plain sight above Dot's mantelpiece. Their stubborn ancestors had defeated one man with wild ambitions and deep pockets before, and now it was time to do it again. The people of Peridale would not go quietly, not for James Jacobson or all the money in the world.

They may have lost the fight at the committee meeting, but together, they would win the battle against the Howarth Estate. Julia did not doubt it.

Thank you for reading, and don't forget to
RATE/REVIEW!

PRE-ORDER! The fight for Peridale is on...find out what happens next in the thrilling conclusion to a year of linked stories in Mince Pies and Madness, the special edition 30th Peridale Café mystery. You won't want to miss this one...

. . .

(And for long-time fans of the series, this is not the end, so fear not! Every ending is a new beginning... Peridale **will** return and continue throughout 2024 for a round of brand new cosy adventures! **Pre-order Sangria and Secrets, the 31st book, now!**)

Thank you for reading!

DON'T FORGET TO RATE AND REVIEW ON AMAZON

Reviews are more important than ever, so show your support for the series by rating and reviewing the book on Amazon! Reviews are **CRUCIAL** for the longevity of any series, and they're the best way to let authors know you want more! They help us reach more people! I appreciate any feedback, no matter how long or short. It's a great way of letting other cozy mystery fans know what you thought about the book.

Being an independent author means this is my livelihood, and *every review* really does make a **huge difference.** Reviews are the best way to support me so I can continue doing what I love, which is bringing you, the readers, more fun cozy adventures!

WANT TO BE KEPT UP TO DATE WITH AGATHA FROST RELEASES? *SIGN UP THE FREE NEWSLETTER!*

www.AgathaFrost.com

You can also follow **Agatha Frost** across social media. Search 'Agatha Frost' on:

Facebook
Twitter
Goodreads
Instagram

ALSO BY AGATHA FROST

<u>Peridale Cafe</u>

31. Sangria and Secrets

30. Mince Pies and Madness

29. Pumpkins and Peril

28. Eton Mess and Enemies

27. Banana Bread and Betrayal

26. Carrot Cake and Concern

25. Marshmallows and Memories

24. Popcorn and Panic

23. Raspberry Lemonade and Ruin

22. Scones and Scandal

21. Profiteroles and Poison

20. Cocktails and Cowardice

19. Brownies and Bloodshed

18. Cheesecake and Confusion

17. Vegetables and Vengeance

16. Red Velvet and Revenge

15. Wedding Cake and Woes

14. Champagne and Catastrophes

13. Ice Cream and Incidents

12. Blueberry Muffins and Misfortune

11. Cupcakes and Casualties

10. Gingerbread and Ghosts

9. Birthday Cake and Bodies

8. Fruit Cake and Fear

7. Macarons and Mayhem

6. Espresso and Evil

5. Shortbread and Sorrow

4. Chocolate Cake and Chaos

3. Doughnuts and Deception

2. Lemonade and Lies

1. Pancakes and Corpses

Claire's Candles

1. Vanilla Bean Vengeance

2. Black Cherry Betrayal

3. Coconut Milk Casualty

4. Rose Petal Revenge

5. Fresh Linen Fraud

6. Toffee Apple Torment

7. Candy Cane Conspiracies

8. Wildflower Worries

9. Frosted Plum Fears

Other

The Agatha Frost Winter Anthology

Peridale Cafe Book 1-10

Peridale Cafe Book 11-20

Claire's Candles Book 1-3

Printed in Great Britain
by Amazon